❧ RESCUE ❧

RESCUE

A Novel

ELIZABETH RICHARDS

POCKET BOOKS
New York London Toronto Sydney Tokyo Singapore

This book is a work of fiction. Names, characters, places and incidents are products of the author's imagination or are used fictitiously. Any resemblance to actual events or locales or persons living or dead is entirely coincidental.

POCKET BOOKS, a division of Simon & Schuster Inc.
1230 Avenue of the Americas, New York, NY 10020

Copyright © 1999 by Elizabeth Richards

Library of Congress Cataloging-in-Publication Data

Richards, Elizabeth, 1959–
    Rescue : a novel / Elizabeth Richards.
        p.   cm.
    ISBN: 0-671-02397-7
    I. Title.
    PS3568.I31525R47   1999
    813'.54—dc21   98-43727
                                                                        CIP

First Pocket Books hardcover printing March 1999

10 9 8 7 6 5 4 3 2 1

Designed by Liane Fuji

POCKET and colophon are registered trademarks of
Simon & Schuster Inc.

Printed in the U.S.A.

For my mother

❧ ACKNOWLEDGMENTS ❧

I thank Ann Rittenberg, my agent and dear friend, for seeing me through the writing of this book, and Emily Bestler, my editor, for wanting it.

Thank you, Richard Craven, for reading and encouragement.

I am most grateful to Elisabeth Macrae for her loving guidance and to Sarah, Dilly, and Seth, the children in my life, the best people I know.

We cannot sleep, and drop by drop at the heart
The pain of pain remembered comes again,
And we resist, but ripeness comes as well.
From the gods enthroned on the awesome rowing-bench
There comes a violent love.

—THE CHORUS, AESCHYLUS' *Agamemnon*

And I will rebuke the devourer for your sakes, and he
shall not destroy the fruits of your ground, neither shall
your vine cast her fruit before the time in the field . . .
And all nations shall call you blessed: For ye shall be a
delightsome land, saith the Lord of hosts.

—MALACHI, 3:11-12

He makes the woman of a childless house
to be a joyful mother of children.

—PSALM 113, v.8, *The Book of Common Prayer*

❧ RESCUE ❧

❧ ONE ❧

"Mrs. MacGowan? I'm afraid I've got some disappointing news about your son Malachi."

"He's not my son," I say for the thousandth time. I hand the phone to Ian and watch his face harden against the details of Mal's latest. A minute later he bangs down the receiver and mumbles something I'm glad I can't hear.

"What?" I ask.

"Pot," he says. "Three strikes, he's out."

I'm about to commiserate, but the phone rings again and Ian's on with Mal's mother, who, I gather from what's being said on our end, is throwing Malachi out too.

"You think throwing him out is going to keep drug sales to a dull roar?" Ian yells into the phone. Ian's a lawyer: the odd puff is one thing, sales quite another. "What kind of a message are you sending to the kid? Never mind you haven't stayed home a single day in his life."

Again, the receiver crashing down. "Christ," he says.

"She's asking you to take him," I surmise.

"Asking?" he argues. "No. Dorothy doesn't *ask*. She *informs*."

I give myself a minute to form a response, all the while conscious of his watching me for a sign of letup.

"I'm not sure I know how to care for a delinquent."

Tiny smile. Hope. There's a chance I'll do it. Not that either of us wants this, wants our world so altered. And I barely know Malachi. He's a teenager, and he keeps to his friends from school, a campus way out on a promontory of Brooklyn.

"Let me talk to him," Ian says. "I'm not sure what to do here."

I start bustling, as is my wont in times of strain. I decide to make brownies. If he's coming, there'll have to be some decent dessert on hand. I retrieve my grandmother Birch's recipe from the back of *Fannie Farmer*. I follow the loopy script, scrawled generously across the yellowed piece of lined paper, conscious all the while of Ian on the phone with Mal, his even interrogatives, his outrage eloquent now that he's not directing it at his ex-wife. The recipe calls for "pinches" of this and that, elements "to taste" and baking "until done." As a child, I watched Birch put things together, guesswork, but now I'm nervous I won't be able to duplicate her success. I'm sure I'll make some small mistake that will amount to disaster.

"You've got a lot to make up for." I'm struck by the irony of what he's saying: so many of our discussions have centered on how much *he* feels he has to make up for.

How will we do this? I wonder, once the brownies are in

the oven. Perhaps he'll just get absorbed in all the household activity. I'm hard at work on the books by six-thirty, then in the afternoons the littles come. There are four of them, Ralph, Electra, Winifred, and Kyle, and they're all in first grade, hardly *little*. But I get away with calling them so because sometimes Kyle's younger brother comes and he's sixteen months, too fat to walk and, on rough days, a good reason for me to go on living. They all get picked up by six, except for Winifred, whose mother is pathologically late, and I've got time to straighten the apartment before Ian gets home.

He appears in the kitchen doorway, puts his glasses down on the counter and rubs his eyes.

"Well?"

"He wants to come here. I said I'd talk to you."

"Maybe he can help me with the kids in the afternoons," I say.

"Don't bet on it." Ian, my Eeyore. Although he strikes a pessimist pose as a rule, there is justification for this kind of thinking. There's a theory being bandied between the households that sibling rivalry is the reason for the drug infractions. Dorothy and Jeremy had a baby about a year ago. Once in a while they take time away from adoring the new extension of themselves for a brilliant deduction.

"Where else could he go?" I say, certain, the minute I say it, that I've sealed my own doom.

"It would only be for a little while," Ian says. "But he pulls any of that sort of garbage in this house, and he'll find himself in an SRO."

"Will Dorothy be visiting much?" I ask lightly, meaning *over my dead body*.

He laughs. "Just for breakfast."

"When's all this going to occur?" I ask.

"Soon as possible. She's already packed his things for him."

Determined, that's Dorothy.

"He's old enough to pack for himself," I muse.

Ian takes me in his long arms, kisses my ear. "You're a wonder," he says.

I draw back, look at him, his handsome height. "Don't speak too soon."

I turn on the oven light. I think I smell fire.

I wrap the brownies in wax paper and put them out of reach of the ravenous four, who will no doubt complain about having to eat plain Teddy Grahams in a house that smells like chocolate.

"You *never* give us anything good to eat!" Winifred often wails.

"Yeah, *Pager*," Ralph scolds. My name is Paige. He got the nickname from his doctor father, who has money enough to send him to an accredited after-school program, but gets me instead, for half the price and no decent snacks.

They've been coming to me for over a year now, so I've learned to anticipate meltdown and switch quickly to an absorbing activity or outing before Rome falls. I do miscalculate from time to time, and then I have to beg Kyle to use his words instead of hitting, or bodily restrain Electra from a disruptive dance number, or apologize to Winifred for my imperfections, or tell Ralph that he can't sue me for malpractice. These times are eased if the baby's around because I can always hide in some problem he might be having. I toe the line, count to ten instead of screaming, go in the other room for three deep breaths, pray to the God I've neglected since forever to still my temper. That something I do or say could cause their parents to stop bringing them, stop depending on me to gather them in from the world of formal school each afternoon, *be* three hours of their lives, is too sickening a thought to entertain.

"God, these are good," Ian says, on the Brooklyn Bridge. "What did you do that was different?"

"Nothing," I admit. "I just followed the recipe." We're inching along through merciless rain. We've had four each. *Nervous eating*, I call it, as when Ralph gobbles up a doughnut faster than I can get it on the plate, then asks for the box.

"I'm telling you, they're different," he says. "Best ever. Hand me another."

I tell him that will make five. He says he has to keep the tire about his middle inflated.

"I don't think of it as a tire," I say, passing him one. "It's more like a love zone, there for me to squeeze."

I reach over and squeeze gently. What he has there can hardly qualify as fat. Tall and lean as he is, it seems a mere interruption.

"Thank you," he says. "Apparently the more there is of me, the better you feel."

"Something like that."

"Okay, I won't eat any more." Now his tone is mournful. The whole way it has vacillated between this and furious.

"We could save one or two for Mal."

"Ha!" he shouts, slapping the steering wheel. "You don't think he's been making his own?"

I should probably be more on my guard. An observer of the way Ian manages his duties as absentee father and of the way Mal manages Ian, I have felt oddly safe. They seem to fling themselves around and occasionally collide, armed with tempers so fierce that they can render any space untenable for all involved. I stand by with the quick answer, making mental notes as to the whereabouts of the first-aid kit, the Domestic Incident hotline. Caring for the fabulous four and volunteering at St. Luke's have taught me, in part, to think this way, although help of this nature has not been called for to date. There have certainly been cuts and bumped heads and, once, a tooth penetrating a lip, but no surgery so far.

"Who the hell does he know can get him the stuff?" Ian says, amazed and injured. I look out at the soaked periphery, the encroaching dark. It's the end of September, but it feels much later in the season, largely, I figure, because we're traveling above open water, where it's cooler. "I don't think you have to *know* anyone," I say. "Maybe it's just people hanging out at the Seven-Eleven." *And in this dreary weather*, I'd like to add, *who wouldn't be running contraband?*

"I guess this means you've decided against the second house," he jests.

"Was it going to be up here?" We've been having trouble scraping together the maintenance each month, after Mal's tuition, even with my baby-sitting money, which I don't declare. A second house would equal ruin. The car we're riding in is our second home.

"I think it's going to have to remain a concept."

"That's okay with me."

Neither of us grew up with houses in reserve. Our families were inventive and grateful about vacations. And we aren't weekend people. We stay in the city, except for a week at the shore, any shore, now and then. Never vacation in the same place twice, Ian says. That way you avoid boredom and relatives. His years with Dorothy taught him this. "It's because you always had to go to Florida," I said once. I used to stay with Birch in the summer. Her house in western Massachusetts was close to a lake, "the small beach," by family designation. When Birch died, I was already in college and had friends to mooch off on summer weekends. The rest of the time I worked, in libraries, bookstores, restaurants, one summer at a dank little cinema near the college campus.

"When you think about the hell a second house can provide," Ian says, "I judge us pretty lucky."

"We *are* lucky!" I say. It sounds forced, as if I am trying to convince myself of this in light of what is about to happen to our only home. Already Ian has begun making lists of rules for Mal to follow as far as conduct in the apartment is concerned. Suddenly the kitchen has become a sacred zone, the living room a museum, the bedrooms cordoned off by caveats. There is a list for every one of the four rooms. I don't think *I* can keep to form. And I know the littles can't. Barbie's Summer Dream House, which I never take down because the boys love it, has been pushed under the desk. Each afternoon I have to remember to haul it out so no one will get upset.

"What sort of welcome is a house that shows no signs of wear?" I asked.

"If he sees a mess, he'll only add to it," Ian said.

I like mess, to a point. It bespeaks liveliness and fun, in our house anyway. On rainy days, when we can't get to the playground, the kids and I make forts, Winifred playing princess, Ralph and Kyle warriors, Electra, the daughter of musicians, wandering minstrel. When he comes, I keep the baby with me under the card table draped with bedspreads, and we await word from the powers that be. I am at my happiest after a day like this, when evidence of our good time is everywhere and no amount of laundering can destroy it. Why *wouldn't* Mal want to play a role in the destruction?

"These wipers stink," Ian says. "I really should stop."

"We're practically there," I point out. "And you have to order the blades specially anyway."

I know everything about the car. I bring the manual in and read it in bed while Ian works late to meet the payment schedule. I love its smooth seats and new smell and futuristic dashboard. On two occasions, after we bought new CDs, I've taken the littles out to the car because music sounds better in there than in the apartment. With a bag of Cheetos and juice boxes, it's just as good as being at home.

"Figures."

"Oh, Ian, lighten up. Think of this as an end to a bad chapter. We'll start the new one and just see how it goes."

"That's expensive theory," he says.

It was Ian's idea to send Mal to private school. As reasons he cited the crippling homogeneity of the yeshiva, the fact that Mal's grades could not earn him a place in any of the three decent city high schools. At a school where the student-teacher ratio was a little bit more advantageous than thirty-to-one, Ian argued, Mal might stand more of a chance.

This theory was blown to smithereens after the baby was born. Mal had been at Bay Ridge under a year when he got suspended, along with a posse of seniors found smoking pot on the fringe of the campus. When the school psychologist mentioned Mal's need for more attention from his biological parents, Mal ran with it. "It's a king's name," he said, of Solomon. Neither Ian nor I had the heart to remind him that he'd been named for a prophet.

We went to the baby's *bris*, which I found nearly unendurable for nontraditional reasons. The fact of the gathering aside, watching Mal greet guests he might rather have suffered a second circumcision than share air with was difficult. I saw his eyebrows lift, then fall sharply with each extraordinary entrance. I wanted to go and stand by him at the door, but anticipated too much confusion as to who I was or what, given who I was, I thought I was doing there. Dorothy, back in full social swing just eight days postpartum, fluttered around her son as adorably and insensitively as a teenager. I envied her the baby, of course, but I was surprised to find that I envied her Mal. I've kept myself, purposely, at a remove from him that none of my friends with stepchildren can fathom possible.

"Maybe he can finish the degree by mail," I say.

"Not a chance."

He's too disappointed to think about alternatives. The baby thing—ours—has brought this to the fore as well. After the second in-vitro, I begged him to let me start the arduous adoption process, one which threatened disappointment at every turn. I started a Birth Mother Hotline with my other childless friends, but we got more crank calls than real ones. Ian begged me to stop chasing the dream-turned-nightmare. I accepted that he was too depressed, then suspected him of a clannishness that precluded his raising another person's child. I put the literature in my bedside-table drawer and eventually threw it away.

"What about a public school?" I press on.

"He can't get into any of the good ones."

"I went to one of the not-so-good ones. It didn't hurt me any."

"You know what those schools are like now. They'd only foster the worst in him. Anyway, you went when it was safe. That was over twenty-five years ago."

"Thanks for the reminder. Maybe he's just not cut out for study," I say. "He wants to play music. Why not let him?" I've got Electra in mind, gyrating to *The Spice Girls*, which we bought at Coconuts one rainy afternoon.

"I don't want him to *starve*," Ian says bitterly. "You're starting to sound like Dorothy."

Ian slaved his way through Yale as a busboy in a frat house, *watching the finest bulk up*. Why won't his son work?

Whence this aversion to labor, decorum, and loyalty? Ian and I are from bookish families, and we have advanced degrees, if mine in bookbinding counts. Mal's boredom with books is an affront, more so to Ian and me than to Dorothy, who, Ian insists, wouldn't know an academy if she fell over one.

"I can't tell you how it burns me up that I'm driving this beautiful machine the law has furnished us, to go pick up my kid who feels no compunction whatsoever to observe that law."

I think this is too simple and say so.

"You think I'm being unfair," he surmises.

"No," I say. "That's not it." I can't set it up for him, the equation that will define Mal's place in all of our shifting lives.

Ian finds a spot in front of the building. "He won't be ready, you watch."

❧ TWO ❧

A few things are certain, and I cling to these. This boy is going to live with us, in the room that until now has been my office. I've moved my press into the living room, my hand tools, adhesives, and cutting boards to the top of the fridge, out of six-year-old reach.

"What do I care? I only go in there to get things," I told Ian.

I prefer to lay my materials out on the kitchen table anyway, close to coffee and water and the junk du jour, which I buy at the corner deli each morning. This week I sank to Twinkies, but a blast of sugar equals momentary energy and optimism—yes, I can manage Malachi, whatever the circumstances, happy to take him on, happy to part with a fruit pie or two. I suffer from a stupefying conviction, given all my schooling, that if one plunges raw-nerved into life, one will invariably emerge the victor.

"He'll never be able to call *you* Stepwitch," my friend Toni said. "But don't give him *too* much. He'll take advantage."

Toni has three stepchildren who live with her, all girls. They are stunning to look at, with oblong, pale faces and rich, dark hair. Toni brushes this hair for the two younger ones and stays up with Olivia, the oldest, whose insomnia her father can't handle.

"*You're* their mother," I roar, when she's at her wits' end about their oblivious *real* mother, who blows into town without warning and sweeps them up into a whirlwind of shopping, theater, and high tea.

"I can't compete with that," Toni moans.

"What's to compete with? You're there, she's not."

"Just wait. You can be there all you want, and you're still invisible."

In the last year I've lost my father and any prayer of having a child. I do not believe that more can claim me than already has, so I said it would be fine for Mal to have the room. But unlike Toni, Bibiana, and Patty, with whom I gather almost weekly at restaurants, I have been lucky not to have to spend grueling, thankless hours in the company of children destined to hate me. I met Mal when he was thirteen, already man-sized but not filled out, a replica of his father except for his eyes, which are round and long-lashed, like Dorothy's. The three of us convened for a bistro dinner during which the only comment that vaguely resembled a complaint was "She looks like she's in college, Dad." I loved him instantly for that, given that my actual age at the time was thirty-five. I'd felt inspected, to be sure, on my guard, but ultimately vindicated. On my worst days, when my hair won't behave and my face looks gaunt and no amount of activity can dispel the fact that I am pear-shaped and forty, I recall the compliment as, it seemed, my father hung on certain phrases culled from all manner of literature, phrases to remind one of one's place on the planet, small, to be briefly enjoyed. Mal's comment surprised me, a blessing out of the blue.

For five years I've seen him with his father only for brief intervals, at movie theaters, restaurants, museums, the odd obligatory family event. My friends advise attending everything, but these dissolute events have done little to enhance my knowledge of Mal. At dinner, "Hen Night," as Ian prefers to call it, Patty said, "You only know this kid in *public*. And now you're giving up your office for him? I think you're insane."

"Ditto," said Toni.

"It's going to be difficult," Bibiana predicted. The Italian second wife of Leonard, who is, as Mal might say, "way high" at Citibank, she faces her life with his progeny, two horrifically spoiled boys named Jules and Sam, with the sort of quiet courage I'll have to muster, if the prediction holds.

Less dooming was the advice of Diana, my college roommate, an occasional honored guest on Hen Night. She doesn't exactly qualify for the group, as she isn't a second wife and she has real children. She hasn't suffered the in-vitro nightmare the rest of us have.

"Jump in," Diana said. "What choice do you have?"

I feel tense, entering the building.

"You don't have to come up. It isn't going to be fun."

"It hasn't been all that fun yet anyway!" I say.

"No?" He puts a finger revolver to his temple, holds off pressing the elevator button. "You're so sane," he says, holding my face. "How can you be so sane?"

Sane? Busy perhaps. Coping. Charging psychiatrist's

rates to mend wounded books, aided by a steady infusion of Hostess products, competing with *Reading Rainbow* and *Kratt's Creatures* in the afternoon (most of the arguing I do with the kids is over TV, which I maintain, until I'm ready to drop, is noninteractive and inferior, even to arguing), keeping up with friends and my mother, and biweekly visits to St. Luke's, where I push the book cart through realms that assure me I am blessed, despite my infertility. But if every day is a race, a flurry of plan and execution, to stave off dwelling on loss, I don't think I can honestly claim sanity.

"Come on," I tell him. "We're keeping him waiting."

We go in, arm in arm, like people already past middle age, worried about slipping.

He appears in the hallway, right in front of us. He has his hair cut in the new way, shaved below the ears, parted and styled above, half English schoolboy, half homeboy. It must be wonderful, I think, to expose so much of your face and skin, to be that free with yourself. He looks terrific for someone who's been threatening to bring down the reputation of a Puritan stronghold.

"Hey, whuddup," he says. "I see you came armed."

I store this, for Hen Night.

"I brought my wife," Ian tells him curtly.

"Whatever." He ducks into the apartment. He has to duck, as his father does, for standard moldings.

"I hope you're packed," his father says. "We want to get some dinner."

"Cool."

I see the baby on his activity blanket in the living room, the nanny on her knees beside him watching TV.

"Where's your mother?" Ian asks.

"Out," Mal says, heaving a duffel bag into the front hall. "She didn't want to be around for this."

"Such is the nature of decrees from on high," Ian mutters.

I stay in the hall, out of the fray. Out of it, period. I marvel at the art, an original Chagall, a Hockney. I feel quite
downscale. I may as well be wearing milking togs, a long-
sleeved, floor-length sackcloth dress moored to me by a crisp
apron, matching cotton bonnet.

I hear quick, harsh argument, peer in and make a useless
gesture toward the baggage and a number of small boxes of
CDs.

"Here," Mal says. He holds out a basketball. "My most
prized possession."

I take it. He smiles. I think he might be trying to apologize.

"Later, Lizzie," Mal tells the nanny without even entering the living room. One day Ralph will be like this, I think.
And my other doughboy, Anthony. What tragedy.

Ian takes up one of the duffels. I'm glad he isn't speaking.
Who knows what could explode from him at this point.

"I'll come back up for the CDs," he says. God forbid he
should salvage some books from this career. *Jesus*, I feel like
saying, an evening of our ruminating over the book bill
flashing to mind.

"So, like, Paige, to what do I owe this pleasure?"

I hate his tone, the crass assumption that I'll celebrate it.

"I thought you and your father could use some help."

"I can carry suitcases," he reminds me at the building's
entrance. For a second I fear he'll let the door slam on me,
but he holds it open, dropping the duffel to accommodate a
chivalrous sweep of his dunking arm.

"Thanks," I say, then hold the door for Ian.

"What a prince, right?" Ian says, exhaling.

"Easy," I tell him.

We form a line and trudge to the car. Ian heaves the duf-

fel bag in back, then snatches Mal's from him. "Go see to
your boxes," he orders furiously. I set the basketball on the
floor between the seats and get in back.

"What are you doing?" Ian asks.

"Avoiding the fray."

"Don't you dare sit in the backseat," he says. I get out
and wait in the drizzle. I'd rather get wet, I reason, than cross
him now.

Mal brings the boxes over to the car. He seems impervi-
ous to the rain, doesn't hunch his shoulders or bow his head.

"Is that it?" his father says.

"The whole shmegeggy."

I can see how Mal's crispness is hitting Ian, in the jerky
force Ian is lending to all his efforts.

"Do you have *anything* to say in reaction to any of this?"
Ian demands.

"Yeah," Mal shouts. "As a matter of fact I do! Jews don't
go to prep school! In case you hadn't heard!"

"*Jews?*" Ian shouts back.

"Yeah, Dad, I'm a Jew. Remember?"

"Who could *forget?*"

"Guys," I beg. "Let's just go eat."

Both men slam into the car, and I follow suit more
civilly. Then Ian roars around the corner at breakneck speed.

"Kick some game!" Mal says.

"*Speak the language*," Ian orders.

We end up at a pizzeria. "A farewell 'za for the kid," Mal
says, picking up a mushroom slice.

"Change the subject," Ian tells him.

"Tell us about Avi's party," I say. A few weekends ago
Dorothy's father flew in from Israel to be feted at some
Midtown hotel for his seventieth birthday.

"My grandfather's a maniac, what can I say?"

"Was there dancing?" I picture strobe lights and a DJ making announcements about the importance of family, tears smearing the makeup of those who would find the references affecting.

"People *still* can't get enough of Los Del Rio," Mal says. He rolls the *r* forever. Then he brings a fist microphone to his mouth, practically eating it, and puts on a pout: "*I am not trying to seduce you.*"

I laugh, imagining Jeremy and Dorothy and Avi lined up to follow some underpaid dance instructor's Macarena, certain that my afternoon lineup could do them one better.

"What about the drum set?" Ian intervenes. Another walletful.

"My friend Doyle," Mal says. "He's got an Explorer. He'll bring them over next weekend. His dad just gave the school ten million."

"Christ," Ian says, setting his beer mug down.

"They're spreading it out over a few years," Mal explains, "so it looks like less."

"They're spreading it out over a few years," Ian says, "so it will cost them less."

"Dad, Dad, Dad," Mal says. "If they were worried about money, why would they be parting with the ten mil?"

"My son, the financial analyst," Ian sighs. He's teetering on tender, perhaps coming down from the podium of rage for a breather. If he can forgive Mal the financial expertise, maybe he can forgive the other felonies.

"So what music are you playing these days?" I ask.

"Rap, mostly. But it's tough to find anyone who knows anything about it in that school. It's all baloney on Sunbeam bread there. It'll be easier downtown." He nods several slow times at that certainty, and Ian laughs caustically.

"Nothing is easier downtown, Malachi."

Mal smiles. "Rap is."

Electra whirls, rapping into her Baby Spice fist: If you *can* dance, if you can *dance!*

"Don't you have to be a little more in tune with *struggle* to play that music?" Ian asks. "Don't you have to know something about poverty and crime?" He stops himself. Mal is sort of up on crime, lest we forget.

"Get a clue, Dad," Mal says. "All you need to have is your dignity compromised and an ear and some idea about rage."

"Oh, well, in that case, allow me to join up," Ian says.

For Mal rap makes sense: he can hide in it, unprovoked, or no more provoked than he already is.

"I don't know, Dad. The brothers might not be able to deal. You're whiter than I am. It was hard enough getting the *two* black kids at the Ridge to even believe I could play drums."

"White is white," Ian says. "And you're white, no matter what music you play."

"Okay, Dad, take it easy."

"Do you want another slice?" Ian asks Mal with forced easiness.

"No, I'm okay," Mal says.

"You're sure?"

"Yeah, Dad, I'm sure."

He stretches out in back after dinner. I hold Ian's coffee-to-go in both hands, trying to warm up. I feel calmer, after the food and one or two glimmers of sympathy from Ian. He's given Mal his sweater, forced him to put it on. I think Mal might be asleep and turn around to check.

"I'm fine, Paige," he says. "I'm not one of your *littles*."

I let that go. "I just wanted to see if I could put on a CD you'll hate," I say.

"Go ahead," he says sleepily. "Try me."

I put in George Winston's *December*, which right away seems a bad choice.

"If we weren't thinking about winter, we have to now," Mal says.

"Never hurts to think ahead," Ian points out. "And it is nearly freezing." The digital register on the dash says 45 degrees, cold enough for late September, but not deserving of such extreme description. Mal puts his head between the seats to check.

"I love this car!" he cries. "Automatic temperature readings, CD player, fine leather appointments! Good work, Dad!"

"It *is* work," Ian asserts. "Two years' worth of bonuses, and some."

"All right, Ian," I chide. "We know you work harder than a draft horse and you put us all to shame."

"Well said." Ian looks at Mal for a second. "Anything you want to know about this vehicle you ask Paige. She memorized the manual."

"No shit!" He pops me on the shoulder. "Girls don't usually do that stuff."

"She's not a girl," Ian tells Mal.

"Sorry." Mal reclines again. "*Women*, I meant."

"There are a few phrases you'll have to alter, moving from your mother's house to ours," Ian warns.

"Romper Room, you mean," Mal says.

I hand Ian his coffee and lean back. I'm agitated. I don't know what to make of Mal: if retrieving him has made me this tired, how will it be to have him in the apartment all the time? My mother asked the same question when I called to

say Mal had been kicked out of school and he was coming to
live with us.

"Can't his *mother* take him?" Frannie asked. "You have
enough flux over there."

"His mother took him for the first fourteen years," I said,
shocking myself by defending Dorothy. "She can't take him
anymore."

I am beginning to understand why this might be. A
teenager is a different bundle of work, not to be appeased by
jump ropes and snack time, and Mal, with his remote
agenda, delicious looks, and sarcasm balled up into one, is
particularly exhausting. Throw in a stepfather and a new
baby: warfare, on a daily basis.

"I don't know why I've suddenly gotten so tired," I tell
the two of them, as we get off the West Side Highway.

As a rule, on Hen Night, I try to steer clear of group misery, try not to echo the status quo, so my report won't take
the form of complaint. And it isn't awful yet, having him
with us. In fact, it's sort of interesting. It puts me on edge.
And like my father, I do best when on edge.

❦ THREE ❧

When I realized that my profession as bookbinder precluded a steady income, perhaps an income of any sort, I put an ad up in the elevator for tutoring in English, which swiftly took the form of afternoon childcare.

"Well, she doesn't really *read* yet," Winifred's mother said after a neighbor gave her my number. "She's four."

"He's still in pre-K," Ralph's father barked from the cellular phone. "But I can have him dropped off by bus every day. You won't have to pick him up." Dr. Eisman had heard in turn from Winifred's mother about my after-school program that very day, well before I had any idea I was running it. "He's got ADD. Do you have any familiarity with that?"

I knew a little just from an errant diagnosis Malachi once earned, later dismissed in favor of a simpler explanation for his inability to listen to Dorothy: who could?

"Does that sometimes depend on the company he's keeping, by any chance?" The joke was lost on Dr. Eisman, who remains to this day suspicious of everything I do but unwilling to fork over the funds for the bona fide program at Ralph's school.

Kyle came slamming into the three of us, Ralph, Winifred, and me, as we entered the playground in back of the museum one afternoon. His mother screamed at him, then at the baby.

"It's okay," I told her as I pulled Winifred howling from the cement, her knee scraped. "We'll manage."

Kyle's mother burst into tears at that point, said her husband had left them a month ago and she had to go back to work but she had no idea who she'd get to take care of them. The baby she could hand over to her mother on certain days, she said, but Kyle was too much for Grandma. "I'll take care of him," I told her. "I've already got these two. Pay me whatever you can."

How perilous a suggestion this last was became evident immediately, when I realized that my salary for looking after Kyle and Anthony would fluctuate according to New York's need for another freelance art dealer. I end up getting accounts for Johanna, just so I can get paid.

Electra was with her father while he played guitar on a hot day in Riverside Park. We listened for a long time, watched her dance. I got the kids in a huddle and suggested they ask her if she wanted to come to the playground with us. Wordless, she pointed to her dad. I cleared it up with him, said we'd be within sight and he could come get her when he'd finished playing for the day.

"James," he said to me, standing up and holding out his hand. For a musician, he struck me as strangely stern.

"Paige," I told him.

"Pied Piper Paige," he said. "You're good people."

So it's been for over a year. I didn't go off duty in the summer either. Ralph was squirreled away to Long Island for August, but other than that he'd arrive exhausted from three-quarters of a day at a Westchester camp. Electra did some performing-arts thing in the mornings, so I got her for the whole afternoon, and Kyle and Anthony were all-day regulars. The four of us would go collect Winifred from Bible camp at two every day, and then it was off to the John Jay pool or the zoo or a playground with a working sprinkler.

The Hens ask me how I stand it. For the money I'm getting, about six dollars per kid, per hour, nothing for the baby, they say I have to be out of my mind. "Out of my mind was before," I remind them. Before I met these children, I was walking a very thin line. I felt will-less and beat up by things medical—IVF surgeries, Daddy's cancer. Every day seemed a chore, and things between me and Ian were strained at best. The littles pulled me out of that place I kept letting myself go to, where things are random and scary and pointless. With them around, there's no time for this sort of indulgence.

"You're a wimp," Winifred told Ralph one day when he was dragging his heels about going to the Rustic Playground. I cowered as she turned to me, ready to defend myself as Ralph's keeper, certain that had she directed that same statement at me a month earlier, before I knew any of them, she'd have been right.

"Paige," she then said in her definite way, "what's a wimp?"

I write their adages and questions down in a composition book. I buy these by the stack at Odd Job, and on really beastly days we have journal time in the car, which, of course, is lost on the baby. Some day, I promise them, someone will find these books and treasure them, fix their pages and bindings, put them up for sale.

"And make money!" Ralph hoots.

"Money is the sponge of mankind," Winifred reminds us. She says she learned it in church.

"Scourge," I say.

"What's a scourge?" Winifred wants to know.

I think. Some questions really *shouldn't* be answered.

"It's sort of a terrible sponge," I say, my mind on those self-punishing types that fascinated Hawthorne. A surrogate parent's prerogative, helping to invent these secrets. A surrogate child's, to keep them. Sometimes I want to shake the dreariness out of Ian, tell him how lucky he is to have that store of secrets with his son, whatever they are.

We pile Mal's stuff in the front hall. "You can unpack all this tomorrow," Ian says. "We'll need to keep this area free of clutter."

Mal blinks dramatically, stepping back from the welcome into the living room and having a look around. I've meant to have the chairs redone, the carpet cleaned, but in view of what goes on in here in the afternoons, there's no point.

"Does anyone want anything to eat?" I say. "I've got those brownies from the car."

"What brownies?" Mal asks me. "There were brownies and you didn't tell me?"

I glare at Ian.

"No thanks," Ian says crisply.

"I'll take a couple," Mal says. "And a soda, if you have."

I think there's one in the fridge, left over from the Chinese takeout I ordered for the kids on Thursday. I get it, then put the last few brownies on a plate. The kitchen, spotless from my own efforts at welcoming Mal, looks foreign to me, a kitchen out of a different city, the controlled province of another woman altogether.

"Some heavy hitter from her agency is coming," Mal is saying when I come back in. He's slated to be at Dorothy's for dinner tomorrow even though she just essentially threw him out of the house. I set the Coke can down on a coaster on the butler's table that doubles as Fort Dix, and present Mal with the plate.

"I'm not sure what difference that makes," Ian says. "Seems to me you should eat dinner here for a while, if you're going to be living with us."

"She said it was good for the transition," Mal shrugs.

"She does know how to make a decision," Ian observes furiously.

"She's making a brisket, anyway."

Mal's doing what I find myself doing on occasion, grabbing at straws to cheer Ian up, coming out on the losing end.

"That'll be the nicest part," Ian says. "She's pretty angry."

"No, she's not," he says. "She's just tired. She told me."

"Yes, Malachi," Ian tells him, "she *is*. She was shouting at me from the Pepsi set. I know whereof I speak."

It's true. I was home. I could hear her shouting from across the room.

"Maybe that's because you buy Coke!" Mal says brightly, holding up the can, then taking a long, audible swig.

"I don't know how it is that you can make a joke like that, in light of what you've done," Ian challenges.

Mal studies the can.

"Ian, enough," I say.

"You're right, Dad," Mal said suddenly. "She's angry. At you."

"Here we go," Ian said.

Mal works on the Coke, all the time staring at his father. When he finishes it, he crunches the can in one hand.

"Oh, awful," I say. "You could cut your hand!"

Mal pushes at the air, at the huge precautions I'm asking him to take.

"Believe it or not, Paige," he chides, "I've done this before."

"Right," I say. I'm not used to being talked to in quite this way. I get more direct forms of admonition from the littles.

"So she likes the idea of her son selling drugs." Ian's tone is courtroom neutral.

"She thinks it's the wrong market," Mal says importantly, "but she appreciates the spirit of enterprise."

I lean on a chair back. "Is that *true?* She actually *said* that?"

I've taken Ian to task over Dorothy, but never Mal. I rationalize any untoward comment I make about Dorothy by virtue of what I know about her. She comes at you direct as a rocket, and there is no view of life, no way to proceed, other than the one she decrees right. Self-doubt is not in her vocabulary. And self-loathing? As she would say, forget about it. Plenty of others around to take care of that.

Mal smiles to himself, as if the bit about enterprise is something to be proud of. "That's my mother!" he says.

"And Jeremy?" Ian asks, as if Jeremy ever gets a word in edgewise. "I'll bet he's pretty intrigued by that spirit too."

Jeremy works on the floor of the stock market. I know about the stock market only from movies in which it is represented as frenetic and dehumanizing, not unlike marriage to Dorothy was for Ian.

"He wants a list of ten promises I'm making them as their son." With this Mal produces an extreme sneer and flings his arms in the air.

"There's a list I'd like to help you with!" Ian howls.

"Me too," I say. I figure the only thing that's keeping Ian

from the telephone is the fact that child-support payments will stop, now that Mal is living with us.

"Hey, these are killer," Mal says, his mouth full of two brownies. He makes light work of the third, then goes to the kitchen doorway and pitches the can from there. It thuds to the bottom of the rubber garbage bin.

"She appreciates the spirit of enterprise. We should all live so long," Ian mutters.

"You married her!" As long as I live, I won't understand that impulse of Ian's, will not be able to visualize him with Dorothy, contrary to the evidence that is turning my kitchen into a basketball court.

"I think I'm gonna crash," Mal announces. "Is there any particular place I should sleep?"

"I'm sorry I haven't got more of a selection of rooms," Ian says. "But Paige gave up her workroom for you. It's the smaller of the two bedrooms, I'm afraid."

Mal sets his long jaw against his father and turns down the hall, closing the door quietly behind him. What will he wear to sleep, I wonder? Has he given a thought to his teeth? It's so odd having him here overnight. He hasn't slept over except one or two times when I've been out of town. Dorothy never saw a need for it, seeing as we all lived in the same city. In truth, she was so resentful of Ian's finding comfort in me, of all the non-noteworthy people, that she couldn't allow her son to be in my company for longer than a lunch until Jeremy came on the scene.

"Maybe you should ease up just a little," I say. "It's got to be a little difficult for him too."

"We've been over that," Ian snaps.

The thing about other people's kids, when other people are your husband, Toni warned, *is that they expect the same from you as they do from their own mother, which really turns out to*

be more because when you're not their mother it feels like the god-
damn galaxy they want from you.

He didn't so much as ask for an extra pillow.

I can't sleep. I doze only enough to have one disturbing
dream, a fragment of an evening actually spent with Daddy
when I was about eight. He'd taken me down to the law firm
for dinner, cafeteria-style, given for the families of execu-
tives. Mother hadn't wanted to go, so it was just the two of
us pushing their trays along the rails, a new stuffed lion on
mine. In the dream we were picking out food and laughing
at our choices, and then I came to in a sweat, wild to see
Daddy, pick out food, laugh with him. Bed, with Ian snoring
off the travel, oblivious, seems a world of heartbreak, so I pull
on jeans and go into the kitchen and make coffee even
though it isn't yet four.

I fill the coffeemaker to ten instead of six. Usually Ian
has two, and I drink about four throughout the day, to stay
sharp for the littles. Maybe Mal will want some, and won't it
be nice if he does? Then we'll have coffee in common, at
least. Basketball, when Ian is glued to it on the TV, leaves
me cold.

I get my materials out of the wooden box I stuck in a corner of the kitchen and set up on the table with Daddy's
Treasure Island. I'm doing it for Ralph, who loves pirates, but
I won't give it to him until I have books ready for all of them.
Book work steadies me, takes me in like a friend. I separate
the sections that aren't already sundered from the spine and
collate them, then knock out the old joint, as per London
College of Printing instructions. I'm replacing the hollows
with a tight back on this one, a decision based on the cost of
leather and the time required to pare it. I fill the glue pot,
plug it in. Now, trimming the pages for a meticulous fore

edge, I think I can handle insomnia, infertility, and parent death. And stepmotherhood.

The days after no sleep I get firmer with plans for the kids so I won't lag, won't leave any doors open so they can walk in and visit my despair, take that home with them. I think this might be a good thing to do with Mal, too, who cares if he's ten years older. We all need our daily anchors.

"Paige?"

He comes in, opens the fridge, and hangs over the door. I get up and close the window, which I flung wide to keep myself awake. He's wearing the clothes he wore yesterday, and his feet are bare. He shuts the fridge and drains the orange-juice quart in long gulps. A little trickles down from the corner of his mouth, which he wipes with the back of one hand, while he tosses the empty carton into the sink. I watch, speechless.

"You working?" He stands, arms hanging, anticipating an answer to this.

It's after eleven. Ian's in the shower, having swept out an hour ago for a jog. He told me he was going to the office to cram for a trial as soon as he talked to Mal about the day's plans.

"Of course I'm working," I say, surprised by my own ire. "I've been up since four. When I get up that early, I get a lot done."

I've moved on from *Treasure Island*, now drying in the press in the living room, to work I'm actually being paid for by a private collector. There is no latitude here for invention; the man, a professor who became ornery at the slightest suggestion to alter the design of the original binding, wants the marbled endpapers replaced, the gold leaf restored, the French grooves reworked. All this for *Pale Fire*, such an irritating book.

He looks over my shoulder, smirks. How do the teachers bear them, I want to know, these smirking kids who'd rather watch people on MTV pretending to have sex or hanging from cliffs by rubber bands than open a book?

"I read *Lolita,*" he confesses.

"That one's better."

"I won't bother you," he says, and sits down, pretending to find the shaded windows in the apartment opposite of interest.

"No, no," I say. "I'm pretty much done here." It is unreasonable of me to expect him to slide quietly, neatly into place like a book on a shelf.

He hikes his broad, bony shoulders, sets them down. "I just thought we could go somewhere for breakfast."

I just scarfed two Yodels. "I ate already. How about some eggs and toast? I've called around to see if any of my friends with kids your age are in town this weekend. Your father made this list for today. You're a sight with the orange juice."

"Great," he says, yawning. "Another list." He ignores it, picking up the Yodels wrapper instead. "You didn't eat."

"Never mind," I say. "What about having a look at this list?" I've already read it four times and willed myself not to amend it. Now, though, the jogging suggestion seems luxurious, given that Mal has slept so long. I cross it out. Getting in touch with his friend Jessica's father, who might be able to get him some work, would be a better use of time.

Mal attends to the list in the same lethargic manner in which he drank the juice. "Christ," he mutters. "Like Dr. Abrahams is going to hire me. I don't know shit about medicine."

"Not in *his* office," I clarify. "He knows people who put out medical textbooks, and he thought they might have some ideas."

"Yeah, sure," Mal scoffs. "Like, pot cures cancer. Malachi would know about that."

"You're not going to make yourself too popular around here talking like that, Mal," I say. "I, for one, am unwilling to sit around and listen to you complain in this, my remaining workspace. I suggest you get dressed, if you can find anything clean to put on. That way, your breakfast idea will seem less outrageous to your father."

Who is *where?* My God, can he take his time in the bathroom.

Wagging his head, Mal shuffles out. He ducks through the doorway, runs his long fingers along the wall. I stare at the space he's occupied at the table, disbelieving that such a short interview can affect my spirits so considerably, can change the color of the day and put me, a person already challenged by a dearth of sleep, into more strenuous territory.

Ian comes in, putting his tie to rights. He pours himself coffee. "Mal up?"

"Mal up," I report. "But definitely not 'at 'em,' as you might say. He'd like to be taken to breakfast. It appears an English muffin and coffee won't do."

Ian frowns, then sits where Mal sat. "Did he have a look at this?" He indicates his handsome list.

"Do you *mind*, Ian?" Venom wells in me. "I'm trying to work here. If you've got instructions for your son, I wish you'd deliver them yourself. It's enough that you're planning to go to the office and leave Mal to his own devices all day, knowing what those are!"

He considers this with apt sobriety. "We'll see about that," he says. "Let me go talk to him."

I don't want a flare-up between them. It will land Mal in my lap for the day, and the ultimate reconciliation, later, will serve only to oust me once again, and I'll have to go the lonely way of the good Samaritan stepparent, as paved by Toni, Patty, and Bibiana.

"Just let's go into this gradually, okay?" I beg of him. "Don't go off to the office as if it's just a regular Saturday before trial."

He nods firmly. "Right you are."

No matter how many hurdles we've forged, my confidence in my ability to do so is perpetually challenged when it comes to Mal. There's too much I don't know, can't chip away at, about their seventeen years as relatives. Because of Mal, I'll never be certain that Ian and I can manage as a couple. There's too much likelihood of another irreparable rent in the fabric. And yet I stand here, darning needle at the ready, brave and idiotic.

I hear their voices but not their words. There is no shouting, but also, I suspect, no tenderness. I suppose this is only the start of a long fall of negotiating, and that I will be called upon to witness all the upset, to cajole, soothe, mediate, and camouflage my exhaustion and despair as the other Hens do, with even more activity, good works, and forced cheer. *What choice do you have?* I grab a jacket from the closet, find some lipstick in the pocket. It's not a daytime color, but I'm not in daytime humor, so I put it on anyway. I slip on my elf boots and wait for them in the front hall. Ian marches into the living room, thumb raised in triumph, over what, I have no idea. Mal follows, in the same button-down he had on yesterday when we picked him up.

"Laundry time," I deduce.

"I know. I'll do it. I just have to get some food first."

Patty would flip: *He does his own laundry?* Her (his) two are older than Mal by nearly a decade, and when they got wise that Patty wasn't a servant, they started bringing their clothes to a one-day laundry and charging the service to their father.

"Come on," I say. At this point I don't care that his hair isn't brushed or that he doesn't have clean clothes. I just want to feed him, watch him like the food, and be surprised, as I am with Ralph, by a sudden brimming over of his enthusiasm and energy. As if he's six, and there's still time for me to make a difference in his life.

He plucks his jean jacket, shredded at the cuffs, from the clothes tree. "You sure you don't mind going out?"

I face him. "Are you kidding?" I say, not at all myself. "I'm alone so much, I'm looking forward to the company."

Ian looks at me with suspicion, but Mal grins hugely, satisfaction moving into his features, coloring them. "Yeah?"

I feel like crying. "You bet."

☙ FOUR ☙

He seems young to me now, cutting his pancakes into fourths and devouring them.

"You're no fun," he tells me, "unless you eat this."

He holds a forkful in front of my face.

"Fantastic," I say, taking the plunge. "But in the end, not all that much healthier than a package of Hohos."

"You eat like a high-school student."

"I know people who love the way I eat. They're short, God knows, but they're wise."

"You're obsessed," Mal says. "Don't you ever stop talking about those kids?"

"At least someone else can talk to her about this now," Ian says. He's ordered nothing. He checks his watch. "Listen, son, I've got to get some things done by this afternoon. If you want, you can come along with me." He glances at me for approval.

"Nah," Mal says. "I've gotta do clothes."

"You're sure."

"He's *sure*," I say, suddenly worried that if Mal accepts, I'll be stuck with his laundry.

Ian kisses me on the top of my head, saying tenderly, like a lover leaving at dawn, "I won't be long."

"We'll be fine," I say. I actually feel charged, by the coffee or the pancakes or the different spirit we've found in the diner, I suppose by the possibility that Mal won't mind a day with me alone, even if I can't keep him free of talk about the children.

"Seriously," Mal says, once his father has left, "why do you eat that shit?"

"I like to. Isn't that why you smoke dope?"

"I *don't* smoke dope," he says.

"Excuse me?"

"I told you last night," he goes on. "I was just trying to make some money."

"But you don't need *money!*" My mind is on Dorothy's high six figures per annum, reported last month in one of the newspapers.

"I want my own money," he explains. "Not Dad's or Mom's or Jeremy's or yours."

"Well, you've got nothing to worry about on *that* score," I tell him. "I don't make enough for a beggar to sneeze at. But no one your age has their own money, Mal. Unless they're related to that person who gave the academy the ten million."

"That's what I'm *talking* about," Mal says. I love his pure intensity about the issue. Teenagers are so intense about everything, so hard core. "If we had our own money, we wouldn't get parked at the Ridge in the first place. Anyway, you make your own money, whatever it is, so you should understand."

"Yes, but at your age I didn't! I was practically penniless when I met your dad! And had I bagged school I'd probably be mopping the floor in this place instead of eating here."

"Is that why you married him?" His eyes get rounder with the accusation.

"Oh, I get it."

"Don't get crazy, Paige, I was just making a comment." He taps his fingers on the table's edge. He has short, filed nails. I suppose this is necessary, for dribbling and drumming.

"You're crossing a line," I tell him.

"*Okay.*" He pushes his empty plate away, toward me.

"Could we get something straight?" I push my coffee, undrinkable, toward him. Chess, with dishware.

"Shoot."

"We're *living* together now, you and I."

"So?"

"So don't appear from battle and expect everything to be how it never was. Your dad and I manage fine, whatever you think of us."

He puts his elbows on the table and presses the heels of his hands into his eye sockets. Then he looks up, focusing.

"You're managing like I'm managing, you know?"

"No," I say loudly. "I *don't* know."

He smiles into the chrome tabletop. "Sure you do. He's never home, is what. And all you do is talk about other people's kids."

"Malachi," I begin, "*you're* other people's kids. And I'm a big girl. Your dad's home plenty. He's home *enough.* Whatever grand failing it is that you perceive in him, let me assure you, he worries about you around the clock, and if he seems inattentive now and again, it may be because he has to work so hard to get you what he thinks you need. What, we now find out, you resent."

I saw Toni soften when Theresa, the middle stepdaughter, called in the middle of Hen Night. Toni treated us all to evidence of her claims about the children by talking at the table on the cellular phone. Theresa was at her wits' end because she couldn't get Laura into the tub. Toni ordered her to put Laura on. "Laura, my love," she said, "what is it about baths? Could I have a detail?"

However hard he wants to push me away, to make me suffer as he has, I've learned from Toni and Patty and Bibiana and Diana that I mustn't give him his way.

"Mal?"

"Yeah?"

"You want to go shopping?" My idea. This is *me* talking.

"What for?"

"You need a new jacket. I'm going to insist that if you don't get one, you borrow one of your father's. There's really no excuse for those cuffs. You're the son of a woman whose income gets reported in the newspaper."

"Is this what you do with the *littles*? Take them shopping?"

I must keep to form. "Sometimes we go shopping, yes. But usually it's for markers or candles or Beanie Babies. The kids tend to arrive at the house dressed."

He turns his wrists in the cuffs, giving my suggestion further thought, balancing it against Lord knows what else is on his private agenda for the day.

"Sure," he says. "I'm there."

"Great," I say. "We'll go to Modell's."

He grimaces, and counters with Patagonia.

"Just give this one a chance," I say. "Your dad bought his parka in there."

"Okay, if you're buying," he says.

"Hold it," I tell him outside the diner. "I'll put it on a card, but you're paying me back. Is that clear?"

"Crystal," he says. I charge on, he lopes along beside me. We proceed thus down Broadway, Mal chatty and animated for a change, myself, host to suspicion but determined to help him to a productive day.

Mal's presence in the store invites the detailed help of a man in a knit vest over a tie too elegant to be concealed under wool. "Nothing belted," Mal instructs.

"Of course not," the man says, busy searching. He retrieves something dun-colored from one of the racks, and Mal puts it on and strides over to the three-paneled mirror. In the mirror he turns one way, then the other, keeping his focus on himself. He's beautiful, but the jacket is seedy. Faux, shiny leather. What they call "pleather."

"Brown?" I ask.

"Pretty low-rent." He hands it and the hanger to me. *What in God's name am I doing?* Entering the realm of the beleaguered stepparent, one halting, misguided gesture at a time.

"How about something more sporty?" I ask. "Something waterproof?"

The salesman jumps in with a Gore-Tex suggestion.

Mal shakes his head. "I only wear that stuff to practice."

Which is a moot point, I keep myself from saying.

"Give me a second," the salesman says. He searches, brings forth a black jacket, lined, leather. Mal puts it on. It comes to his waist, accentuating shoulder breadth and his general trimness. Again he turns in the mirror.

"I'm thinking yes," the salesman says. "Not to would be a sin. Don't you think so, Mom?"

I nod, thrown. I don't approve of the leather, but I'm not up for a public disagreement right now.

"She's not my mother," Mal says.

"His mother is famous," I add. "I am not."

"I beg your pardon," the salesman says with a slight bow. He grazes the jacket at the elbow, redirecting. "It'll be warm in the winter. And the lining is removable for this kind of weather." He rolls his eyes, then shuts them against the painful unpredictability of early fall.

"We'll take it."

I fish for my wallet, slide out the Amex and give it to him. He stands for a moment, then pivots and goes off to perfect the transaction.

"I'm wearing it," Mal says.

"Evidently."

"I'm never taking it off." I might find this charming, but I'm annoyed and feeling sorry for the salesman. I wonder if Mal does this with the girls his age, makes promises he has no intention of honoring. I wonder if he behaves this way in front of his mother.

He bites the inch of plastic that secures the price tag, which falls to the floor. I pick it up, my stomach fluttering. One ninety-nine, ninety-nine. With tax it will be about two hundred and fifteen. The leather is of a lesser variety, rough and a little bumpy, something I'd have predicted would not be permissible.

"What's the damage?"

I can see him shopping with Dorothy, not having to ask this question. I tell him the price without tax.

He nods, unimpressed. "No sweat." His jaw works the way Ian's does when he's concentrating. I fret, pray he isn't cooking away at more drug deals. Then, in a second, he's circling me, posing: Marlboro Man, VH1 rocker, Bad Prepster.

Ralph and Kyle will be in heaven, meeting with such cool. And the girls, I suppose I have to let myself think of them as *girls* now that they're six, will back away with big eyes, wonder who let him in, then fall in love.

"How many people can you *be?*" I ask.

"I am the soul of the people, señorita," he announces. I have no idea whom he means to imitate now. Che Guevara? He worries me.

"Here we are," the salesman, much recovered, chirps. He holds out a thick catalogue as hard surface with the slip for me to sign. The poor creature has brought a shopping bag for Mal's rejected jean jacket, and he proceeds to stuff it in.

Outside Mal shakes my hand and says we have to celebrate. I allow him to drag me into Dunkin' Donuts, where he buys us an assorted dozen.

"You want?" he asks, pointing the cruller at me. "What is this anyway?"

"A cruller," I explain dutifully.

"Here, have it. It sounds like something *you'd* eat. It sounds like *crumpet.*"

"Why do you associate me with *crumpets?*" I ask, happy for the attention. As long as he's not on me about the littles, I can take whatever he's dishing out.

"They're probably things people eat when they're reading," he says. "Which is pretty much all you do, right?" He winks, but I feel pressed to defend myself all the same. We're sitting at the counter, looking out on the street. I have coffee. We have time.

"The people who eat crumpets," I begin, "and I do include myself in their crew, meaning that were I offered one I would certainly eat one, do so at teatime or at breakfast. And because they would most likely be at a table with family members or in a parlor with guests, they would not be reading. They would know that it is impolite to read in the company of familiars, of anyone really, unless one is on a train or a ferry or an airplane and those who surround you are total strangers and there is no prayer of conversation. Now, in the event that you want to know"—I hold up the cruller—"this is not a crumpet. It is drowning in sugar, which a crumpet would never be. A crumpet, in the true sense, is not sweetened. One puts jam on a crumpet."

"*Does* one!" he laughs, licking bits of doughnut glaze off his fingers.

"Indeed," I assert. "And one doesn't lick one's fingers. *Ever.*" I have hosted a few tea parties during after-school, and I've been informed by my guests that certain of their parents lick their fingers while eating. Brought up short by that information, I could only think of one thing to say, something Birch used to say to me: *You mustn't.*

"One has a lot to remember," he says with mock gravity.

"If one is not to be a barbarian," I say. I hand him a napkin. "Please."

"O-kay," he says. "For you I'll try not to be such a pig. But just for you."

"I'll be forever indebted."

He leans away, looking down from his full height at me. "You're not as boring as I thought you were."

"Thank you so much," I say.

"You're a little out of your mind, though," he says. "Do you consider yourself an eccentric?" His sudden seriousness indicates that he's aping a talk-show host—I wouldn't know which—but I sense he really might want to know the answer.

"Not really," I tell him, with like sobriety. "I'm more of a personal-shopper type."

*   *   *

We walk north in the strange heat the Modell's salesman alluded to so gloomily. Indian summer irritates me as well. Last night it was cold, and now we're back into T-shirt weather. Still, Mal keeps the jacket on. Outside the building Ramone, Mal's baseball friend and the most romantic of our doormen, is having a cigarette.

"Ramone! My main man!" Mal shouts.

"Mr. MacGowan, Jr.!" Ramone says, smiling widely. They update communication about the New York Yankees. Ramone comes up weekly to convey his anxiety to Mal via Ian's E-mail.

"Go on in," I tell Mal. "Start that laundry. I'm going to put the car in the garage. It's supposed to rain again later."

"All she thinks about is that car," Mal tells Ramone fondly. He probably won't make it upstairs before I get back. They'll be going over player status, who's being traded where, who hit what when, what the likelihood of a future is for this or that coach, how many millions will be offered a certain recruit for a life of play.

"I know, right?" Ramone says.

I get the car and drive it to the garage, where a woman is waiting for her car to be drawn out of the basement depths. A little boy stands by her and the assortment of durable luggage. I bring the keys to the office, where Harold is sitting in his director's chair talking on the phone.

"*Excuse me!*" the woman says, glaring at Harold, her lips pursed.

I step away, closer to the boy. The woman is telling Harold, clearly without help today, that she's been waiting for her car for more than fifteen minutes. Harold slams the phone down and storms out of the office into the gallery of cars that he takes an unusual interest in caring for. I don't move. I watch the boy, now kneeling over a shopping bag of toys. He's about four, I gather, picturing him between Anthony and Kyle. The woman returns, boot heels calling out victory. She looks at me.

"Is there a problem?"

"No," I stumble. "I was just worried he might wander off, where the cars come in and out."

"He would never do that," the woman assures me.

I look at the boy, who now has a wooden circus wagon out on the concrete and is taking all the animals out of it.

"I thought you were standing here because he was doing something *wrong*," the woman goes on, happy, I think, to find a new victim for her venting.

"He's just so adorable," I tell her.

"He can be," she says without expression.

I climb the ramp into the sun, prickling from the exchange. When I see people throwing tantrums in front of their children, I want to steal them, make them part of our company, already too big and various for the space I have. But I don't know what it's like to have a child around all the time. I don't know whether I'd love not being able to send the littles home at the end of the day.

There's a message from Ian, saying he'll be home around five. He sounds energized by productivity and the upcoming trial, a discrimination showdown in the suburbs. The wider the spaces, the narrower the minds, Ian has taken to saying as he is sunk further and further into disbelief by the facts of the case. And one from Dorothy, calling to put off dinner until tomorrow. Solomon has a stomach virus.

"Knock knock," I say at Mal's half-open door.

He's watching wrestling, lolling in the armchair, one sneakered foot tucked under him. It distresses me, seeing him glued to the TV.

"The littles will be here soon," I tell him. "We'll be going on a march."

"A march?" He comes to attention. "But this is Saturday. Don't they come on weekdays?"

"Yes. But we're practicing for the Veterans' Day parade."

"You want company?" He means it, I really believe he does.

"I do," I admit, "but first you should call your mother. She wants you to come tomorrow night instead because Solomon has a stomach virus."

"Figures," he said. "Kid's always sick."

"Hey," I say. "Promise me something."

"What?"

"You'll also come with me to the hospital tomorrow? I could really use your help taking books around to the folks in quarantine." If I make things sound threatening, maybe he'll come.

"You mean, like, AIDS people?" He's sitting forward now, his elbows on his knees.

"Exactly."

"Do I have to wear some kind of *space* suit?"

"Not exactly a space suit. But it will require a mask."

He puts his thumbs up. I'm exaggerating, in part. We'll get to the AIDS Unit, but my primary customer is a man named Marekki in the Metabolic Unit, not nearly as glamorous.

Marekki has chronic diabetes and has been in the hospital for a lot longer than the few years I've been volunteering. He hasn't seen its exterior in the time I've known him, except on pamphlets. Medicaid pays his bills, and, as far as I know, I'm his only regular visitor other than nurses and doctors. Still, Marekki maintains an eagerness, a level of involvement in matters political, athletic, and literary, that is surprising for a man doomed by his own glands.

I think about what their first meeting will be like, Mal's and Marekki's, what vestige of worry will flash over Mal's face, what delight will appear on Marekki's. Marekki will take in Mal's beauty with the solemnity it deserves, Mal Marekki's misfortune with camouflaged fear. Drama, threat, danger. That's what Mal likes. He's keeping the promise any-way, I think, as I rummage in the closet for hats and batons. And, for the moment, the one about never taking off the jacket.

"It'll work," I tell Johanna, who's come with a broken stroller and some string, her two sons hanging on her like fruit bats. "I'll get my stepson to help me rig it."

"It's just *too much*," Johanna moans. "I got a call from Carson's lawyer. I don't even *have* a lawyer."

"I'll be your lawyer, Mom," Kyle says brightly, at his tallest beside Anthony, sprawled on the tiled floor, wet Zweibach packed in his fat fists.

"Thank you, honey," Johanna says, nearly weeping.

I pick up the baby and tell Johanna to go.

"I don't know *when* I'll get back," she says. "I've got to go to a gallery in Tribeca, and there's something wrong with the subway."

"*Go*," I urge. "We've got things to do."

We watch her leave, as always, while we wait for the others.

"Mom's really sad," Kyle says matter-of-factly.

"Yes," I agree. "But she'll be okay."

"The good thing is they don't fight anymore," he asserts. "The bad thing is Daddy's gone."

Kyle has a good-thing-bad-thing way of seeing, which I haven't sought to amend. He needs to put things somewhere, in two boxes, good and bad. Whatever works.

"He's getting cookie in your *hair!*" Kyle screams, flustered as ever at Anthony.

"So he is," I say, trying to finger it out. Give me Anthony in any form, however, and I'm happy as a clam.

"When's Ralph going to be here?"

"Now," I say, spotting the Maserati as it pulls to a stop in front of the building. Ralph gets out, gives an exhausted wave to his father.

"Hey you," I say.

"I'm vanished," he tells me.

"*Famished.*" It would take a lot for Ralph to vanish. I take his backpack from his sweaty shoulders. "What have you got in here, Ralph? Rocks?"

"Flashlights," he says. "It's my collection for show-and-tell. I wanted to show you first."

I look inside, incredulous. Flashlights fill the space, all sizes, all colors, all, I'm assuming, values. Kyle crowds me, Anthony wants in.

"Keep your distance," Ralph orders. "I beg of you. They're worth a lot of money."

"Okay, guys, we'll do lights later," I say.

Ralph now begs to go upstairs, reminds me of the hunger factor. Winifred and Electra drag in with Ramone, who watches them as they come from the corner. The bus doesn't turn down our street.

"Hello, ladies," Ralph says, in a tired imitation of me.

"Hi," they say at the same time. They've had another fight, I can tell. Like little old ladies they are, kvetching at each other about this and that, forgetting they ever fought five minutes later.

"Listen up." I move Anthony to my other hip, out of my face. "There's someone upstairs I want you to meet."

"Who is it?" four times.

"He's a big kid. His name is Malachi."

"Oh yeah," Ralph says with confidence. "The guy in all the pictures."

"That very one."

"How come he's here?"

A perfectly reasonable question. Hard to answer cheerfully. Mal hasn't expressed any interest in meeting the littles. The one time Ian suggested it, Mal countered with the observation that he had enough little kids in his life, Solomon earning plural status.

"He's living here now," I state plainly.

"But you're not his mother," Winifred says.

"Ian's his father," I say.

"But where's his mother?" Winifred says.

At work, I want to say, but Ralph saves me with, "Who cares?"

"Does he have a Sega?" Kyle asks, jumping.

"He has a drum set," I say. "But it isn't here yet."

"Does he have a girlfriend?" Winifred wants to know instead.

"Oh God." Ralph shields himself from the question, from the effrontery that is Winifred.

Electra reaches for the baby's foot, affixed, prehensile, to my waist.

I herd them into the elevator, nerves a-jangle.

❦ FIVE ❧

"Hey," he says, shy as they are, no adult to hide behind.

"Hay is for horses," Winifred quips.

"I know where you got that," he says, and looks at me.

"Nuh-uh," Winifred argues. "No sir."

I announce that Malachi will lead the march to the boat basin.

"Who said anything about that?" he asks me.

"You said you wanted to come along," I remind him, patience draining. "I thought you might want to be first in line. You're the biggest."

He chews on this, and all of us watch for signs of cooperation. Even the baby is rapt.

"I'm not wearing a hat," he warns.

"Everyone has to wear a hat," Winifred tells him. "It's the rules."

I step in with a condition. "Since this is Malachi's first time marching with us, maybe we'll forgo the hat."

"Anthony can wear the hat!" Ralph offers, to group laughter.

Mal actually smiles at Ralph, who affirms their new collusion with a raised fist.

"Okay, good," I say generally. "I'll get all the food together, and we'll go. Mal, will you entertain this lot while I operate on the stroller?" I don't dare take him away from them by asking him to fix it instead.

He runs his fingers back through his hair, imitates a shiver. "Whatever you say, chief."

Electra and Winifred giggle at their new prospect, and Kyle and Ralph are already at the batons, dueling away for Mal's pleasure.

"Here," I whisper to him. "Take this baby."

Anthony reaches for Mal's shoulder, and I pass him on. Mal attempts to look pained, but that's not what I see.

"Bring me something to wipe this kid off with," he tells me, and my nerves and I make haste for the kitchen. There are moments that approach history-in-the-making stature, which I can't believe I'm witness to. This feels like one of those. I can't wait to tell the other Hens about how Mal takes care, assumes a role he may not want, for the good of all. As I hand him a damp cloth for the baby, I'm careful not to intrude.

"Anthony's a pig," Ralph despairs. "He always looks like that."

"You're a pig," Winifred says. "You eat too much."

"Shut up." Ralph sits on the sofa, covering his ample middle with angry, crossed arms.

"The good thing about Anthony is he sleeps a lot," Kyle explains to Mal, who nods.

"The bad thing is he's a *pig*," Ralph adds miserably.

"Let's just assume we're a motley crew and not call names," I advise.

We're even more motley with the addition of a teenager, making our merry way down the wide avenue in Riverside Park. Ralph's ahead with his largest flashlight, which looks like a gun. Kyle and Winifred keep in step behind me and the mangled stroller, which works by virtue of one cord tied every which way. I do my weak imitation of a drill sergeant, trusting that Mal is in back of Electra, who heeds, as always, her particular drummer. After a short spell we stop, and Mal comes over to me.

"Is she always like this?" he asks.

"Like what?"

"Like she's retarded or something," he whispers. "You talk to her, and it's like she doesn't hear you. She's like that guy in *Rain Man.*"

I don't want to talk about Electra in front of her or the other kids. "Things flip her out," James confided. "*Words.* She's been around, seen some stuff other kids haven't seen." *Fighting words*, he must have meant.

"She hears music in her head," I whisper back. "And that guy in *Rain Man* was a genius."

"Somebody should test her," he says.

"For brilliance?" I wink at him, something I never do.

"*For brain damage,*" he says fiercely.

I don't know whether to be touched or offended by his passion about this matter, so I let the whole thing go.

"Come here, troops," I shout. "Sustenance!"

I open the satchel of food and set it all out on a bench: Fig Newtons, string cheese, juice, Rice Dream for Electra. "Here," I say to Mal, handing him an orange soda.

"You're kidding, right?"

"You don't like orange soda?"

"Does anyone?"

"What about *lollipops?*" Winifred whines. "Those big lollipops you promised us, like in Candy Land?"

I love it, all of them at me about the dearth of good treats, about my sorry lack of attention.

"Fuck up your teeth," Malachi tells her.

"Speaking of low-rent," I mutter.

He cups his hand over his mouth. "Sorry. I forgot."

"He said *fuck!*" Kyle squeals.

Electra stops her swaying, stands still, eyes round with terror.

"He didn't mean to," I say quickly. "He won't say that anymore."

She then takes off at a run, to go find refuge behind a tree, the Styrofoam hat landing on the pavement.

"Stay here," I tell Mal. "This may take some doing."

"I said I was sorry," he calls after me. "What do you want from my life?"

I promise her he didn't mean it, it had nothing to do with her, but she won't stop crying. "It's just a word," I say. "A not very nice word. And he was talking about people's teeth anyway, not about you."

Electra's crying, like everything about her, is unusual, a high-pitched moan I don't know how she breathes through.

"He's," she says, after a few gasps.

"What, sweetie."

"M-mean."

"No he isn't," I tell her, although I may be wrong. "He's just sad."

I force her to look over at Mal, in the middle of the other four, now straining to lift Anthony, who's pitching a fit, out of his stroller. "See? He's trying to help the baby."

"Okay," she hiccups, bursting into tears again.

"Hu-ut!" I call out, imagining formation, turning up wrong again.

At the boat basin we watch the boats bump around in the waves.

"So this is what you do? Every day?" He's incredulous, shaking his head so his fine hair falls forward. I feel sorry for her, the woman he's destined for, whoever she may be, that she'll be subject to such judgment.

"Yes."

I know what I'm being accused of. Double escapism. Hiding in two worlds: the books and the kids. Compared to people who hold *real* jobs and qualify as *real* mothers, I am a pathetic imitator, a wannabe. A *non*-Dorothy.

"Don't you get tired?"

"Of them?" I indicate the lineup at the railing. Ralph and Kyle are arguing over the status of the sailboats, whether they're oceangoing or not. "No."

"What about when they get too old? What do you do then?"

"Don't be such a lawyer. Anyway, there are always more kids. And this one," I say, struggling to lift Anthony higher, "isn't going anywhere too soon."

Mal fiddles with the baby's moccasin. "What do they feed this kid anyway? Solomon looks like a famine victim. He's got no hair and all he does is scream."

"His father played professional basketball," I say, wincing. The one time I met Kyle's father, the whole family came, and it was one big putdown after the next. "He's huge."

"The other kid isn't huge."

We look at Kyle, jumping up and down in fury over a point about a boat, and at Ralph, twice Kyle's width.

"He has a growth issue," I report. "They wanted to put him on hormones, but Johanna said no."

"They *all* have issues," Mal complains. "They're all *nuts*. I mean, that thing about the swear word. What's up with that?"

"Electra reacts to strong language."

"Probably something going on at home," he says. "More *issues*."

"More on that later," I say.

I gather the kids for a story, spread the picnic blanket on the pavement, and sit down.

"Please please please don't tell us another one about your dad," Ralph begs.

"Just one more," I say. "Because he was such a good sailor!"

After I pass out more to eat, I begin: "Daddy really hated motorboats. Every time a motorboat cut into our path, sending us completely off course, he would threaten to call the Coast Guard."

We digress into a discussion about the water police, and onward.

"He was convinced that the occupants of large motorboats couldn't share in the subtleties about wind and water that sailors live by."

"What are suttletees?" Winifred wants to know.

Ralph shoots up a hand, as if this is school.

"Yes, Ralph."

"Manners."

"What you don't have," Winifred says.

"Shut up."

"Don't say *shut up*," she cackles. "It's bad manners!"

Mal laughs. "She's *good!*"

"It might be fun to try sailing sometime."

"You might get a mutiny," Mal pitches in.

"A mutiny!" Kyle hoots.

"Anyway," I continue, "when I sailed with Daddy, his tone was so harsh as he gave out orders to pull in the sheet, tighten the jib, come about, that it was difficult to have any fun *at all*. Daddy was in the Navy, and he barked out the orders, and you had to follow them."

I wait for questions, but somehow I've got their full attention.

"One September afternoon, when my hands were sore from holding the sheet—that's the rope attached to the sail—I let it go!"

"Were you *supposed* to?" Winifred wants to know.

"No. Here's the thing. There was such a blinding wind that I couldn't hold on to the rope anymore, and Daddy was up on the bow—that's the front of the boat—taking down the spinnaker, which is an extra sail you put on when you want to go really fast. But we'd gotten going *too fast!*"

"What *happened?*" Electra bursts out.

"She speaks," Mal mutters.

"Well, the boom, that's the metal rod the sail's attached to, swung into me and knocked me out of the boat!"

"Did you *drown?*" Kyle asks.

"Yeah, she drowned," Mal says. "Which is why she's still alive."

"Malachi?" I plead. "I'd like to finish?"

"What *happened?*"

"Just a second, sweetie. No cause for alarm! In jumped Daddy after me. *He saved my life!* But the boat *capsized!* Which means it turned completely over and we had to wait on the bottom of it, which was now the top, until the *Coast Guard* came!"

"Oh my God," Ralph says. "Holy Toledo."

Mal roars at this. "We've got a kid here who says *Holy Toledo!* Where'd you get that one, Ralphie-boy?"

"My dad. My dad talks *all the all the all the time.*"

"Like father like son!" Mal tells him.

"So what's the lesson for the day?" I do this, only because they're all so fond of closure.

"Don't let go of the rope!" Winifred, of course.

"Use a motorboat!" Kyle comes up with.

Ralph: "Stay on land."

"Big boy," Anthony says, pulling up on Mal's shoulder.

"I want to go home," Electra says in my ear.

I tell her I know, that we will. Home means my apartment, in this case.

"Those are terrific answers," I say. "You all pass."

"Do you like it here?" I ask Mal on the way back. "In the city, I mean?"

"Are you *kidding?* It's the only place for me."

And, I'm thinking, for the odd drug deal. And I happen to know, from Ian, that Mal loves camping. Like Ian, he's a parcel of contradictions. Ian says that as a Scot, which he is, distantly, his family having lived in Canada for generations, you have to be happy holding forth in the Edinburgh court and falling apart in a Glaswegian bar at the same time. I think Mal might rather join the Israeli army than admit to his descent from men who wore skirts.

"Me too. I like the *action.*" I'll be the open book, for his sake.

"You call this *action?*" He gestures hopelessly at the children.

I keep my head level, my eyes on his face. "I wanted a baby more than anything."

"I know," he says. "Dad told me."

"And these people," I say, indicating the children, "I need them. They're saving my life."

"They need *you*," he says, and takes after Electra, who's making friends with a distant tree. "Or a doctor."

I crave a chat with my father, whose wisdom was not always apparent but bloomed shortly before his death. After his first bout with cancer, he told me he was letting go of a raft of worries he'd always had about work and marriage and he was just going to do the things and see the people who made him happiest. He was going to sail his thirty-foot Pearson and eat in good restaurants and live in a house instead of an apartment, and he was going to be in the company of the women (Mother, Audrey, me) he loved. From then on, Mother and I, and Ian, when Mal was otherwise occupied, would go out to the house in Connecticut to observe the major holidays. This Christmas, Audrey is going to her son's, as there are grandchildren for her there. The system of visiting that Daddy set up has broken down. He would tell me to set up my own, in whatever manner I like, but I'm not sure how I'll do that. I suppose I could do the Christmas ham in the apartment, and Mother can come over and get horrified by Mal's smart tongue while Ian carves dutifully and stores commentary about the huge license Mal takes with everyone.

"Kids always surprise you," Diana said.

But *kids* are younger. *Kids* are people you know as babies. I walk fast. I'm starving. *Vanished.*

❧ SIX ❧

"Well, come home, why don't you!" Ian stands in the kitchen, his work clothes a mess of flour. He doesn't change clothes when he gets home from work. He lets whatever might happen to his suits happen. He hunkers down to get a look at the young folk. "Did she drive you to the brink of despair?"

"Where's that?" Ralph asks.

"Midtown," he teases. "Where my office is."

Electra approaches and yanks on Ian's tie. "Ding dong."

"Is the witch dead?" he asks. Standard hello between these two. Giggles abound.

"What are you doing?" I'm dizzy from hunger, but I think I can have a short conversation before falling into the refrigerator.

"Making a pie!" His face is red from the kneading effort.

"What an idea," Mal quips with a shrug of filial pride.

"How far did you get?" Ian asks. "Can I fix everyone a diet water?"

"Diet water!" goes the hue and cry.

"The boat pond. All of a mile."

He brings me the water. "For my sleek wife."

I'm embarrassed, thinking Mal must have a question about the word "sleek" in application to me. My shape would best be described as *sloping*.

I'm at the cupboard, hunting down the Wheat Thins, hungry urchins at my side.

"I picked up a lasagna," he says. "Mal, can you do the salad?" He presses the flattened dough into a pie tin.

"Wow," I say. "Crust from scratch."

I cram four Wheat Thins into my mouth. "Did you have a good day?"

"Productive. We'll be ready for trial."

"Work's easier when you've got slaves, right Dad?" Mal teases.

"It's the truth." Ian has an assistant we call Paula the Paralegal.

"Lucky for you Paula has no life," Mal says.

"Can't argue with you there!" Ian says. "Let's go, son, I've got the crust done. We need to put stuff on the apples."

I settle the troops in front of *Sesame Street*. I lay Anthony on our bed, stacking pillows in a square around him like sandbags in a battlefield. When I return to the kitchen, I go for the cheddar.

"You eat all that, you won't have room for the feast!" Ian says as I break off a hunk.

"I ate junk today."

"What else is new," Mal says.

"Hey, look at that jacket! Wowser!"

"It looks good on him," I say. "It was expensive, but."

"So we'll take out a loan." I watch Ian quarter an apple with a too-small knife. "We're going to the game tonight, son. I splurged."

Curious, Ian's amnesia. Yesterday he could have killed Mal, and today he's spent a fortune on basketball tickets and opened a restaurant in our kitchen. I have no grounds for complaint, of course, given my bankrolling the jacket.

"The season started already?" It seems early for basketball, as if this matters to me one way or the other.

"Yeah. Duh," Mal scolds. "It never really stops."

"I'm going to go in and watch," I tell them. The cheese and crackers are rolling about, not doing their job. I waited too long to eat, then I ate too much too fast. I have no justification for it, the bingeing, the near passing out. I know, from recent years, that depression affects the appetite, makes one tired, but I'm not depressed. Overwhelmed, maybe. Domestically challenged.

"You have to *watch* with them?" Mal begs.

"I like to," I say. "*Sesame Street*'s about where I am."

"*Jesus*," he says.

Harsh, I'm thinking.

I can't imagine ever feeling well again. I go directly to the sofa, freeing myself of my sweatshirt on the way, letting it float to the floor. They all want to know when their mothers are coming. "When the show's over," I offer weakly, although I know it'll be seven-thirty before Johanna gets here.

When they call it seems way too soon. I sit up, dizzy and hot, trying to make room for what Ian is saying in my foggy brain. They're at the Garden. It's halftime.

"I slept through dinner?" I vaguely remember greeting

James with a wave. Winifred's mother, whose name, also Winifred, has been helpfully shortened to Freddie, came a bit later, as Ruth Buzzi sang "Put Down the Ducky" for the millionth time. And Johanna spilled in about seven, after which point I must have passed out.

"We came in, turned on lights, danced around the sofa, but you didn't move. I thought about hiring a prince!"

I don't want to think about it, Mal watching me sleep.

"So how is it? Are you having a good time?"

"Here, Mal wants to tell you himself." There's lots of noise, and a public announcement going on.

"Hey," Mal says. "You passed out."

"So I gather."

"So we're at halftime, Knicks trailing Pacers by four. Reggie the Executioner Miller is our man to watch, but unfortunately he's playing for the wrong team."

"Sounds good," I say. I'm thinking of the dinner I missed.

"Can we call you back when it gets crazy? Dad brought the flip phone."

"I got that. Call me back."

I sit a minute longer until I feel steady enough to get to the kitchen. The kitchen is bright and clean, which pleases me. I take the lasagna pan out of the fridge, find a clean spatula, and slide a section on a plate. I take a bite, then several more, wolfing it down. Then I have another section.

I put the lasagna pan back and draw out the pie tin. Ian and Mal finished half of the pie. I don't bother with serving, just get a clean fork and even off the edges, the way Daddy and I did with Sarah Lee's orange cake, until there were no more edges, until there was no more cake. There. Now I don't feel queasy. The food has grounded me. I'll be fat in the morning, but anything is better than feeling sick the way I did when I answered the phone.

Which I have to do again now.

"Eight minutes remaining in the third," Mal says, "Knicks leading sixty-seven to sixty-one. You want the breakdown in traveling violations and fast breaks?"

"It's okay. I'm just glad they're winning." I almost say something else, about what a sin it would be for New York to lose to—where? I have no idea where the Pacers are from. And why would they want to be named for horses?

"Dad wants to talk."

"Did you get some lasagna?" Ian asks. "I put everything away. Just shove it in the microwave for two minutes."

"I got some, thank you. It's wonderful."

"Okay, Sleeping Beauty," he says. "We'll get back to you."

Sleeping Beauty? My sleek wife? Too weird.

I think to go and see if there's anything on television, but when I stand up the dizzy feeling recalls itself and I have to sit back down. And the phone is ringing again anyway. I pick up, wondering what of any import to me can have transpired in that other setting in less than a minute.

"Hi." I can't place the voice. "It's Paula."

"Oh hi."

"I just wanted to tell Ian about something work-related."

"He's at a basketball game with Mal."

"I know," Paula says. "He just called me from there, and I totally forgot to tell him that they changed times on us for the deposition on Tuesday. I can't find the cell number. Can you tell him we've got to be there an hour earlier?"

"I'll tell him."

"Thanks a lot."

Poor Paula, deposition schedules preempting her home life. I will myself into the living room and sit on the sofa. Again the food I've inhaled turns traitor on me. Perhaps I

have flu, I think, channel-surfing. But it's too early in the
season for flu, and I never get sick. In my family there is no
vernacular extant for illness, except "not oneself." I suspect
that a cosmic punishment has been meted out for our penchant for secrecy, in the forms of infertility for me, cancer for
my father. I land on *America's Funniest Home Videos*.
Everyone seems overweight and unkempt, I think as I head
down that same road. Even the babies look ugly.

I should work. I should refine the sample for the Mark
Twain set Diana's mother gave me to rebind and cover. I
want to be able to explain my choice of covering to Mrs.
Alderman, although Diana says her mother is so vague that
it wouldn't matter if I covered them in plastic garbage bags.
There are eight volumes, and Mrs. Alderman wants to
donate them to the Beinecke Library at Yale, in her husband's name.

I turn off the TV. I can't work to save my soul. Why did
I eat like that? Whence this urge to stave off emptiness? I'm
not pregnant, I know that. Sex is too huge an effort. And in
our case, sex doesn't lead to pregnancy anyway. That's all I
can think about. Failure. Sex as failure.

The phone rings again. On the other end I hear shouting. One of them is holding the phone out into the crowd so
I can get the full effect. "*De-fense!*" I hear more times than I
need to.

"Hello?" I shout.

"Oakley missed the foul," Mal tells me, tortured, "so now
we're behind at eighty-five. Ewing's back in, and Wallace, so
we're set, but this Benson Askew guy is driving everybody
crazy. It's really touch and go, man."

Benson Askew?

"Let me talk to Dad," I say.

"Deal."

"Hello?" Ian says.

"Paula called."

"She did?"

"She said the trial time is moved up."

"Oh yes," Ian says. "I know about that."

"So why did she call then?"

"Beats me," he says. "She probably spaced. She's been working long hours, and she has no life."

This is a phrase the Hens have decided to outlaw. It is on our heads to insist that we have lives, even if these are largely determined by other people and other people's progeny.

"Well, that's all."

The noise is deafening.

"Okay, then. Wait! Mal wants a word."

"Hey," Mal says. "Just want you to know. This jacket? The guys on the *court* are looking at it."

"No wonder half of them are losing."

"How'd you know?" I can barely hear him.

I hear the roar of music, cheering, stamping.

"Shit!" Mal yells, right in my ear. "They got it! I don't believe this shit! Suckers!"

"Mal?"

"Gotta go!" he yells. "See ya!"

I pray the phone will never ring again. I feel worse at an angle, so I stay sitting up on the sofa. I haven't even turned on any lights.

The hall light goes on. Disoriented, I squint into it. They're hanging their coats up. Their heads nearly reach the ceiling.

"Paige?" Ian says.

"In here."

He turns on a light. "Are you sick?"

"I think so."

Mal stands slightly behind his father.

"Have you been on the sofa all night?"

"I think I have." I'm so uneasy. My stomach is a saddle of pain and I'm remembering unsettling things from earlier in the day. The near-argument in the diner. The fun in the doughnut shop. The talk at the boat basin.

Ian comes and sits on the far end of the sofa and Mal takes up a post by the mantel.

"We got you a hat," Mal says. He holds it up, one of those caps all the kids, even the girls, are wearing, backwards or forwards, thinking the style somehow distinguishes them.

"Thank you, but you wouldn't wear the hat *I* wanted *you* to wear." I put it on anyway.

"I'm crashing," he says. "See you guys in the morning."

He wanders off to bed.

"I don't like the expression *crash*," I say to Ian. "It's so desperate."

"Teenagers like to exaggerate," Ian says. "Another plea for attention."

"Seems to me he gets a lot of attention," I say. "He's pretty hard to ignore!"

"He's a big kid!" Ian says.

"With a big mouth," I add, grateful that for a second there isn't any anger.

"Do you think you have flu?" he asks. He starts rubbing my feet. I'm aware of not wanting him to do that. I bring my knees up, my feet out of his reach.

"I doubt it. I think I'm just tired. I ate more than any human being should ever have at a sitting. And this wacky weather. I got my summer stuff put away, and today they said it was almost eighty. So I went out and worked up a sweat and came back sick."

"Maybe Mal's making you sick!"

I have to admit that there's a screwy logic to this.

"You want some tea?"

"I hate tea."

"Then let's get you in bed. Tomorrow I'm getting him out of your hair. And he has dinner at his mother's."

I sit up slowly. He helps me to my feet, and I feel it, warm liquid between my legs. I stop in the bathroom and close the door. I step out of my underwear and put it in the sink under a rush of water. My period, which comes every few months, affects me so dramatically one would think it would be easy to predict. I eat like a pig beforehand, feel fluish, don't sleep, and let things affect me to degrees they ordinarily wouldn't. Still, it doesn't occur to me until I see the blood, because of the irregularity, that this, in fact, is what is wrong with me.

"I'm going to bed," I call out.

"Gotcha," Ian calls back.

When I was first informed about the endometriosis, the description horrified me. The specialist likened the condition to having several mini-uteruses within the regular structure, all responding to the menstrual impulse at once, magnifying the pain exponentially. I envisioned pink satellites of tissue wheeling in a small, dark universe, capricious. Malicious, even.

I stash my jeans in the hamper, wash my hands and face, do my teeth, and take my nightgown off the hook on the back of the door. It's a voluminous, cotton thing Mother gave me, and in it I look ageless and sexless and a little wistful, like an angel in a Neoclassical painting. Normally this image of myself might strike me as funny, but my ailment steals my humor. Thank God it comes so rarely.

❧ SEVEN ❧

I wait at the crosstown bus stop, irritated. Earlier, I passed Mal's half-open door and saw the mess of him sleeping on my way to the bathroom, and then, later, as I was gathering my profile of work for Mrs. Alderman's pointless perusal, I heard him thud out of bed and slam into the bathroom himself. I removed the *Treasure Island,* too long in the press, and set it on the shelf at the top of my closet, as if Mal were Anthony and might threaten it if I left it visible. The job is good, but the glue cracked a little when I lifted the front cover.

"Where are you going?" he demanded, as I was on my way out.

"Work," I told him. Wasn't it obvious? Why else would I be in a skirt and blazer?

"Yes," I snapped. "Can you imagine." I was impatient telling him where and why and that Dad was out jogging and

I really had to go now. I broke rules I hadn't imagined myself breaking, making the boy feel unwelcome in the only home currently being offered him.

I pick at the coffee lid, make a mess of that, then just take the thing off.

"Nice day," a man says. He's heavyset, with a reddish goatee and mustache, both well trimmed.

"Glorious day," I say, meaning to sound erudite and odd and to deter him from thinking about trying to sit near me on the bus.

"Well, if you put it that way!"

I've failed, it seems, to create the impression of threatening lunacy. I gulp coffee, praying that bad manners will do the trick.

When the bus comes I sit in one of the single seats. He goes astern, and I open my bag. As we cross the park, I plow through the banana-chocolate muffin and the coffee, so that by the time the bus reaches Fifth Avenue all I have left is garbage. I feel less fluttery, having eaten, and guilty for having been so rude to the man. I turn around, thinking I should apologize, but find he's gotten off already. The rear doors come together, the bus hisses, and we go riverward. I'm relieved to be on my way to Mrs. Alderman's, to be headed for a different sort of demand on me. Calmer. Less wrenching.

On my previous visit I came away with a rare sense of continuity about a certain fading ethos of New Yorkers, one to which my own family, had its disintegration not been so overt, might have remained attached. The decorative character of Mrs. Alderman's stunning apartment is familiar. Similar fabrics and furniture and wallpaper and room design embellished the large, numerous rooms of the apartments of one of my girlhood friends. On a more limited scale, the same taste prevailed in the apartment where I grew up. The tea, brought by the antique servant, evoked the enviable, occasionally tragic, lives of people in English and American novels from the turn of the century, leather-bound versions of which sometimes make their way into my workshop. My kitchen, that is.

"My dear," Mrs. Alderman says in her shaky tenor.

Seated in the rose chintz chair that is fitted with an orthopedic pillow, she lets go the cane, puts on her bifocals, and smiles triumphantly. "There. That's the ticket. Let me get a look at you."

I told Mother about Mrs. Alderman, and her jaw fell. "She has *millions!* How did you ever hook up with *her?*"

It isn't unusual for Mother to get so overwhelmed by fortune that she pays no attention to what she's saying. I reminded her that Mrs. Alderman's daughter was my college roommate, and that she has a son Mal's age. "Oh!" Mother said, abandoning the topic, preferring, as always, to stand scowling on the periphery of any scenario that involves him.

"You look *wonderful!*" Mrs. Alderman says. I can't think she remembers what I looked like the first time she met me. "Now show me what you've done."

I take the *Huckleberry Finn* out of its protective wax paper sleeve. I lay it on the small cherry table to Mrs. Alderman's left.

"I haven't touched the spine yet," I explain, "but the threading between the sections has been replaced."

I did it with a nylon so thin I could barely keep it in sight. Surgical nylon I procured from the hospital. I haven't used it before, and I like the effect, strong and invisible. I open to my favorite illustration, of Huck and Jim on the raft, with the quote below it: "It's lovely to live on a raft."

Mrs. Alderman nods. "You're quite a talented young lady.

I look forward to seeing *all* of it. Apparently the people at Yale can't wait to get their hands on it!"

I don't imagine that this is true. As an undergraduate, I entered the Beinecke Library with trepidation, as one does any restricted area where there's an attempt to preserve delicate things. I gazed at the climate-controlled glass cases and felt both wonder and regret for their ephemeral contents.

Mrs. Alderman sits back, exhausted from the effort of complimenting. "Do let's have some tea."

I pour for both of us, and ready Mrs. Alderman's with lemon and two rectangular lumps of sugar. I put it on the table and hold out a small plate of Social Tea cookies.

"Thank you, dear, I'll have one or two," Mrs. Alderman says. "Now you must tell me about your life. I want to know all about you!"

I choose the same innocuous details I related when we met before. "Well, my husband's a lawyer. And I work at home, as you know. We met through Diana at a Yale gathering."

Drunk as skunks, I might add, landing in a club downtown where, group assumption, we thought we could blend in with a twenties crowd.

"Oh yes, of course," Mrs. Alderman says as she settles her cup onto the saucer at a tip. Anything Yale is good news here. My parents are Harvard people, which I'm not about to mention. I went to Yale instead, claiming that Cambridge was too cold, in climate and character, a decision both my parents interpreted as a blatant act of rebellion. "But what about your son? I know he's about the same age as my grandson Robert. How does he like school?"

"*Loves* it!" I sing out.

"What are his strong subjects?" Mrs. Alderman goes on. "Robert seems to be up to all sorts of computer studies. He's just *mad* for computers!"

"Mal likes that too," I concur. Stop at *mad*.

"Will he be going on to Yale, do you think? I know it's too early to tell."

"He hasn't really decided what his first choice is," I tell her.

"I hope the boys will see a lot of each other in the coming years," Mrs. Alderman says, taking up her cup and saucer again.

"That would be nice." The gap, already Magellan in scale, will widen. Robert will be elected youngest-ever head of the C.I.A. while Mal stands in the unemployment line or calls us collect from prison.

I lay the *Huckleberry Finn* gently in Mrs. Alderman's lap. I found an extraordinary blue shimmery fabric in a bath supplies store, as iridescent and changeable as fish scales, and I attached it temporarily with a paper clip to the cover.

"Gracious, if this isn't the most heavenly blue!" Mrs. Alderman cries. "You are too clever. Well, and why not! It's the river, right here in my hands!"

My throat wells up for no clear reason. I'm moved, I suppose, because Mrs. Alderman is.

"You've probably got all sorts of things cooking for the others!" Mrs. Alderman says. "I can barely wait to see them!"

I smile carefully, so as not to displace tears. "Thank you," I say.

I make it a habit not to buy hardcover books except off the discount tables or from street merchants, and these only when a pang sets in about Mr. Marekki. But with the idea that a new book might inspire Mal toward reading, I pick up some thrillers, heavy as sin, from Barnes & Noble for him. Not risky purchases, as Ian will race through them if Mal won't.

It's what I would do if he were mine: return to thoughts of him after taking care of errands. He'd be built into my day. My heart. He'd be habit. Comfort.

I hand him the bag, point to the TV.

"For when you've had enough of that business," I say.

He pulls the two tomes out of the bag. "Thanks," he says, and puts them aside. "You want to watch this?"

"What is it?"

"People killing each other," he says, his smile a dare.

"I'll pass."

"I thought you would. No Big Bird in this."

I sit in the chair opposite, wishing he'd turn off the set. I'm hoping the sheer fact of my presence will make up for the ugliness of earlier.

"What, they're not coming today? No band practice?" he says.

Were I sixteen I'd probably find his form of quickness appealing. I'd follow him down the long halls at school with my eyes, hoping for another quip. "Later on today," I say. "They have to spend a *little* time with their parents."

"No shit."

"Why don't you turn that dreadfulness off?" I say. "We can think of something else to do."

He sits up, somehow managing to be graceful, arranging his long arms and legs as economically as a dancer. "You got any quarters?"

❧ EIGHT ❧

Diana calls to find out how I'm managing. "What's he doing?"

"Laundry. I was thinking maybe we could get him and Robert together later. I thought they could go play basketball."

It occurs to me, as I make the suggestion, that Robert might not be at home on a public basketball court, whereas Mal, with his love of tough talk and living on the edge, will fit right in.

"They're not *eight*, Paige," Diana says. "Anyway, Robert wouldn't know what to do with a basketball. He and his father are going to the Javits Center later to look at stamps. How are you managing?"

"All right," I lie. "The littles like him. He doesn't like them much, I don't think. He's a package, though."

"Of course you're thrown," Diana says. "Look, I have the world of help in this house, but do you think I've brushed my hair today? No. I put in four different sets of braids for Lydia, and she *still* went off to the Sky Rink in a fury. I told her that chances are good that while she's ice skating the braids will come loose anyway. You have to give this time, Paige."

As difficult as Lydia can be, I envy Diana the Herculean task of dispelling her moods, finding ways to send her into the world with all of her clamoring idiosyncrasies tamed.

"He puts me on edge," I say.

"Why don't you all come over for dinner? I think there's a stew planned."

"Mal's going to his mother's."

"A breather!" She laughs.

"I know! Listen to me!"

"He's disoriented too. It'll smooth out after a while."

How would I know this? Lydia and Robert are *her* children. She *knows* them. I don't *know* Mal, and I can't trust that things will smooth out.

He stands over my shoulder, reading a line Daddy under-lined in a Robert Graves collection.

"This is the meter." I point to the marks above the words. "It's called trochaic meter because the strong stress is first, the weak stress second, and the pattern is repeated seven times in the line. Each of these bits of the pattern is called a metrical foot."

"It looks like Japanese." He seems perplexed, his eye-brows a flat line of suspicion.

"It's just something to know," I say. "It's the kind of thing you could throw at some woman at a party when you're older so she'll put you above the other guys. When I met your dad, he was spouting poetry in a crowded restaurant. *The*

MacGowans are a race of clods, / Loved by men and scorned by Gods."

"I know," Mal says. "I've heard the story a hundred times."

"I want you to do me a favor."

"All these promises, Paige," he says. "I don't know."

"I want you to learn about meter so that when I'm ancient like Jeremy and I can't remember anything you can tell me in a big booming voice all about it. In front of your wife and kids and everyone."

Mal laughs. "I don't think I'll ever have a wife and kids, Paige."

"No?"

"No." He shakes his head definitely, several times.

"Too hard?"

"Yeah."

Who does he have as models, after all.

"So, did you find any free machines?" I ask.

"All full. I have to go back down."

"I'll go with you," I say. "We'll read stuff."

He frowns. "Yeah?"

"Sure, why not?"

"You want to go read in the basement?"

"Yeah. You know, sit on the machines, chanting trochees. What else do we have to do?"

He stretches, grazes the ceiling with his fingers.

"You missed it, Paige," he says.

"What now?" I moan. I've heard about it from the other Hens, the endless criticism, the unfailing eyes of the young, how they zero in on a weakness and attack it.

"You should have been a teacher," he says. "If I had someone like you at the Ridge, who'd have class in the laundry room, I might have stayed."

I'm amazed he can talk about his staying there as if it were up to him.

"Go back downstairs," I order. "I'm going to get some books."

"It's your party," he says, and loafs out.

I haul the box of Daddy's favorite books from the back of my closet, choose the collected T. S. Eliot and the Salinger stories and throw in Sagan's *Contact*, thinking it's a guy book. I take the legal pad from the kitchen table and the Waterman pen Ian bought me for my fortieth birthday. When I get down to the basement, Mal is taking someone else's wet laundry out of one machine and piling it on top of another. He looks huge and out of place, but I like watching him do this. It gives him a new dimension, one that takes care of basic things. A dimension I can reach.

"Just give me a couple minutes," he says. "I gotta sort all this shit out."

I write down the second phrase. We may as well start with that. Sort of dactylic, I think, assigning the stresses. Then I open the collected Eliot to "Prufrock." This will be an ongoing project, I decide. The meter is changeable, establishing itself anew, according to the whim of scene. A total wild card.

"I hate that poem," Mal says.

"You haven't read it in a laundry room yet. See? Here's our table. Now lie down."

I thump the table meant for folding.

"Excuse me?"

"You be the patient. That's the easy part. You get to be *etherized*, which means you don't do anything but lie there."

Mal laughs. "Like I needed *that* explained to me."

He hops up on the table and stretches out, hands under his head. "Does Dad know you're certifiable?"

"What do *you* think?"

"I think you're *both* nuts."

"You're entitled to your opinion." I perch on one of the machines. "You listen while I read, and then you tell me why this poet bothered about evening being like some guy knocked out in an operating room."

"Aren't *you* supposed to supply that information?" he gripes.

"You're the pupil."

I read the first stanza, then the couplet about the women coming and going and talking about Michelangelo. He puts a hand in the air. "Time," he calls, and sits up.

"What?"

"Got it," he announces.

"Tell me."

"It's how he feels," he says, shrugging.

"Who?"

"The guy."

"What guy?"

"The guy who's talking. This Prufrock character. The one who's inviting her to go with him."

I look at the page. "You think so?"

"Well, don't *you*? Why else would he be talking that way if he didn't feel like shit?"

I smile hugely. I can't help it. "That is *so* wonderful."

He raises both fists, straight-armed, into the dingy space above us. "And you thought I was illiterate."

"*No,*" I object. "I never thought that. I just thought—"

"It's okay," he says, lying down again. "Keep going. I like the way you read it. Mr. Thayer, this alcoholic at the Ridge, he just sits at the desk and makes everyone read ten lines and then gives us a test. Like that's going to make us go home and read the rest!"

"That doesn't sound very brilliant."

"*Duh*," Mal says. "Now do the part about the fog. I love that part."

This must be what Diana meant. If you stop counting on them, stop wanting them to be otherwise, kids come forward and surprise you. We do three loads, read the whole poem. Mal rolls his jeans, tries to part his hair behind, pretends to eat a peach.

"Gotta get me some of those flannel trousers," he says, as we're folding. I notice he has two pairs of jeans besides what he was wearing, and the knees are worn through on both.

"You aren't that sad," I venture.

"No one's that sad!" he says.

"You think he's a loser."

"Nah," he tells me. He starts to put the piles back into the duffel bag.

"You *don't* think he's a loser?"

"No! Why is he a loser? Because he admits he isn't Hamlet? That's pretty harsh, Paige. What, everyone you know is so good at everything? They can all come back from the dead?"

I feel pinned. Examined by potential enemies. Like Prufrock, *formulated, sprawling on a pin. Wriggling on the wall.*

"No," I say, stuffing the last pile in. "Obviously not."

He snatches up the book. "*I am no prophet—and here's no great matter; I have seen the moment of my greatness flicker, And I have seen the eternal Footman hold my coat, and snicker, And in short, I was afraid.* See? *Greatness.* Anyone who's known greatness is *not* a loser. Anyone who's had a fucking *footman.*"

"I'm sorry," I say. "I didn't exactly mean *loser.*"

"Well, then don't say shit like that."

*　　　*　　　*

He's crashing about the kitchen, putting the kettle on, searching for tea bags.

"On the left." I'm going to have some, his way.

"So," he says, his back to the flame, "don't you get bored?"

"With reading?"

"With, like, working in this kitchen?"

"I don't think about it," I say.

"Seems kind of lonely."

"Not anymore!"

He laughs. "Now you got me." He flips sugar into both cups, sets the milk carton before me, sits down heavily, drums on the table. "I gotta get stuff going," he says. "I gotta find some people who want to play some serious music. I'm not good at hanging around."

On the contrary, I think.

"So?" he asks me.

"It's okay." I've drunk a third of it.

"Sugar water. I drink it instead of coffee to stay up all night," he said.

Given his grades, I don't know why he'd think to do this.

"Want to play chess?" he asks. "While we wait for them?"

"Something easier." I always mix up the players in the advancing army, can't keep the lowly pawn's path clear from the formidable rook's.

"Backgammon?"

"You're on. I'll make popcorn."

He wins two games while I eat most of the popcorn.

"Way to go!" he says, pointing at the bowl.

"Sorry. I don't know what got into me."

"That's easy," he says, sweeping all the men back into their starting positions. "Boredom. People eat when they're bored."

He sends the dice crashing onto the board. Double sixes. When he's completed the furious tour, he looks up and says, "Why don't you just let yourself be normal?"

"I don't know what that means," I say. "*Normal.* Would I be more normal, in your eyes, if I worked for a corporation? If I liked basketball? If I never opened a book?"

"It would be a start," he says. He shakes the dice importantly, ready to determine my overall fate.

After he wins again, I suggest we watch something on TV. "Is that normal enough?"

"I gotta get ready. You go ahead."

He rummages in his room awhile, then comes back out in the clean, shredded jeans and a crew shirt.

"This looks like a chick flick," he says, of Audrey Hepburn for the thousandth heartbreaking time chasing her cat through an alley treacherous with garbage cans and rain.

"I like it, so I guess that makes it so," I say. *I'm a chick,* I think, pleased. I adjust the sofa pillow under my head.

"So we'll watch it," he says. He rolls into centerfold posture, propping himself on one elbow.

A half hour later I shut off the set. "I can't bear the ending."

"Why not?"

"I don't know. It's overwhelming."

"You're a control freak," he says, wagging an instructive finger. He turns the set back on, and we watch love sort itself out.

"What does that make you?"

He lifts his diver's watch for both of us to see. "Late for dinner," he says.

Or five hours early for dinner, depending on who's cooking. I don't know what he thinks he's escaping, going from one romper room to another.

I stand in the doorway while he waits for the elevator. "Have fun," I say.

"Sort of a tall order."

I stay put after the doors shut, listening to the elevator whiz down, thinking how lucky Dorothy is to be entertaining her son for dinner, how I'd rather he not have gone. I think of Mal moving through crowds, his mind electric. The jacket as decoy.

I take out the cold lasagna, don't bother with a plate. The boy is going to make me fat, is what.

"Bad mood," Ralph observes, as I spread out coloring books, crayons, markers, and clay on a plastic sheet.

"Not really," I say. "Just tired." Not used to having them seven days in a row either.

A decrease in zest is always apparent to them, even when I'm most conscious of covering it. And at these times, I wish I *were* one of them. I could say *I'm tired, I don't feel well, pick me up, stroll me around, wake me when everything's different.* As it is, Winifred's sound asleep on the sofa and Electra's in my bed with a fever. I sent Johanna away with Anthony because of it. Kyle, on antibiotics for an ear infection, won't catch anything. Sometimes I suspect the parents of inventing emergencies.

"So, guys, what do you want to draw today? Castles? Pirate ships?"

"Chicken pox," Kyle says. "On you."

"On *me?*"

He nods importantly. "The good thing about chicken pox is that you don't have to go to school. The bad thing about chicken pox is that it itches and you have to put lumpy oatmeal all over you."

"I draw the line, ha ha, at the oatmeal." I hand him all the red markers.

"You're really nuts, Pager," Ralph, Malachi's soul mate, tells me.

"How'd you make out?" Ian says, "And what, for the love of Mike, are you watching?"

"Your son insists that I'm not normal. So I'm watching this to see if I'm really beyond hope."

It's an action thriller with Mel Gibson. I don't know the name of it and think the plot a stretch, but Mr. Gibson's face is enough to force me through to the end.

"Did he drive you over the edge?"

"Almost. But then we did laundry and he helped me to a new understanding of Eliot."

"You're kidding."

I laugh, deep and healthy. A knowing Mother laugh. "I am absolutely *not* kidding."

"What's all that on your face and arms?"

"Illness," I tell him. "Kyle's version of the chicken pox."

"Saint Paige. Come, I bought sandwiches. Let's sit in the kitchen."

"I already ate, but okay." I can't believe I might actually be able to swallow a sandwich after my Italian feast for one. Mal is making me want to do everything, know everything, eat everything.

"You didn't order in with Paula?"

"Paula doesn't eat *food*. More like sawdust. Gourmet sawdust. Meat sends her into a frenzy. If she weren't so helpful, I'd fire her for her eating habits. They remind me of Dorothy's."

Dorothy's food has to pass the inspection of the rabbinical elect. I am to this day unable to imagine Ian putting up with such detour.

He sets us up with a half of an enormous hero each, a pickle sliver, Russian on the side.

"Beer?"

"Sure."

He decants two Pete's Wickeds. "I don't want you to worry about Mal. Let me do that. I'm looking into the GED option."

"Good," I say. "He's too smart to be a dropout. I'm sorry for suggesting it."

"I've just got to think of things to keep him busy during the day. I'm not going to have him around here bugging you all the time."

"Don't worry about it. We're fine. He said he'd come with me to the hospital. There's a whole universe of stuff to do there. And he's looking for a band, he said."

Listen to yourself! I can hear Toni scream.

Ian leans back in his chair. "You look good, despite the dots."

"I do?" I don't like to think about my looks all that much. It makes me feel old.

"Yes," he says, as if it surprises him too. "You look, I don't know, full."

"I am full. I've been eating all day."

"That's not what I mean."

I wait for him to go on.

"You look like you had a good day."

"I did."

Again I'm not sleeping. I pick up the mended *Treasure Island*. Ian's snoring causes me to stop every third word, so I go into the living room and cover myself with the afghan. It's only eleven, but I'm already wondering why Mal isn't back yet. To be sure, dinner at Dorothy's doesn't occur until nine, so Mal is probably still at the table, eating something chocolate and bucking Jeremy's worldly chat with his arsenal of sarcasm.

I try to concentrate on the entrance of the Old Seadog, the verbs of which Daddy underlined, probably at a very young age. They are, as he must have noticed, the most affecting words in the paragraph. But the Old Seadog's entrance doesn't seem as grand scale as any of Mal's have. I put the book down to wait for his next one.

I check the door to see that it isn't locked, then get a different book, the Salinger, thinking that a less remote century will fit the evening better. It does, but again, and especially because of the private school venue, I have Mal in mind, his voice over Holden's, his gripes just as earned. As the hour trudges on to midnight, I begin to feel tortured with waiting, not that I have any idea what I'll say to him when he appears. And what will he think, finding me up, nothing on my mind but him? What will he see?

He'll see, according to the bathroom mirror's current findings, a pale woman with wispy hair, unkempt, large teeth faded from coffee and overbrushing, a long neck still relatively safe from falling wattles, large blue eyes. Exposed collarbones, which might be dismissed as unfeminine, too Spartan. You're forty, you crone, I scold.

I hear him in the hall. To intercept him and ask how dinner was would be far too brash, so I steal back into the bedroom, cursing myself for being such a chicken, and dive into bed. I listen to him in the kitchen, cracking open a Coke, sending the fridge door back into place. I hear the slight creak of the floor as he passes our barely open door, mortified at Ian's behemoth snoring, no doubt. *Old people*, he probably thinks. Then I hear him in the bathroom, taking a long pee and running the water. Then he shuts his door.

Maybe it would be better, I think, not to have done this. Not to have trusted in powers I don't have. Not to have said yes.

❧ NINE ❧

"*I* don't *want* an organizer," Mal is saying. "So I don't *care* which kind you get!"

Ian's voice is much lower. I can't make out what he's saying. It's after eight. I haven't slept this late in years.

"Forget it, Dad. Just forget it."

I put on my robe and take my time in the bathroom, hoping they'll sort things out before I appear. As I'm getting out of the shower I hear the front door close. He's off to work, and I'm day care. I go back in the bedroom and put on pressed khakis, a blouse, and a thin sweater. A string of pearls, even. If Mal sees me tidy and presentable, perhaps he'll be inspired.

At least he's reading the newspaper. I take in the egg pan, the streaked plates, the crumbs.

"Good morning!" I crow. "Dad off to work?"

He lets go the sports page.

"He's unbelievable. He wants to get me this thing that I, like, don't even want and he's getting it anyway! An *organizer*! Like I work in Midtown and commute to the suburbs! What am I supposed to say? Fine, get me ten of them?"

"An organizer isn't totally useless," I offer. "You can keep track of phone numbers and job interviews and birthdays and such."

"Whose birthday."

"Mine," I say. It's already past.

"Oh yeah?" he says. "What day?"

"I'll give you plenty of warning," I say. "How'd you sleep?"

"Like a rock." He sifts through some of the weekend mail. "Christmas Revels! I'm getting tickets."

With whose money, I find myself wondering. "Good. You can put it in your organizer," I say. "Listen, Mal, I have to go over to the hospital. Why don't you shower and get dressed in something that isn't falling off you and come along. You can't just sit here all day."

"I'm bugging you," he says, grinning.

"Right."

He stands, a skyscraper, and goes down the hall to his/my room. I busy myself with phone calls, confirming appointments and lunch with Diana, then guzzle cold coffee instead of rinsing the dishes from their breakfast.

Mr. Marekki is chronically diabetic, chronically overweight, chronically lonely. It breaks my heart to know how he hangs on the moment when I'll wheel the cart, full of pitiful paperback offerings, most of which he's already read twice, into his stuffy room on the Metabolic Unit. Occasionally I stick a new book on the cart just before I get to his room.

"He eats books," I whisper to Mal before we go in. "He's the biggest man in the world."

Mal is still enraptured by the regulation yellow paper gown. He keeps smoothing it down and shifting the disposable plastic belt at his waist. We both have on cellophane gloves.

"I feel like I should be serving French fries," he whispers back.

"Not on this unit."

We go in.

Mr. Marekki is upright, expectant, prepared not to be amused, like a massive king ready to receive the court jester. He has a pendulous chin, and huge, dark eyes, the sole feature it doesn't pain me to look at.

"Hey, Mr. Marekki," I say. "This is Mal."

"Hello, Mal," Mr. Marekki says. "Welcome."

"Thanks."

"I have done with the mysteries, Ms. Austin," he says, pointing to a neat pile of four paperbacks on his bedside table. "I must confess to not having enjoyed them as much as the nonfiction." Now he indicates a separate pile.

"Any recommendations?" As if I'll ever read anything again, with Mal around.

"I found A Brief History of Time extremely compelling, the French thing a bit of a bore, and, if you'll forgive me, the Kennedy book ridiculous. Who cares? Who cares? I kept asking myself. Obviously quite a lot of people do. But I have never subscribed to celebrities. They are mere persons like ourselves, wouldn't you agree?"

All three hardbacks I bought on discount at Barnes & Noble for him.

"I might," I hedge. It is not easy to slip Mr. Marekki into the category of mere persons.

Mal is busy with book collection and wheeling the cart over for Mr. Marekki's perusal.

"You are extremely tall," Mr. Marekki tells him. "You strike me as a sportsman."

"I play basketball."

"You don't say. I often watch the game on television." He motions toward the oversized television. "I invested in a big screen for just such purpose. Perhaps when you come again we can discuss the latest tragedy. I find myself frequently disappointed."

"You must have missed the last game," Mal says. "That was awesome."

"But certainly not stellar. If Indiana can win by such a margin, I ask you, what sort of a team *are* we?"

I see Mal teetering on the rim of hysteria, probably over the use of the plural pronoun. I come to his rescue with a Paul Auster novel I'm fairly sure Marekki hasn't read.

"Yes, fine. That will do nicely," Marekki tells me, barely looking. "And I think something less ponderous to balance out the week."

Two books usually keep him occupied between visits, but they have to be fairly long. I hunt down an Anne Rice.

"Lovely," he says. "I'll savor the gory outcome, as always."

"See you in a few days," I say. "You have a good week."

"I shall do my best," Marekki says. "And I do thank you for bringing this young man to visit. Tell me, what does Mal stand for?"

"Malachi."

"I should have suspected. You have conflict in your eyes. I've always thought that book, while the shortest, was as difficult as Job. So little light. So little light. In any event, good-bye." He raises his forearm ceremoniously, as if it wields a scepter. Mal waves.

"He's a trip!" Mal says outside.

"He's brilliant. He's never getting out of here."

Mal stops the cart. "*Why?*"

"He can't live on his own. And he's got no relatives."

Marekki has two 4x6 frames of his parents on his bedside table. His father, hefty and studious, wears a yarmulke, a tallis, and glasses. His mother smiles into infinity, petite, beautiful, like Rita Hayworth. "Both dead," he said to me once. Like me, like Mal before King Solomon, who Mal would like to think doesn't count as a sibling, he's an only child.

"How is that possible?" Mal demands, upset.

"Join the androids," I say, hoping it's the sort of thing he'd say. "We've been expecting you."

"He's that sick?"

"Look at him!"

We take the elevator down to a ward where all the signs on the doors read "Hazardous Waste" and the garbage bags are red instead of clear. "AIDS?" Mal asks quietly. He stretches the wrist of one of his gloves and lets it snap back.

"AIDS," I confirm. "The gloves are sweaty, aren't they?"

"They're awful."

I stop us outside a semiprivate room, its door wide open. "Masks on."

"We're in such danger?"

"No, silly. The patients are. The masks are to keep *our* germs away from *them.*"

"Oh." Disappointment reigning, he follows me in.

"Do they really feel like reading?"

"Sometimes," I say. "Some people believe reading can save your life."

"We know who *those* people are," he whispers. "How come you do this?"

"You met Marekki. Now don't tell me you're planning to disappoint him by not showing up next time. Anyone want something to read?" Through the paper mask, my voice is just as clear as it would be without, so it's hard to feature that such a thin film of paper can block germ passage.

Someone moans opposite the plastic tent. Mal pushes the cart over.

"I want the nurse," the woman says.

I press the call button anyway and grab a magazine from the bottom shelf and leave it on the nightstand, then dart among the beds, leaving books and magazines. The other patients are sleeping or comatose. I point to the door and Mal backs out with the cart.

I barrel past him, and the automatic doors burst apart. "You might want to skip the next one," I say, pulling off my mask, talking to him over my shoulder. "Obstetrics."

"Yeah," he agreed. "I need to start slow. This is pretty hard-core. I can't believe you do this for no money."

I think it's crass, his assignment of dollar value to everything.

"Find your way home, then," I say. "Make the phone calls your dad suggested, get some exercise, and put your mind on dinner. Your dad tells me you know how to make tacos."

"You want me to make dinner?" He seems amused by my quaintness.

"Is that so extraordinary?" I ask. "I've got a lunch date, and all afternoon I'm with the littles. I can't imagine anything nicer than sitting down to a Mexican meal."

Like Dorothy, I sound. Like a sergeant in a MASH unit. I'm stern, in anticipation of where I'm about to find myself. With women who've just had babies. He may not have required such urging.

"Tell me," Diana says, sipping water.

We're at the Whitney Sarabeth's, being ignored by the help.

"I can't concentrate. All I think about is whether he'll like it with us, whether he'll stay. I think about myself in comparison to Dorothy, which I never used to do. I think about how *dressed down* I am, as if what I do demands some sort of a wardrobe other than a smock and jeans."

Diana sets her menu down. "Such a tragedian. It's about time *something* happened to push all that bleak business aside. As for *dressed down*, you don't qualify." She looks around at the other tables. "Excuse me," she says, loudly and to no one in particular, "do I have to go borrow a waiter from across the street?"

A man about our age, parked behind an empty champagne flute, applauds. "*Brava!*" he cries, and keeps clapping.

"*Neil!*" Diana hoots. "No one I know is ever around when I do that!"

"One of Tod's colleagues," she explains. "Divorced. Likes boys. You want to see screwed up, have lunch with one of *his* kids."

"Do they know?" I ask.

"Know what? That he's gay? *Honey!* I'm surprised you haven't seen him—he just moved into your building!"

I hunch forward. I love gossip.

"One of his sons found him in the apartment with a male escort," Diana delivers gravely. "His wife finally went back to Costa Rica, which she'd been threatening to do since their wedding day. So now the boys have established little drug cartels for themselves in the schools they landed in after getting kicked out of their European boarding schools."

"They should get together with Mal," I moan. I'm glad to be hearing, despite how sorry I feel for the whole crew, that other people are having trouble managing, even the ones with, as Mal would say, *sick money.* "Did Neil tell you all this?"

"Are you mad? I have a son who can get all the information there is. Everything. You want controversial scientific research, he can access it. You want insider trading, no problem. You want tales from the yuppie infrastructure, Robert's your man. I'm fairly certain he can tap into phone lines." Diana does not seem displeased with Robert's nosiness.

"He knows these kids?"

"They used to live in *our* building."

"Downward mobility," I observe. "Horrible."

Neil is looking in our direction, but his expression is vague.

"Very little fazes me," Diana says. "But the thing that bothers me is that so little fazes Robert."

"He'd probably be fazed if something like that happened in his home."

Diana laughs frivolously, and Neil goes back to the crossword.

"Has it?"

"Well, I don't know about Tod, of course," Diana says, brooding. "Oh, yes I do. He's halfway around the world a lot of the time. But since we're almost never together, we haven't gotten past the dating phase. An occasional transgression overseas really wouldn't impress me that much. I've certainly thought about doing same. I just haven't gone ahead and done it. Who has time?"

I have time. Or I could certainly *make* time. But an affair is hard to imagine. I don't know anyone I want to have an affair with. And how sad, really, how melodramatic, to sneak around behind Ian's back, convinced that the world still lies in wait, lovely and gentle, for my romantic cameo.

"It doesn't bother you?" I ask Diana. "I hate longing. I'm convinced there's no way to endure it. Mal and I spent Sunday afternoon in the laundry room reading Eliot. I just want you to know, I'm Prufrock. Speaking of longing."

"He reads Eliot?"

"He pretends to be a drug-dealing, basketball-dunking moron, but he's smarter than anyone I know, with the exception, perhaps, of his father."

"So you like him!"

"I don't know why. He's incredibly annoying. He sits around so much! What is it with kids these days, they don't get up when someone enters a room? You have to beg them to clear their plates off the table. Mal arrived with a mountain of laundry, and he wouldn't have done it without urging. Perfectly content, he was, to stay in last week's jeans and T-shirt. I went out and bought him a jacket, for God's sake, even though it's ninety degrees, because you should have seen what he had on when we picked him up. His mother makes nearly a million dollars a year, and she lets him out of the house in rags."

"You sound like Toni," Diana says. "Don't worry so much. Lord, I'm hungry." She glances around, desperate.

⊰ T E N ⊱

*H*e's out, as promised, but has left notes all over the house. The first is taped to the telephone in the kitchen: "I'm here" with a number. The second I find when I open the fridge for a snack. He's made pizza English muffins, it looks like. "Don't even think about it." To the remainder of the lettuce I bought last week he's taped "A Better Choice." On his door is "Demolition Zone," a lie I find evidence for when I peek in and see he's straightened for a military inspection. Above my face in the bathroom mirror he's written in soap capitals "BEAUTY."

It makes me want to run, hide somewhere, wait for whatever this is to blow over. At the same time, I can't get to the phone fast enough.

Instead I pull the notes from their perches, ball them up and put them in the trash. Think of something, think of something. Work? Here? Yes. Okay. All right. Try.

But I've run out of the coated paper I've been using to reinforce pages of *The Celebrated Jumping Frog of Calaveras County*, and I've gotten the idea to repair the gilding on the cover, which will require gold leaf I don't have. An article in the *Times* suggested I could raise my fees to forty dollars an hour if I can provide this sort of extra embellishment. I call Mrs. Alderman.

"*Anything,*" she answers. "When do you think they'll be ready, dear?"

With money no object, I promise Christmas. But at the rate I've been working these last three days, this is totally unrealistic.

The phone rings. I unfreeze after the fourth ring.

"Paige," someone says, not him. "It's Jeremy. Is Mal around? His mother wanted me to get a message to him."

"No, he's not here," I say. Jeremy, the yutz, has become his wife's social secretary, and I've become Mal's.

"Ah. May I leave word with you?"

"Certainly."

"Tell him that the only available flights are for December eighteenth, going, and the thirtieth, returning. Avi's going to be renting a house in Florida for the month, and Mal expressed some interest in visiting."

Instantly miserable, I take down the information. "Got it."

"How is it going over there?" Jeremy asks me.

"Just fine. Mal's fine."

"Good to hear. We thought that by the holidays you might need a break. He has friends down there."

"I'm sure he'll enjoy it." I anticipate descriptions of relatives in unflattering swimsuits.

"So he seems all right?" For a man who works at the stock market, Jeremy has surprisingly little on his plate this afternoon. Where is all the trading noise, the roar of Reuters, the alien aggression?

"Definitely," I said. "He's fine."

"Dorothy and I worry about Mal a lot. He's been very put out since Solomon was born."

I could bring up their refusal to let him live with them, but now I wouldn't want a reverse offer. "That's pretty normal." As if I know. I just see how Kyle reacts when Johanna melts at the mere sight of Anthony, how he hangs on me, begging for attention.

"At dinner the other night he was very unresponsive."

"Jeremy?" I say, trying to keep my voice down. "He just got kicked out of school. Did you expect him to appear with wine and flowers?"

"Of course not." Ultimately, there is no love lost between the households, and neither I nor Jeremy sees any point in disguising this fact.

"I've got to get downtown," I tell him.

"I just wanted to tell you to be especially alert. He can convince anyone of anything, Mal. Even that he's doing all right when he isn't."

"I'll take that on advisement."

"Paige? I mean it."

"Is there something further I should be doing, Jeremy? Other than meals and beds and general bucking up? Are there prescriptions to be filled? Is there a counseling plan in the works?"

These would have been my questions had anyone come to me the *first* time Mal went to the discipline committee at Bay Ridge. Lord knows the hospital can provide a big enough database.

"You take care," he says. "I'm here if you need me."

"The day I need *him*," I mutter, after hanging up.

I pick through the kitchen trash for Mal's number. I count on its being a Manhattan exchange and dial. A girl answers. She sounds sleepy but not surprised when I identify myself.

"Sure. Hold on."

"Yeah" is how he answers. As if he were waiting for a call about a cocaine shipment.

"Where are you?"

"At my friend Jessica's."

"Jessica?" I know who he means, but I want details.

"Jessica Abrahams? She goes to NYU?" College girl. Dorms. Freedom. Uh-oh.

"Oh! Jessica. Right." Medical textbook liaison. "Okay, well. You left this note. I thought you wanted me to call."

"I did."

Perhaps so that Jessica could see him as sought after, not that there could ever be any doubt about this.

"Well, I'm calling."

"Hi."

"What are you doing?" Hey, why not. There's such huge background silence, all I can picture is Mal and the mysterious Jessica wound around each other on an unmade bed. Does he carry condoms? I can't bear to think about it. *You're too young!* I want to scream. *Too young!*

"Hanging out. We're going out later, hear some music."

"That sounds nice." My mind races ahead to postconcert entertainments, Mal's wee-hour return, if, in fact, he's coming home at all. I'll never sleep again.

"Okay. Well. Bye."

I hang up, desolate.

What do I expect? That he'll be forever mooning around the apartment waiting for the next opportunity to admire me in another of my demanding roles? *You don't want that,* I tell myself. But I'd prefer it to the sting of childlessness that is threatening to overturn my day, remind me that if I had my own kids I wouldn't have a moment to think about this one, to imagine ridiculous scenarios in which I, a nerdy nonrelative, feature as important to him.

I go downtown, buy more coated paper, the gold leaf, book cloth, baby-soft leather for the doublure inside the covers of Mrs. Alderman's books, manila card and shellac. By the time I leave the supplier I've spent over three hundred dollars. I walk briskly back to the train, the wind rattling my shopping bags. I'm cheerful from the errand, happy about the speed of it, the heavy result. On the train I peer into the bags, rearrange their contents, feel proud to be a person who knows how to use all this stuff. An artisan.

I get off at Eighty-sixth Street and walk home through the park, now soggy and empty. The park is the place I remember being with Daddy the most. I learned to ride a bike around the great lawn, my parents taking turns running alongside, holding on to the back of the seat. I hung limp and nearly weightless from the cherry trees, watching through the blossoms for Daddy, who would feign ignorance as to my whereabouts, then surprise and relief at finally finding me among the branches, taunting me, daring me to come down and follow him to the Sabrett stand for hot dogs. I was stubborn then, not wanting to come down, because we'd be that much closer to the end of the park venture if it was already lunchtime. But we stayed late, sometimes, playing Frisbee and kickball and torturing Mother with detours. Daddy didn't give me the impression, despite his work, which was international in scope and required him to be gone more than home, that he had other things to do when there was a day for him to spend with me. Being in the park now is a form of sad communion, since there is virtually no

one to whom I can adequately express—and to what end?—
how terribly I miss him.

I pass the pond where we let an oversized goldfish go free
one summer. It was either that or watch the tank explode.
I'm hurrying now. The kids will arrive soon. Mal won't be
home for hours. I don't want him to come home, but I'm
dying to see him.

"You got company," Ramone says, leering. He tells me
Ian has just walked in. It isn't even six o'clock. But today was
the deposition for the trial, so he's probably given himself a
work reprieve until tomorrow. The elevator seems a cell of
shame, so actual is my disappointment that it's Ian who has
come home and not Mal.

"In here!" he calls.

He has papers all over the bed. "I had to get out of the
office for a while. They're renovating the floor above us. I
don't think I've ever had such a headache."

"I hope you're not getting sick too," I say. That will be
the end of me. Having the two of them at home, darting
between requests, between loyalties.

"Oh that's right," he says. "You had that *Mal* bug."

"Mal bug?"

"The mysterious virus. The one you caught just in time
for the basketball game!"

He's lit up with teasing.

"I didn't know you'd bought me a ticket," I say. "I would
have gone, Mal bug notwithstanding."

"So tell me," he says. His long legs stretched toward me,
crossed at the ankles, a dark corduroy river through the yellow plain of legal pads. "How's it going? I've hardly seen
either of you. Are we still a united front?"

The thing about Ian, I hardly need reminding, is that he

can be so oblivious. How was he supposed to pay attention to what is going on in his own house? Scots are strong, outdoor people, I've learned, as opposed to my English, who spend half their short lives sick indoors, watching rain aggravate into snow and praying for a dry day.

"I took him to see Mr. Marekki. He's with his friend Jessica now. Remind me about Jessica?"

"Daughter of Arlene and Adam Abrahams."

Friends of Dorothy's. Or, they'd been friends of Ian's and Dorothy's until the divorce.

"The one he's known since he was a baby?"

"The very one."

He and Jessica are probably out having hamburgers somewhere now, complaining about her two parents and his four. Harmless sibling stuff that won't waylay my efforts toward his reformation.

"You should have seen him with Mr. Marekki. And in the AIDS ward. I don't think that lacrosse and chapel were ever things he really cared about. Maybe if we let up, he'll find his own way. I've got half a mind to call up that dean and thank him."

Ian bites on a pencil eraser. I set to rearranging the few frames I keep on the bureau by taking them all off and putting them on the radiator cover.

"He's an angry kid," Ian says. "As talented as he is."

"He's got things to be angry about," I say. "You're angry too."

"About this, yes."

"That's what I'm saying, Ian. That's what he's picking up on."

"Of course you're right. You're always right. Come sit." He pats an untenanted space by the pillow. "You don't need to change the bureau cover right now."

I sit.

"I have one concern," he says.

"Which is."

"This is sort of a honeymoon period we're in. Just a few days out of prison, he's at his best. But he's going to start to flounder unless I get him into some kind of a program or schedule. The kid needs structure. All kids do."

Laundry lit., hospital rounds, band practice, provided he finds one, occasional booster dates with Jessica. This seems enough of a schedule to me. Healthy, too. But it's a selfish schedule, one that entitles me to keep total track of him. Out of my ken, Mal becomes unreal, a figure in a dream I don't want to end, someone to remind me that life can be fun, surprising. In the sort of program Ian is suggesting, Mal will enchant others, always be elsewhere.

"Ian," I say. "He's not exactly a kid anymore." I'm not sure how I mean this, I just want him to leave well enough alone for the moment.

"Yes, he is," Ian says, his voice stony. "He's my kid."

I stand up. "He's your kid, yes. But you don't know him. If you want to serve him with a schedule, make it one that includes you now and again. I listen to you gripe about Dorothy's never having been home to raise him for a second, but I don't see you bowing out of duty so you can find him a job or a band or another school or anything that would indicate *to him* that he's amazing and you adore him."

"Are you suggesting I quit *my* job? Because that's what shirking duty in a law firm amounts to. In your line of work, you can shirk pretty much without consequence. But we cogs in the corporate wheel can't do that. We can't bring our baggage into the office."

Again I take my place by the bureau. "Children are not *baggage!*" I shout. "I can't believe this!"

"Nor can I, Paige."

"We can't afford to fall apart here," I say, as much to myself as to him.

"Are we falling apart? I was not aware of our falling apart."

"That's just it! If we *were* falling apart, you'd be hard put to notice!"

I have worse times in mind, trips back from the hospital by subway. No baby. No father. He's not falling apart. *I* am, have been for a while.

"Paula warned me about this," he says.

"*Paula* warned you? About what?"

"About bringing my son into our home. About what it would do to you."

"And what does Paula know about it? Has she got a stepson? Was she around when Atreus fell?"

He smiles. I've amused him, midchaos. "She's a single mother."

"Then she's a lucky woman," I say, keeping myself tall.

"All I meant to convey," he says gently, "is that it's understandable, what Mal's being here all of a sudden is doing to you."

I breathe, groping for words that will weigh against Paula's, tip the justice scales in favor of *our* home. "You have no idea what it's doing to me. You have no idea about that at all."

I leave the apartment. Things are beginning to feel unsafe inside. I hate the idea of Paula peering in and making comments, uninvited and busy as a Greek chorus. More difficult, however, is the fact of my turning away, from Ian toward Mal, and were he not approaching from Broadway, sudden from the bus, I'd turn around before he sees me.

"What's goin' on?" he says. "Paige? Why are you crying?"

I shake my head, against all of it, him, Ian, all the things

I go through with my afternoon five, my dead father, the evening closing in. Then he takes over, hugs me, says, "It's okay. It's okay. Come on. Where were you going, anyway?"

I press my cheek into his shirt. He tries to get another look at my face, which I do not allow.

Here. Right here.

"I spend too much time in this place," I say, of the diner. He shrugs. "What are you going to do? You don't want to go back to the apartment, you want a place to sit down, you're in a city. This is what there is."

"I drink too much coffee."

He isn't having anything.

"Why are you beating yourself up?"

"Why did you leave those notes around?"

"I don't know. I didn't want you to think I just left. Without saying anything."

"You must think I'm pretty pathetic, if you have to leave a sign that says *Beauty* on the bathroom mirror." I felt flattered for a second. Beyond that, suspicious. Because he couldn't have meant it.

"No, Paige," he says. "I don't think you're pathetic."

"What is it then? You think I'm so desperate for attention that you have to provide it in these insidious ways?"

"God!" He whirls around, helpless. "I'm sorry! I thought you'd think it was funny!"

"*Funny!* You have to be more careful, Mal. You can't imagine the power certain words have over people."

"Fine," he says. "I'll never leave you another note. What do you want me to do? Is there some big rule I'm breaking here? You want to throw me out too?"

"No," I tell him. "I don't want to throw you out. I want to tell you where I'm going and promise not to eat Yodels and take you every place I take the others. But what would be the *point*? I'm not your mother, and soon you'll be gone."

Instead of getting up and leaving me in disgust he reaches across the table for the napkin in my hand. "Let me do that."

"No. Please."

"Give it to me."

He takes the napkin from me and dabs at my face. I have to be looking like a clown after a rainstorm, lipstick down my chin, mascara streaking my jowls. There's a terrible pressure in my chest. My throat. Maybe I'm having a heart attack. Women have heart attacks. Even those who aren't grandmothers.

He comes and sits on my side of the booth.

"You think you're alone. I'm out here flapping in the breeze."

"No you aren't."

"Why is it such a big deal to need someone anyway?" he wants to know. "What's *wrong* with that?"

"It should be the other way around," I say.

"Oh, so what. Maybe it is. You don't know *everything*."

I laugh at this. "You're right. Is that why you came back so early? I thought you were going to hear some music somewhere."

"Jessica has some shit to do."

"What did she say about your getting kicked out of school?"

"She said stuff like this happens all the time. She says everyone has their own pace, and mine's different."

I'm suspicious of kids who are too savvy, who carry around the big truths with seeming effortlessness.

"Did that make you feel any better?"

"How could it?"

"Maybe you should have talked to us instead," I say.

"Like that would help."

"You can talk to me, Mal." If I leave Ian out of the equation, I might have a better shot at trust.

"I sort of was, with the notes." Now his focus is down, on the flatware, the chrome. "Anyway, I figure pretty soon you guys will tell me to get my own place." He beats out some finality on the table, both hands.

"We're not going to do that," I promise him, thinking I'd sooner throw myself in a river. "Let's go back. It's almost three."

❧ ELEVEN ☙

"What about this," I tell the crew. We're disease-ravaged, Electra and Winifred having succumbed to the flu and ailing, one on each sofa. Neither James nor Winifred's mother could afford to take the day off, so the girls were sent to school loaded with Children's Tylenol and cough syrup, only to arrive here on fire with fever. I have no plan at all for them, but I know I'm good for one by sentence's end. Mal stands apart, listening, but, I'm fairly certain, ready to bolt.

"Instead of a fort, we set up a MASH unit."

The littles love emergency. I've been witness to this in the park, where, for almost an entire month, the play revolved around incapacity, maiming, or other illnesses of an incurable order, all of which demanded furious help, usually on the part of Ralph, who is happy to take after his father in any context. The three more verbal children would send

Electra off in search of sticks to serve as crutches, rocks for pillows, jackets for bedsheets, and pails of sand or dirt for mixing potions. The impromptu hospital was set up under the double slide, and some of the adults wouldn't let their charges get involved. These were messy, wonderful days which required me to plunk everyone in the tub later on, then dig into the drawer where I keep their extra clothes.

"What's a MASH unit?" Kyle asks Ralph.

"Where they take care of people in a war," Ralph says nonchalantly. "After they've been hit by cannons and stuff."

"Cannon*balls*," Mal corrects. "Except they don't use cannons anymore."

"Whatever," Ralph says. At least he's picked something up from Mal.

"Is it *outside*?" Kyle wants it to be outside and ever so tenuous a place.

"It's in a tent. And there's blood everywhere. It's a real mess." Ralph coughs, pleased with his delivery and, no doubt, its effect on Kyle. "It's called triage."

"Can we make triage, Paige?"

I gesture sweepingly at the contents of the living room and beyond. "Go for it."

Winifred lifts a weak hand. "I get to be sick."

"You are sick, stupid," Ralph tells her.

"*Children*," I command.

"I don't feel well," Electra moans.

I do the tummy test for her fever, having hoped the cold washcloth on the forehead would help some. "I have to get you in the tub," I tell her. "Boys, you set up the triage tent, get the patient comfortable, check for vital signs, while I deal with this. Malachi, do you mind letting some lukewarm water into the tub?"

He stands still, as if he hasn't heard me.

"Malachi?"

"Don't you have a thermometer?"

"Not one that works," I say gruffly, my hand back on Electra's fiery tummy. "What about the bath?"

"*Jesus,*" he says, and turns down the hall.

I'm not sure what the expression is meant to insinuate, my sloppiness or the intricate demands of the setup here, but I am sure that I don't like its tone. I resent his hesitation to help; in fact, I find it appalling.

"What's *wrong?*" Electra whines, her eyes registering panic.

"Nothing, sweetie."

"Why do I have to take a *bath?* I don't *want* to take a bath."

"Just a short bath," I say. "To get the fever down."

"Can we use this?" Ralph asks, reappearing from the bedroom, dragging the bedspread.

"Of course," I say, although Winifred is sleeping, and unless I volunteer, they're fresh out of triage victims. "Get the kitchen chairs, and use these pillows." I toss them the cushions Electra threw off when she first lay down.

I hear the rush of water. Malachi's door closes.

"Come on, baby." I gather up Electra, a limp bundle of heat and tears. I can't bear to think of putting her in water, how she'll shiver, how unfair she'll think it is.

"I'll be back," I say to the others, who are just as happy to operate on each other.

I want to tell Malachi how to survive, but this is all I know:

You slog through. You take it on the chin. You're in a family one year, the next thing you know it's a different arrangement. You lose an ovary one night, expecting to lose an appendix. You go back to work. You meet someone funny at a party and marry him. You try to have a baby and can't. Instead, you make friends in waiting rooms. You keep working. Events punctuate the stillness of your days, reminding you: Stay alert, don't dwell. You see your father through illness, and the journey is not all horrible, but one day he slips away, ship from shore, and you stand there reeling.

"You want me to make that into patties?" He points to the mess of onion and burger in a bowl. At one point, this all might have transmogrified into tacos.

"Sure." I can't give in just yet.

"Feel this," Mal says, his hands in the burger, his smile a dare.

Raw ground beef, with its whitish suggestion of crushed bone in with the bloody animal flesh, has never held much appeal for me.

"No thanks."

"You're such a *girl*," he says.

"Jessica's a *girl*," I correct.

"I guess."

"Tell me about her. Why you like her, blah blah."

"We talk," he says. "I told you."

"You don't—?" I can't help smiling, although, like a *real* mother, I don't want, ultimately, to know.

He gives me the dishtowel. "We have. We don't anymore."

"My God, Mal, *when?* Before you had sex education in school?" It's terrible what I feel. Betrayal. Absurd, unnatural, but betrayal all the same.

He laughs out loud. "I've been hitting on girls since I was ten, Paige."

"Oh, really, Mal. I can't bear it."

"Don't worry about it," he scoffs. "I'm always careful. Come on, help me make these things."

Something about slapping meat around, at this interval, seems crude. "I'm going to let you do that. I'll hunt up a salad." I go into the crisper for lettuce and tomatoes and pluck a bottle of dressing from the refrigerator door.

"She's always at me," he volunteers.

"*Women.*"

"No, I mean, it's like she thinks I'm the only guy on the planet."

"That may be true for her." I'm batting for Jessica, Lord knows why.

"Yeah, but, like, get a clue. I'm over it already."

"Oh, Mal, don't talk that way." At some point, I'm sure, he'll be telling Jessica that *I'm* at him all the time, a monstrous source of irritation, a person undeserving of authority. A person without a working thermometer.

"That guy, Marekki? He's cool," Mal says, squeezing and patting.

"He's an emperor," I say. "He'll teach you much."

"Yeah, like what?"

"Like how to speak, read, and act. Like how to *see.*"

"Has he taught you that?"

I shrug. "I think so." Since I've gotten to know Marekki, to talk to him about books, I believe I've learned to consider things with more measure, more scope.

"Cool."

I tear the lettuce, exasperated. "This weekend we're going after bigger game."

"Yeah?" He's done six patties and is at the sink, washing again.

"*Yeah.* Marekki says that if you resist Shakespeare, you are only circling the world of literature. Because so many people refer to the plays, you will never make sense of anything unless you read Shakespeare first."

"I've read most of them," he says.

"No you haven't. Not until you do so in a cellar."

"Okay, but I'm supposed to be getting the drums this weekend. Doyle's coming over in the Jeep."

"There's a part for Doyle," I argue.

"The king, right?"

"No. Polonius. Someone will have to stab him behind the dryer."

"Who will I be?"

"Hamlet, stupid. Fresh from university, home for the Thanksgiving break. At the ready with criticism."

"*Okay*, Paige, I'm *sorry*. I just don't see how you can take care of kids five days a week and not have a thermometer."

"And I don't see how you can *have* kids," I argue, "and not let them live in your home."

I've heard about this from the Hens as well, this pitting real mom against stepmom, the rage that results therefrom.

"Back to Hamlet," he says, as neutrally as his father might. "Two problems. Dad's alive, and it's not Thanksgiving."

"We'll work around it. As you say, he's not always present."

"Yeah, well," he says. "Should I cook these?"

"Probably." I get out the large frying pan, the splatter screen, and the apron I wear for holiday cooking. He lets me tie it around him. "So you don't get all greasy."

He holds the screen in front of his face. "I don't think this will be much help."

I sit at the table, watching him cook, until I hear Ian's key in the door, his crashing in.

"A hearty Bardolino, to go with our venison!"

He unsheathes the bottle ceremoniously and I rip into it with our lame corkscrew, pulling out the cork with a satisfying, resonant pop. I pour Ian's and then a glass for Mal.

"Yeah?" he says.

"Yeah."

"Cool."

We eat in relative silence. A few comments about Ian's trial, Mal's anxiety over a band, who's sick. After dinner Ian gets out Scrabble. Ian is a Scrabble tyrant. No peeking in the dictionary, no slang. I manage against him fairly well, but tonight I have lousy letters and have to stick to monosyllables while he and Mal establish an architecture of words that have mostly to do with science. Ian wheels out *porous* and Mal puts in *oxidize*, capitalizing on prime placement of the *x*. They're teaming up, it seems, to combat my idiocy. *Dust*, I add miserably, to Ian's *solvent*, Mal's *tremor*.

"I'm winning," Mal calculates, tallying the rows of numbers.

"Not so fast," his father says. He stacks letters toward the top of the board, branching up from *tremor* into *enema*.

"Nice one, Dad," Mal says.

"Paige?" Ian says. "It's your go."

I put in my usual two letters. *Son*.

Mal looks at me. He adds *net* to that and wins.

❧TWELVE❧

I sleep past nine, wake up with a screaming headache, slosh four Tylenol down with a handful of tap water. The apartment is silent. I go directly to the coffeemaker, which hasn't been touched.

I deduce that Mal left after Ian, perhaps has not even seen his father this morning. I shed the T-shirt I can't remember putting on and get in the shower. I feel lopsided, fat, but for some reason not upset about that. As if a larger force, at work on latent parts of me, deems some changes necessary for my personal evolution. If I must be fat to survive, I must be fat.

I work fiendishly at repairing the shredding spine of *A Connecticut Yankee* until lunch, when I take myself out for Ring-Dings and some air. I'm feeling almost righted, looking at the newspaper after Ring-Dings and coffee when the phone rings.

"Listen, do you want to get away for the weekend? I thought maybe we could go up to Mohonk and spend a fortune on ourselves. Mal can manage in the apartment alone. We could even just go for one night. That wouldn't be leaving him too long."

He doesn't want me to get swept up, I'm thinking, by a child who can never be mine.

"I don't think this is a good time," I say. "To leave him at all. And I've got a ton of work. It's a really nice idea, though."

"You're sure."

"Positive."

"Well, then, I'll just be around a little more, to help with dinners and laundry," he says.

"It's okay, Ian, really," I say. "I'm fine. It'll work out."

"You're terrific," he says, and hangs up.

I'm so terrific I've run out of ideas for my sick squad, so we sit in the car for a spell and pretend we're at the drive-in. I put Ralph's Sony Watchman on the dashboard and tune into a very fuzzy version of *Wishbone*.

"Aren't we supposed to be having food at the drive-in?" he asks, happy to be in front, out of range of the truly infirm.

"No one feels much like eating, Ralph," I remind him.

"I do."

I tell him about the tiny White Castle burgers you can buy frozen at the supermarket and promise that next time we do this (God forbid), I'll microwave a few and bring them along.

"Why do we have to have those?"

"Because that's what people eat in drive-ins. Burgers and milkshakes."

I hand juice boxes and pretzel rods around. Then I pull out of what will no doubt prove to be the only parking spot in our neighborhood and we tour the upper city arguing for a good twenty minutes about whether we qualify as an ambu-lance or an ambulette.

"This day is also helpful in terms of your futures," I explain as we wait in stopped traffic in the Ninety-sixth Street transverse. "It will teach you that you must get a job that doesn't require you to commute by car."

"I have to go to the bathroom," Winifred whines.

I grow more anxious. What does a boy with nothing to do do all day in a city by himself? He can't be alone. I wanted to appear fresh and victorious for Hen Night, but know that I will sport a gaunt face. Once the children have been picked up, I take an age to get dressed, hating everything I try on. I wait until the very last minute to leave the apartment, in the event that he should turn up and give me one of those end-less adolescent excuses I am now convinced I cannot live without.

Everyone is there already, even Bibiana, who is usually dropped off late by a chauffeured limousine. The wine has been ordered, the bread basket plundered.

"Ciao, Bella!" Bibiana says, out of gray Chanel and fea-tures that have no doubt been celebrated at a spa earlier in the day. We're all past the age where vanity counts against one, instead are to be commended for it as a way to stay aloft of drudgery and hagdom.

"What's his name?" Toni asks.

"Diana's not coming," Patty says, pouting. "There's a benefit dinner for Sky Rink."

"I saw her a couple of days ago."

"So we hear," Toni says.

"What," I say. "What did she tell you?"

"Nothing!" Toni sings. "Except that it isn't horrible with Mal. Which is why, everyone, Paige doesn't show up looking half dead or like she wants to kill someone."

She sips her wine, pleased with the synopsis.

"Lighten up, Toni," Patty says.

"What's for dinner?" I ask.

"Bibi ordered," Toni says. "In other words, we don't know."

"I did my best," Bibiana admits. "I can't say it will be real Italian food!"

We always begin this way, pleasantries and teasing, before hunkering down to more wrenching subjects.

"What's our topic for tonight?" I ask.

"Wattle-ectomies," Toni says, pushing the loose skin from her neck up to meet the tighter skin of her cheeks.

Bibiana winces. "You really shouldn't do that, Toni. It makes your skin get looser."

"My skin couldn't be looser if I was eighty," Toni tells me. "Olivia calls me Accordion Neck."

"Olivia *e molto viciata*," Bibiana determines.

"If that means she's full of vice, then you're right," Toni sighs.

"That's exactly what it means," Bibiana says. "And, believe me, I know."

Leonard's boys wouldn't notice things like wrinkles, I figure, being too busy with revenge ploys to waste time on the simpler sorts of insults.

"Sam and Jules want to divorce their father and Bibi," Toni explains to me. "Someone at the Yeshiva has actually been goading them into believing that this will be possible. They've sought out the school counsel."

"They could have called Ian!" I say, not at all surprised, wondering whether the boys sat Leonard and Bibiana down in the parlor at the back of the brownstone or shouted their intentions from the top of the staircase.

"Kids!" Patty says.

"Back to tonight's topic," I say, not sure I can bear one more generalization about *kids*.

"You're our topic for tonight," Toni says. "Diana said there's a lot to talk about." She raises her penciled eyebrows. She must have gone home after work and redone her makeup. It looks way too sharp.

"Well, Mal came home. I mean, we drove him back from that prison. He's been helping me with the littles." I'll stretch his goodwill, in the interest of not falling into the gripe zone.

"She looks like the cat who ate the canary," Patty says, in obvious collusion with the others.

"What's it like, to have him there?" Bibiana does look tired. Beautiful, in her done-up way, but tired.

"Very interesting," I say.

"How old is this kid again?" Patty asks.

"Seventeen. He'll be an adult in March."

"Hah," Patty says. "Bill, Jr., is twenty-four going on four."

"Patty," Toni warns. "Let the woman speak."

I seize the floor. "He's remarkably mature. He does his own laundry and reads Modernist poetry."

"And you didn't invent him," Toni says. "He's real."

"*Madonna,*" Bibiana says. "This is the best story of them all."

If the entire store of tales were being considered here, then it could be heralded as accomplishment. Hard to beat the one about wife number one sending a lawyer to inspect Toni's apartment to see if it was suitable for her daughters to live in. This, from a mother who was leaving her children for a singing career in Europe. Or Patty's husband having to be evaluated by a psychiatrist in order to retain visitation rights when the children's mother was taking Prozac.

"I love this," Toni says. "I get the Valkyries, Patty gets to have every vacation spoiled by drunk college kids, Bibiana has to live with Romulus and Remus. But *Paige* gets Superboy dropped into her life and comes to dinner looking better than she has in months."

"It's a little less glamorous than that," I say, a little stung.

"I defy you to make it appear so," Toni challenges.

"It's complicated," I explain.

"*Tell* me about it," Patty moans. "Bill just bought Bill, Jr., a BMW. Now he can run me over at will."

"I feel very strange, is all," I say. "I *worry* all day. But I *shouldn't*. He's not mine."

Toni sits back, looking at me. "It's happened, ladies. She's a *real* stepmother."

"I feel—" I search for the word, "*caught.*"

"Between," Toni urges.

"Oh, come on, Toni," Patty gripes. "A rock and a hard place. Yes and no. Love and fury."

"More like between what is and what isn't," I hazard. "All the things I want converge in one place, the book work, the full house in the afternoon, the baby thing, Mal's stuff, and there's no way for it all to get sorted out, to *happen*. I *feel* so much, *too* much. It's not right to feel this much. I must seem so overbearing to him."

"He may not see you that way," Bibiana says.

Toni pours out the last of the carafe. "Bibi, would you mind summoning the camaretto, or whatever you called him?"

"*Camariere*," Bibiana corrects. She flags yet another statue type. "*Ancora di vino, per favore.*"

"*Prego, signora*," the waiter says.

It seems particularly fitting to me that Italian is being

spoken tonight. For me the language is synonymous with longing. The words are the ideal. I can only reach for them.

"I can't stop thinking about him. Where he is. What he's doing. What he's going to have for dinner. Whether he brushes his teeth. What kind of girls he sees."

"What I wouldn't give for a kid like that," Patty says sadly. Her husband is nearing sixty, and she isn't yet thirty-five. Of all of their marriages, Patty's makes the least sense to me. Patty is good-looking in a solid, horsy way. You can tell she came from a wealthy suburb where she'd have been better off staying. She met Bill during a corporate training program. An upscale student-teacher situation which all of us try not to insist has been doomed from day one. In a moment of intense generosity, I think how nice it would be to trade stepkids with Patty, but I wouldn't want Bill's parcel of three, two boys and a girl, none of whom will ever understand why they have to share air with Patty.

"He thinks I'm odd," I brag.

"You *are* odd," Toni says.

They move in closer.

"Maybe there's hope," Bibiana says.

"Maybe," I say. "He leaves me notes, wants me to know where he is."

"Where is he?" Patty asks. "What about the drugs?"

"Oh, good Christ, Patty," Toni says. "I think we're intruding, don't you?"

"*Madonna*," Bibiana repeats into her place setting.

"I'm in awe," Toni says.

"Me too," Patty says. "Not to mention green with envy."

"I wouldn't get carried away," I say. "He'll shatter my heart in some way, you watch."

"Listen to you!" Toni hoots. "You're like another person.

You've become unhinged, Paige. You even *sound* like someone's mother!"

"Hey, are we eating?" Patty asks.

"He's coming," Bibiana assures us. She points to two legs approaching under a pile of large, oval dishes.

"I don't think I can eat," Toni says. "I'm too excited." As if I've announced that I'm pregnant.

"We need more wine," I decide.

Bibiana rolls out a reminder to the camaretto, who admonishes himself with *"cretino"* and whizzes away with the empty carafe.

"She's so *together*," Patty says. "It isn't fair."

"I changed clothes six times before I left the apartment tonight," I say.

"But that's *fun*," Toni insists. She's forty-four, the oldest of us. The department store has become her chief comfort zone, not that her stepdaughters object.

"I'm forty, people," I say. "Lest we forget."

"You're a *baby*," Toni reminds me.

"None of us are babies," Patty says, agitated.

"We're just having fun, Patty," I say.

"*You're* having fun," Patty corrects.

"Let's be fair," Bibiana says. She pours refills.

"I'm so tired of being fair," Patty says. "I want to have fun. I want to go out and flirt. A *lot*. Just not with Bill."

"Let's have a toast before we eat," Bibiana suggests. The veal and pasta dishes are no longer steaming.

"To young men!" Patty says, raising her glass, much recovered.

"To boys!" Toni says, because she'll never have any.

Bibiana rolls her enormous brown eyes and sets down her glass.

"I didn't mean *them*," Patty says.

*   *   *

Again I've had more to drink than is good for a person who eats as badly as Mal claims I do, but I decline an offer to ride the three or four blocks home in Bibiana's limousine. Across the street from the restaurant I make good friends with a traffic-light pole, steadying myself, then march forthrightly home with only two slips into zigzag in front of a nondoorman building. Perfect. No one notices. I pass into our building at a comic clip, earning one of Ramone's best ogles.

"Can you make it all right?" he asks, amused.

"I'll be *just fine!*" I push the Down button and then have to wait, once the elevator arrives, for the doors to shut and open again. Up we go, and then wheee, into the apartment, letting the door fly shut behind me only to find myself smack in front of Mal, who is stretched out on the sofa with the headphones on.

"Hello there!" I salute.

He removes the headphones and holds them in his lap. "You wasted?"

"No," I lie. "I am not *wasted*. And whatever happened to the auxiliary verb? I sort of miss it."

"You *are* wasted," he says. He's staring at me as if I have food splattered all over me or have grown another limb. I suppose I'm out of my league here, in the mind-altering-substance department.

"Define 'wasted,'" I continue.

"'Out of it,' 'zoned,' 'trashed,' 'plowed,' 'inebriated'—"

"That one I recognize," I interrupt.

"So these hens can put it away, eh?" he asks.

"Don't call my friends 'hens.'"

"You do!"

"That's another matter," I decide.

"You're incredible," he says. His disgust hangs between us, actual, a wall.

"And why is that?" How long, I wonder, will I stand in the middle of the living room?

"You're acting so bitchy."

"Excuse me for living," I say calmly, "but I'm in a bit of a state."

"Well, we know *that*."

I feel flattened. Flung out. This is the part about young people I've erased from my memory of being one. Affection comes easily and can lose its significance just as quickly.

"I'm sorry to have disturbed you," I say.

"Don't worry about it." He puts the headphones back on. I go into the bedroom, a dark terrain of shame. I put on the light and sit on my side of the bed and weep for the sad creature I've become to ever think I'd constitute an object of Mal's affection.

❧ THIRTEEN ❧

I choose to combat the new hangover by going mad with housework after an infusion of Advil and coffee. My attire is a statement of indifference aimed at Mal, still in his room. I am taking an angry hand to the issue of bathtub grime when I hear the refrigerator door thud shut. Under no circumstances am I going to alter my charwoman's demeanor in order to secure an approving glance from him whom I have now cast into the category of ingrate sloth in order to assuage my self-loathing.

"Paige? What are you doing?" One would think, given the consistency of Comet, that the vicious scrubbing I'm administering to the tub could be heard two apartments away.

"It would appear I'm cleaning the tub."

"So early?"

"The tub doesn't think it's early, actually," I go on. "The sun came up about four hours ago." I turn on the hot and let it roar, scalding my already red fingers and rinsing the green paste out. He takes a seat on the toilet. I hang over the tub's rim, fuming.

"You didn't get any sleep, did you?" he shouts.

I turn off the water with a satisfying squeak.

"Why is that of any consequence to you?"

"What is *with* you, man? I'm just asking you how you are!" He bends his head down to rest in his palms. Purposeful gesture, I think.

I shift around, exposing the wet front of my overalls. "You say you'll do things, and you don't do them, witness the tacos. If you're going to live here, then make a stab at *living* here. Now, if you'll excuse me, I have an apartment to clean."

"I never said I'd make tacos. *You* volunteered me for that."

"Another thing to regret." He's right, of course.

I rise, pulling at the flanks of my overalls. I collect my sponge and abrasive and march into the kitchen.

He follows me. "You're pissed because I was gone all yesterday, aren't you?"

I start in on the kitchen sink, sprinkling and wiping large circles in the stained porcelain. "What about the other stuff, at least the phone calls? You might want to put a little effort into making a new life for yourself, now that you threw away the old one. As for your being out yesterday, frankly, I was relieved. I got some work done, ran the infirmary alone, and then I had dinner with friends."

"Boy, did you."

"You watch yourself," I say. "You're living in *my* house now, and you are not at liberty to say whatever you want to me. So you can get with the program here, help out, or you can find other lodgings."

Incredibly, he's laughing. "I'm sorry."

"You see? That's what you do. You humiliate. You scoff. You don't care."

"I'm not laughing to humiliate you," he begs, his arms at his sides, useless. "I'm laughing because you're funny."

"Now you flatter, thinking that I might have a shred of sympathy left for you."

I toss the sponge against the splash guard.

He shakes his head. "I don't expect that. I don't expect anything. I'm just trying to figure out what to do. All day yesterday I was with Jessica looking up courses they have at night, seeing if there were any I could take."

"You have to have a *diploma* to take those courses! You can't just waltz into a university and *qualify*." Outer space. If you're this stupid, there's no helping you.

"I know that now," he says quietly.

"I don't understand you, Mal. If you wanted to take courses so badly, why didn't you stick it out a few more months at Bay Ridge and get yourself into college?"

"*Because,*" he says, "I don't think it's the way to learn."

"Well, if you have some privileged notion of what that way is, I'd love to know about it."

"You know about it already. I told you. The stuff has to feel like it's alive. Otherwise it's dead!"

"Look," I say, "if you want to go be Hercules, go be Hercules. But you can't expect your teachers to fly along with you."

"Why not?"

"Because they're *too old*. They can tell you how to get it together. But you have to do that on your own. I'm no teacher, but I am not going to watch you sleep late every day and moon around this kitchen. Or decide when to be nice to the pre-K set. Or hear about courses you can't take. It's all too *half-baked*. So here's the plan. You hop aboard, come to Marekki with me today, keep up the study as we've laid it out, get yourself into a band, and don't lay on any more garbage."

"Jesus," he says. "You can be such a Nazi."

I suppose I might deserve that one, for issuing all the directives. "Marekki," I say. "In ten."

"You remember Mal," I tell Mr. Marekki, who's had a shave and is sitting in a chair by the window in a brown terry wrapper, his short thick legs bare, his alabaster feet in leather slip-ons.

"The boy needs no further introduction," Marekki says with a dismissive wave that takes a loud gasp to execute. He recovers from it and goes on, "I don't suppose you've had your eye on St. John's of late."

"Sure I have!" Mal says. He abandons the cart for the other chair. "Everyone's got their eye on that team. But Syracuse'll crush 'em, trust me. Boeheim's better than anything St. John's'll ever have."

"I may be in agreement with you," Marekki says. "What goes around comes around, of course, and Mr. Boeheim has a courtside manner that none of these other fellows exhibits. I do enjoy a good fight, mind you, but I don't care to have it occur out of bounds. In any event, it will be satisfying to see him reach the playoffs this term."

Term. I stop my shelving. "Mr. Marekki, you were a teacher. Maybe you could tell Mal a little about that."

Mr. Marekki turns back to Mal. "That I will save for another time. But I will preface that discussion with the detail of my having taught Classics for my entire career in a small boys' school in the Midwest."

His eyes are bright and watery.

"So how come you're here?" Mal asks.

"My body has betrayed me," Marekki says grandly.

"I meant instead of a hospital out there."

"Another time," Marekki says again.

"You want some new books?" Mal offers. He gets busy looking.

"Naturally. Books are my staple food."

I keep my eyes on Mal, who is attempting to look efficient, rifling through. He holds forth one slim leather-bound book, the least ratty of the hardbacks.

Marekki makes a production of donning his bifocals, in which he looks almost elegant. "Of course you chose this one," he says, pleased.

"Of course," Mal agrees, clueless.

"*The Oresteia*," Marekki says. "How timely." He looks from my face to Mal's, then back to mine.

"Next time you visit," he says to Mal, "perhaps you'll do me the honor of having read 'The Libation Bearers.' It's the middle play. You needn't consult any secondary texts. I am all you will require in that department."

Again the hefty wave, and out we go, renewed.

The rest of the rounds amount to a slow meandering, will-less, fatigued. "I can't read that stuff," Mal complains on the bus home.

"You can't *not* read it. Think of what that would do to him."

"You better help me."

"That's what I'm here for, apparently," I say.

I send him to the corner to stock up on fruit pies and bottled water. Alone in the apartment for a second, I call Mother. "I miss Daddy," I say.

"I know you do," she says. "We all do. Is it difficult for you, having the boy there?"

Marekki would ask what was a little domestic displacement stacked up against the tragedies of Aeschylus.

"No. Actually, yes."

"I think your father would be very proud," she says. "That you've taken this on."

"He took on Audrey's kids."

"But they never lived in the same house," Mother reminds me. "Even if they had, he wouldn't have said a word about it. He was so *good*, in that way. A true stoic. I'd have fallen completely to pieces."

"I can see how that happens," I say.

"Where is he now? Mal?"

"He's at the store getting some things for me."

"Sounds like you've already got him well trained!"

I laugh. "There's no training this one, Mother."

"Murder! I hope he'll be civil at Thanksgiving. I've already told Audrey he's coming."

"He'll be civil," I promise, no grounds whatever for the statement.

Against all instincts except the most true, I enter Mal's kingdom. I need to know more in order to help, proceed, manage. I go right for the bureau, wherein, among the distinct piles of underwear and socks, I find an unopened box of condoms, some packets of rolling papers, and a tin of Pastille candies. Whatever he's using the rolling papers for is not in evidence, and I rest on the dim hope that maybe they're just decorative, a convenience for friends, something to carry around, like the condoms, for image's sake.

Onward: a journal, leather-bound, in his shirt/jeans drawer. I lift it out, note scratches in the surface, shredding edges. What would Dorothy do, I wonder? Would she blare in and read, bring him up short later with her concerns? Whatever she'd do, I don't want to do. I don't want to resemble her, to him.

I flip back the hinge and let the pages whir, stopping on none but seeing they're all full, front and back, with a wild black script that suggests unbridled inspiration, if not mania. Every line is full, up until the end.

I hear the front door open and close, the rustling of a plastic bag. Quickly I slip the journal back and slide the drawer closed. Almost as quickly, he is behind me.

"I was thinking," I fudge, hand to chin, "that maybe we ought to clear off the desk in here. The TV could just as well go on the bureau. What's your view?"

"My view?" he says. He looks thrown, perplexed at having found me here. He shoves hands into pockets, shrugs. His hair settles over his forehead, in his eyes. "My view is that it doesn't matter. It's just furniture."

"Right," I say. I should go on, I suppose, for credibility's sake, but I'm frozen by his uncomprehending stare, and by the fact that I've broken a rule and he knows it.

⚔ FOURTEEN ⚔

*I*an suggests the new Woody Allen and dinner out. "Come on. You and I need to get out together. I can be a lot of fun, I promise you."

"I'm trying to get through this play so I can help Mal with it. Mr. Marekki is going to give a talk," I say. I hold up my paperback *Oresteia* as evidence. Mal is out running. Doyle is three hours late with the drums.

"Bring it along," Ian says. "You can read it in line. The movie just opened so you might want to cart along some Sophocles too."

We take the Broadway bus. Ian is his chatty, date self, going on about the probable horror of Audrey's for Thanksgiving with Mal in tow.

"I just hope he can leave his street self in the coat closet," Ian says.

"He'll be fine. He knows when to turn on the charm."

"Oh believe me, I *know*," Ian says. "You should have seen him with Paula."

"Must you bore me with Paula all the time?" I beg. Mal went into the office with Ian to try to get his academic history embellished on letterhead for a GED program Ian found out about. When he came home, focused and hopeful from the effort, there was no mention of Paula.

"He thought she was cute."

"He didn't say 'cute.' He wouldn't say that."

"No. You're right. I believe he used the words 'hot' and 'fine.'"

This description doesn't jibe with Ian's, which has established Paula as a driven but sage stick figure with a large, broken heart.

"That's just guy talk," I say. "Lyrics."

"He's taught you much!"

"He's a total handful. I can't rest!"

"I must admit to feeling a bit upstaged," Ian says with mock sadness.

"Word has it that's what kids do to marriages," I say, as lightly. "Ask Paula."

He sticks out his jaw in my least favorite of his expressions. In the beige raincoat that has never quite fit him, he looks dorky, a handsome man who has sartorially misfired. All he needs is a shoe polish mustache and a toy gun.

"You forget that I haven't lived with this version of him either. I'm not exactly looking forward to the drums."

"I'm sure he's not thinking of practicing in the apartment."

"I wouldn't be so certain of that."

Over dinner at the Hunan Balcony I fawn. I have to test myself, perform, find the right, wifely words. The Woody

Allen has inspired me, urged me into a more generous view of people and their foibles, of myself just stumbling along. I'm glad we saw it.

"So is Paula really hot and fine?" I ask. "I don't think I can take the competition."

"Hot and fine and dull as a summer day!" he says. He tips back his free glass of wine. "What sewer do you suppose they tap into to get this?"

"Don't tell me she's dull if she isn't," I say. Every time he speaks of Paula, he throws a jab into the description. I'm starting to think this is purposeful.

"She's dead sound," he says, winking. "She reminds me of architecture."

"What?"

"Yes. A great building. Something with a flawless foundation that you know will remain standing, regardless of force majeure."

The image is so drab I don't know how I'll continue the ruse of envying Paula.

"And I'd crumble," I say.

"Yes. You'd be the victim. The Crumbling Wife. But I mean that in a good way."

"I don't see how you could," I say. "God, this wine is awful."

"Men like women who crumble," he goes on. "It makes them feel useful. Sometimes I look at Paula when she's mid-flurry and I have a horrible idea that her husband, or significant other or whatever he was, left her and the kid because he knew he *could*."

"You mean, if I suddenly up and founded a company and bought myself a Corvette, you'd seek asylum in the arms of someone like me?"

He thinks about that one. "After a tour of the city in the Corvette, yes."

"I'm glad I'm a failure," I say.

"Don't ever say that," he says. "You're anything but. I can't believe how Mal's taken to you. I've never seen the kid care about anything or anyone before. You've got a boy who was selling pot a month ago taking books to people in hospitals and taking care of six-year-olds. You've got him thinking about what to buy at the grocery store, whether there's enough milk for breakfast. I seriously don't know how you've done it. In a matter of *days*."

"I had to," I say. I don't like to take credit, now that Mal has caught me snooping.

"Not everyone would say so. You could have refused to have him in the house."

"People don't do that."

"Dorothy did."

"Dorothy's not 'people.' Dorothy's his mother. That's different. There are layers upon layers of reasons, I'm sure, for doing things when you're somebody's mother. But that's something I'll never know about."

I stare out the window at the busy evening street, people in new coats, their eyes up, their hands full, heading into the most difficult season.

"I disagree." Ian's eyes are full. "You already do."

"Don't, Ian," the Crumbling Wife warns. "Don't even think it."

He gathers himself to say, "Do you think we'll get back to something familiar here? This détente is starting to work on me."

I'm across the great divide, paralyzed. I can't even reach for him. He means, in part, the sex. But I can't summon it—sexual desire—when it feels so pointless, ridiculous even, and bound up with sadness.

It doesn't go away, the despair about not being able to

have a child. It dulls. The feeling, I've thought about this so much, must be a little like the one a drowning person has when he or she thinks survival is still possible. Keep trying, keep reaching up into the air, out of the heavy water. There, where it's brighter. But then the arms, now someone else's, out of control, so heavy, start to sink, sharing their impossible weight with other body parts—neck, shoulders, trunk, hips, thighs, ankles. Then the head, under, down. Release from the effort, no more struggle, forget about it. Go down.

He buys me flowers on the way home, a bunch of carnations from the corner deli. And ice cream. Mint chip. My hold on the evening, on the two of us wandering around in it buying things, is tenuous at best. I'm confused, wrought up, remembering being comforted in similar ways by my father, unable to separate Ian from the image of Daddy beside me, trying everything on earth to improve my spirits.

"I'm so worried," I tell Ian.

"Tell me."

"I'm so worried I'll never come out of this," I say.

"You will," he promises.

"How do you know that?"

"I'm watching," he says. "I see it." He squeezes my waist, holds the flowers to my face for me to smell.

"What do you see?"

"I see how you are with Mal," he says. "You're like a young kid. Hopeful. Funny. Upset. Beautiful. It's no wonder he's up to his eyeballs in you. You're the woman I met at the party."

I start to cry. "I am so sorry," I say.

"For what?" he laughs. "For being this wild movie I get to watch from the minute I wake up until the minute I fall out? You're my entertainment! You're the reason I wake up in the first place! I don't want to miss the show!"

I look at his strained face, and at the gray flecks in the hair at his temples, and I just want to wail over all that's happened, interrupted us, hurt us. "Oh, Ian," I weep, "you are so very, very dear."

He gets out his handkerchief, gives it to me. "But you're so very far," he says, his eyes watery, "away from me."

We walk north for a while, then back down West End toward the building. It's finally getting cold. The air could almost be called fresh.

"Sometimes I feel like he's been sent to us," I say. "Cosmically sent."

"Why is that?"

"To shake us up. Enrage us and love us and drive us so crazy we don't know what to do."

"Prophets do that," Ian says.

"Kids do that." Kyle, Ralph, Electra, Winifred. Fat Anthony.

I stop outside the building, not wanting to go in yet, but Ian has work to do.

"The party already started," Ramone tells us. "You late. I got a lot of complaints."

Ian takes the news without issue. "How many kids?" he asks Ramone. I wouldn't have leapt to that, numbers of kids. I have the drum set in mind, being dutifully carted upstairs by Doyle.

"I don't know," Ramone says. "Eight? Ten? I didn't count."

"Girls?" Ian asks.

"Definitely."

We ride the elevator in silence. The thumping bass becomes audible on approach, before we get to our floor.

"Oh God," I say, disembarking, worrying for our ancient neighbors and the ones with infants.

"Prepare ye," Ian says, leading the way.

We couldn't have warned them if we'd wanted to. The door is unlatched, the music louder than the doorbell. No intercom buzzer could penetrate the merrymaking, no air of reason the smoke. The apartment is unrecognizable, and there are large strangers everywhere. I hold on to Ian, afraid for him and for myself, and somehow, despite the huge betrayal that the scene foists on us, for Mal.

We wander, as persons through the smoky aftermath of musket battle.

The living room is host to the drum set, now being exercised by a boy in a Tommy Hilfiger jacket, so intent on his playing along with what is blasting from the stereo that he fails to notice Ian and me staring at him. There is a couple on the long sofa, their clothing loose but not off, I could cross myself. There are beer bottles on most of the flat surfaces, ringing the wood with water stains, to be sure. Whatever music this is, with its minor key, its dark, urban message, resounds from every inch of wall, every corner of furniture, every cared-for space of the room I have until this moment thought of as a portion of home. Mal is not in evidence.

A girl, her hair cruelly cropped and dyed caramel, in an undecorated black jumpsuit that makes me think of a cartoon villain, stops in the kitchen doorway and scrunches up her face, in disappointment for us, I believe. A sympathy grimace, perhaps. More earrings than there is flesh for decorate her ears and face.

I follow Ian past her, down the hall to our bedroom. Around the bulk of him I catch sight of bare feet, bare legs on the bed. He turns quickly to me, tells me he'll handle it, and closes the door between us.

It can't be, I think. He *can't* be doing this. In *my* house. He may as well sock me in the stomach. My stupidity faces me, a jeering stranger. How could I have presumed to know him? How could I have thought I occupied a coveted place in his heart, now filled by that pair of white legs laced into his? Even during the brief glimpse into the bedroom I knew which legs, which feet, were his. I've memorized him, head to toe.

That Ian is shouting and that Mal is shouting back is clear because someone in the other room has had the decency to shut off the music. I stay in the dark hallway, safe against the wall. I do not want to proceed with cleanup until all of them have made themselves scarce, so my reaction, whatever form it takes, will not become public. I hear clattering and movement in the outer rooms, and I marvel at the slowness of the guests to leave. I don't think I'll survive the sweet, barnyard smell of the dope, and it takes me to task, how I ever inhaled something so putrid, so historically stupid.

"I mean *now!*" Ian thunders just before Mal throws open the door and strides past me, pulling a girl in noisy heels behind him. Jessica?

He stays in the bedroom. I stay in the hallway. I listen to drawers opening and slamming shut, and I'm acutely aware of the girl's silence, as if this exit of Mal's is something she expected all along, something she planned with him.

I sink down, hug my knees. And in the way of people paralyzed by event, I tell myself it isn't happening, that he'll be back tomorrow, all smiles and apology, begging to go to the corner deli to store up on junk before we descend to the basement for Greek lit.

How stupid I've been is only beginning to dawn on me. I thought that with enough study, with the proper degree of devotion and, yes, love, if love is what I actually feel for Mal, I'd be able to create an equation into which he fit and behaved predictably. Palatably. I have tried to put him into the *category* of child, and I've prepared myself to stand vigilant over him until he behaved. I've been unwilling to lend credence to the possibility that he cannot be controlled, does not want to be, that his school troubles are unusual, that his mother's fierceness is merited. That there will always be something in the way of his joining us, something more than circumstantial.

I'm aware of drastic movement around me, of Mal throwing things in his room and the girl pleading privately with him, a role I actually envy. I sense that the other friends have left and that Ian is seeing to some of the mess. But I can't bring myself to join him yet. In the way of people who don't know that their hearts have been broken, who don't believe it is possible for that to happen again in their lifetime, I stay still, literally holding myself together.

If you ever think you've hit rock bottom, you're wrong. Rock bottom is not recognizable. Rock bottom is next.

We work until two in the morning. I collect garbage and rinse bottles and Ian tends to displaced knickknacks, water stains, ashes and crumbs, and the issue of the bedclothes. I try to be chatty, to summon him back from the deep, mean place he disappeared into the minute he found Mal with the girl in the bedroom.

"We're like those sad souls picking through the mess after Agincourt," I say.

"Those people had some inkling as to a reason for the destruction," he spits back. There's no fixing it. I have to let him be furious. But I do feel as I imagine people do after a battle: out of context and exposed, the very earth they trusted churned up by the enemy.

I shut off the stereo and sit on the floor, no idea of how we'll muddle through this.

I'm aware of the silence, a hole in the place. Good thing I didn't kill myself to get through "The Libation Bearers." Where will we store the drums? The bin in the basement is full.

I wish he'd call, just so we'd know where he is. He was careful to take all his clothes, even the dirty ones he was letting pile up in the closet. The CDs he can replace or send one of his army for. He wore the jacket. There'll be no need for him to come back.

"You have to try to find him," I say to Ian.

Ian looks up, annoyed. "No I don't. I don't have to do anything. I've done what I can to keep him on course. He's defied me on every front. He's even tried to turn my wife against me. So I think I can rest now."

"*Turn your wife against you?* Ian, that's *crazy!*"

"Don't you agree he turns on the charm to get his way?" Now his face is hard with certainty.

"Who doesn't? I'll admit he's pretty unleashed," I say, "but he's just not that calculating! And what would be the *point?*"

"To get at *this.*" He gestures inclusively, so as to indicate our life through our material holdings.

"Oh God, Ian. That is just *so* naïve. He's been with us a week. Ruin takes longer than that." What am I *saying?* Two seconds!

"Then he's put finishing touches on what was already there."

"You're letting him do this," I say, steely.

"*Letting him!*" He shakes his head wildly. "Did I order this mini-Armageddon tonight? I took my wife to dinner and a movie. I was anticipating a quiet bowl of ice cream in the kitchen after a pleasant evening. Instead, I got a protest rally. And a very poorly organized one at that. Could someone explain this to me? Could someone explain how long the average person can sustain blame? If he ever comes back to stage an apology, I know what I'll get. I'll get accusation. I'll get 'you divorced my mother,' *quod erat demonstrandum*. Do you know how sick I am of this? Of him and the things he does? Do you have any idea?"

"I'm getting one."

"I was married to someone I never saw except briefly on weekends to fight with, and I will be taken to task over not adoring her for the rest of my life by this child of mine."

"Boo hoo, Ian. This is such a seriously old story, I don't know if I can bear to listen to it anymore. You have to shift into the present. You have to examine the evidence *as it is now*. Maybe this isn't *about* Dorothy. Maybe it's about you and him."

"I knew I could count on you for support."

"I think I've done all right, under the circumstances." Something old is building in me, a familiar rage.

"I believe I said as much tonight. I didn't realize there was a limit."

"There's always a limit, Ian," I say. "You've reached yours."

"Ditto."

I stand for a minute staring at him. Then I can't do that anymore. I locate my coat, put it on, and leave the apartment.

❧ FIFTEEN ❧

At the West End I sit at the bar and order a glass of Chardonnay. Basketball is on the TV, and I listen more attentively than I ordinarily would, picking out some of the names Mal rattled off the night he kept calling me from Madison Square Garden. I munch a few pretzels, dry and pointless.

I drink the wine fast.

"Another?" the bartender asks. "We're closing up soon."

"I think so. I think that would be the ticket."

"If you fancy drowning." He's pouring anyway. I like his Irish accent, and I ruminate momentarily on what my life might be like if I lived with him, an Irishman instead of a Scot, presumably without a child. I conjure a hazy urban bedroom full of his smiling approval and his work clothes, slung passionately over a chairback.

"I don't like the idea of drowning much," I say, lifting the Chardonnay. "But like it or not!"

"You've got a look about you," he says.

"What look?"

"Like you're thinkin' too hard about somethin'," he says. They're all over, the experts.

"It's the game," I explain, pointing up at the ceiling TV. "I can't watch." I hold my head in misery.

"You're a Lakers fan, then," he says, with the smile.

"Diehard," I tell him.

The girl, I learned from Ian, wasn't Jessica. Who was she, and how did he dig her up so fast?

I do need a vacation.

The next morning Ian and I don't speak. I walk to Liberty Travel, where I land a low fare to a place I've never heard of. The agent says that the place is perfect for single parents, and that all the food and entertainment you could possibly want is included in the package. The name of it, Turkoise, suggests a colorful mindlessness I'm sure I can benefit from, and the brochure pictures of the beach, accommodations, and sports facilities bespeak an Eden before sin. I book the second week of December, not a blackout week, and walk out with a battery of vacation tips. I'll tell the kids' parents that I have to get away, and that for one week they'll have to fend for themselves.

I catch Toni mid-movie. "He took them to the theater," she says. "How's Superboy?"

"He lasted here a week," I tell her. "Now Ian and I are at each other's throats."

"Did something *happen?*"

"Mal gave himself a welcome-home party. He trashed the apartment."

"And *then* he left."

"Ian didn't care for the crowd."

"I'll have my mind around this one by midweek. Diana is taking us to the Terrace."

"Oh, that's nice." It will suit my new penchant for luxury.

"That's all you can say? She'll be spending a college loan in one evening!"

"I guess she must want to."

"Are you *alive?*" Toni complains.

"I'm sorry," I say, although I'm not exactly sure what for. For not getting flummoxed about the extravagance, but how dare I? "See you Wednesday."

"He'll be back, you know," Toni says.

"Joy and rapture."

"Honeymoon over?"

"*Way* over. You know how short they are!"

"He'll be *back,*" Toni repeats.

All that's left in the junk cupboard is a package of fairly hard Twinkies. I bite into one. The spurt of vanilla inside does nothing for me. I spit the thing into the trash, throw out its twin, and rinse my mouth with tap water. "Hell," I snarl. I call Diana.

"I'm going on vacation. *Alone.*"

"And here I sat thinking about work I can get for you. Mother says she's waist-deep in volumes of original Bentleys. If this is true, and I do need to verify it, someone's got to repair them."

"I'd be lost without you," I say, even though I'm a little out of my depth with art books. In college, I *would* have been lost without Diana. She was the perfect friend: funny, available, outraged over the slightest upset to come my way.

"How's Mal?"

"Absent."

"Welcome to teenage boys. He'll manage."

True, how Mal can temporarily right himself. Wherever he is, I know he's arranged for his current comfort. In terms of company and surrounding, he's able to rig things. Who is going to say no, other than Ian and Dorothy? And, when the trashing of apartments came into play, myself?

"You're a good friend."

"Shucks," she says, and hangs up.

Again, to the dreadful business of how to fill the empty moments. I wish it were a weekday. We'd all be off to the zoo or the park. No time for introspection or bewilderment, time spent, as Birch said, *in selfish pursuit*.

At seventy, my grandfather moved out in a silent hurry, taking only his clothes and his file boxes full of records and press about his accomplishments as director of a small museum. From two towns away, he kept in touch with Birch by telephone from the upper floor of a two-family home, the downstairs of which was occupied by an art-history professor who had been a friend of theirs for years. The logical assumption, that Andrew and the professor, Tom Lucas, were lovers, didn't get mentioned. Although she claimed to be fine, busying herself at her easel, the summer after Andrew left, I found Birch at the kitchen table crying. I sat down and asked her what had made her decide to marry him.

"I don't know," Birch told me. "I suppose I wanted to."

She wiped her eyes and went out to fill the birdbath.

I adored my grandfather for his humor, the doggerel he scribbled on my birthday cards, but I did not understand what he did until now, how he could dismiss Birch like that. He was drawn to Tom because there was something lacking with Birch. He believed he had reason.

Likewise: I am drawn to the littles, to Mal, away from Ian.

*   *   *

Monday I touch up the cover of *Frog* and chart the path through the next six volumes, marking on my calendar the days I have left to finish one to get to the next, making notes about the specific needs of each on a legal pad. I don't stop until Ramone rings to say that Johanna's downstairs. As I get out of the elevator a football grazes my cheek. I toss it gently back to Kyle.

"Where's Mal?" he demands joyfully.

"He's not here today."

Kyle turns into his mother's skirt. "Instant tears," Johanna says. "All he talked about all weekend was *the big boy*. Thus the football."

I apologize and make the criminal promise that Kyle will see Mal soon.

"Do I get both today?" I ask, gesturing for the baby.

"Can you?" she pleads. "I've got a ton of paperwork."

"Give me *this* big boy," I say. Anthony smells like shampoo. His bath has made him sleepy. "No stroller?"

"Next time," she says. "I have to get a new one."

She bends to comfort Kyle, tells him she's bought the fried-chicken TV dinner with the speckled pudding in it. She hands me the bag of two dinners.

"Anthony will eat this too?"

"What *won't* Anthony eat?" Johanna says. She smiles, for the first time all fall. She must be getting used to the new stress level. She kisses both kids and backs away, a spring in her walk. She's finally doing it, I think: *more* than enduring.

"I want to talk to Dad," Mal says. Everyone's in front of the TV. I had to go buy more of those TV dinners because the other three kids pitched a fit.

"Where *are* you." My tone is raw, all wrong.

"Just let me talk to him, okay?"

"Try the office." It breaks me, to be barking at him like this.

"I did. He's not there."

"He's not?" Odd. He usually stays until well after six, which it is. I remark on this from a distance. Right now I don't care where Ian is, when he'll be home.

"No one is."

"What do you need, Mal?"

"Money."

Figures. "I'll let him know when he gets home."

"There's a place in an apartment," he goes on. "A friend of Jessica's who lives up on Riverside, near you."

My heart leaps. Close by. At least there'll be that. "Is it the one we met at the party? Because I can tell you right now, I don't think that'll go over too well with your dad." *Or with me*, I might add. I can't help imagining how they must speak to each other, Mal and this girl. Mal and whatever girl. Monosyllables. Quick interrogatives and declaratives. Surface decisions. A haze of sexual innuendo that might not even be recognized as such.

"Doesn't matter who with," he says. "I just need a place to live. It's four hundred a month. I'd be out of your hair. I got a job, by the way. At HMV. I start Thursday."

"The one on Eighty-sixth?" My interest in the logistics are second to my displeasure over the roommate issue.

"Whatever."

"I'm sure he'll be very interested in that. I'm sure he'd be glad to split the first month's rent with your mother."

"Yeah, like *that's* going to happen."

"It has to, Mal," I say. "I'll pass on the message. Thank you for calling."

Where there are no checks and balances, you invent

your own. I have no idea who has built the sudden moat around me, but I like its offer of safety. And the five honest attendants at the castle gate.

Electra comes into the kitchen in tears.

"What?"

"Ralph called me a *fucking bitch*."

I wait. I don't want to react as I think I'm going to.

"Don't say those words, Electra, no matter who says them to you." I don't mean to be harsh. I just can't stand the idea of Ralph's poisoning her.

I march into the living room, haul Ralph up by his arm, take the chicken leg out of his hand, and toss it into his aluminum tray. "How dare you?"

"Paige!" he screams. "That hurts!"

"So do those words you called Electra."

Now Anthony, in my other arm, is aware of difficulty. He joins in the din with his baby wail. Kyle is up like a shot. "Leave my brother alone!"

"I'm not doing anything to your brother! Now sit down and finish your dinner!" I drag Ralph with me into the kitchen, realizing I have less justification for my behavior than I do for his.

"Paige!" Winifred whines. "Why are you being so mean?"

"What is it with you?" I demand from Ralph. "Why do you talk like that?"

He's crying, wiping his face with his sweater sleeve. "Electra said I'm stupid!"

"Where did you learn that language?"

"At school," he sniffs. "All the kids say it."

Electra, cowering under the kitchen table, bursts in with, "That doesn't mean you have to say it!"

"All right, all right," I say, trying to calm myself into a civilized grip on Ralph, on the situation. "But Ralph, just because other kids say things like that doesn't mean you should. Or *can*. I can't let you talk that way in my house. Now, apologize to Electra."

"You apologize to *me!*" he yells, showing me two pink dents on his upper arm.

I sit down, jiggle Anthony, now past wails and into hiccups, on my knee.

"I'm sorry, Ralph. I lost my temper."

"My dad's going to fire you."

"That will be my tough luck," I say, recognizing the distinct possibility of this.

Kyle looms in the doorway, hopeful. "Did you lose your temper at Mal too?"

"Yes," I say.

They often point me in the direction of the truth, these five.

"Is that why he went away?" Now, with the trembling chin. Of all of them, Kyle cries the least, so his crying is most difficult to witness.

"What makes you think he went away, Kyle?" I ask.

Kyle shrugs. "His stuff's gone."

"Come here," I say. "All of you."

I pull them all into a huddle, all ten arms, five heads of different hair, all the smells of school and food and outdoors. "Sometimes people do things they wish they didn't," I say.

Ralph draws back, smiling. "You can say that again! Jeez!"

Ian doesn't come in until after ten. He's gaunt from the commute uptown, his face shiny.

"You look wretched," I say, watching him sift through the mail on the hall table.

"Thank you," he says. "I suppose I am, a bit."

"What was for dinner?"

"Noodle something."

"With?"

"Salad."

"I meant who with?"

"Paula."

"Ah." I swallow. What possible further understanding can Paula be offering him? I don't want to think about it. "Mal called."

"Did he."

"He got a job, starting Thursday, at HMV Music. And he found a place in an apartment near here. If you can float him half of the first month's rent."

"How is he planning to pay the other half, I wonder. Surely his millionaire mother won't be participating."

His dinner with Paula hasn't had much of a prophylactic effect after all. "Ian, he's trying. He's putting into effect that program you were ranting about last week."

"I fail to see that."

"Well, open your eyes, then. He called you at the office. He didn't *want* to involve me." Of this, I'll never be sure, but as long as I'm going to bat for him, I may as well paint everything in the best possible light.

"I was at the office all day," Ian argues. "He tried to call me when he knew I wouldn't be there."

There is something final in his tone, something irremediable. When I met Mal for the first time, at a bistro on the East Side, he and Ian were so jovial and hands-on with each other I could not have foreseen this rift, any rift. They made a handsome duo, sitting at the small table, laughing, healthy. It was July, and Mal was off to a summer program for young musicians at Chatauqua the next day. We'd bus him in for the wedding, a month later, to a friend's house in the

Hamptons where he'd get the idea to smuggle a bottle of rum from the bar and turn up later, passed out next to a fence near Georgica Pond.

I was too elated after the wedding to think anything of the incident other than it's a normal reaction to act out when one's parents remarry. I considered myself as responsible for the bender as Ian. But I may have been wrong to assume any responsibility. I was just as angry at Daddy when he dropped Audrey so permanently into my life. I couldn't blame Audrey: who in her right mind would have refused him, a divorcé with assets, humor, and good looks?

"Did you tell Paula about what happened with Mal?"

He finally sits down, resting his general despair in the armchair opposite. "I didn't need to. She guessed."

"How clever," I say.

I get up, a ghost in my own house, and search the other, frantically neat rooms for something to straighten. Ian stays in the living room, catatonic, in front of a political program. I'm too exhausted to sleep, but I get into bed eventually anyway and turn out the light, fated to lie watching the car beams decorate and redecorate the walls until their light becomes indiscernible from dawn's.

❧ SIXTEEN ❧

We've talked about it, the other Hens and I, the waiting we all did, the hideous, shaming effort, the bottomless disappointment and rage. When I met Toni, we were waiting to consult with the same doctor. She had Olivia and Laura with her, and I automatically assumed she was just greedy for more kids and had run into some infertility problem that couldn't possibly compare with my own.

Olivia was doing her homework, and Toni was reading to Laura in a tone so strained I knew she wouldn't get through the short book.

"Honeybun," she finally said, "I'm going to have to let Olivia finish reading this to you."

"No way," Olivia said.

Toni looked at me with big eyes, as if I could help, but I was having none of her despair.

"Sartre said, 'Hell is other people,'" she announced, getting up and depositing Laura on the chair. She straightened her skirt. "But he hadn't met their kids."

I understood, at that moment, what her predicament was, but I didn't know until now that the sidelines are easier to bear when you *choose* them.

Walking up Amsterdam to the hospital, my copy of *The Oresteia* tucked into my coat pocket, I can't remember exactly what I've done the last few days. They seem as if they occurred years ago. I'm not looking forward to seeing Mr. Marekki's third chin sink into his chest when I tell him Mal has bailed out of his lesson. If Aeschylus were alive to witness the impending disappointment, he'd certainly make note of it for a future work.

Alice, the spinster saint who runs the hospital library, shuffling volunteer schedules and cataloguing the pathetic donations, greets me with vigorous surprise.

"Oh! I didn't think you'd be here!"

"Why not?"

"I just sent your son out with the cart."

"He's here?" I gasp.

"Arrived about twenty minutes ago, ready for duty! Charming boy. She'll be a lucky one, that gets him!"

"But he shouldn't be up there alone, Alice. He's only been around with me twice. Did he put on a gown?"

Alice pats my arm. "He seemed to know exactly what to do."

"He has no badge! Do you know where he went first?" Stupid question. How would she?

"I gave him a temporary. He seems old enough for you not to be so *anxious*, Paige!" Alice winks, then hops up on a half-ladder to shelve something that has no spine at all. She reminds me of a butterfly, frail but busy, impossible to tack down.

"He's my stepson," I explain. "He's a bit of a loose cannon."

"Family's family," Alice tells me. She was a nun once, but there's been no discussion about why she left the order. "You're lucky to have him."

"Thanks."

I hurry up to the Metabolic Unit, using all the dismal shortcuts there are, employee stairwells and surgical units. My hospital ID card slaps against the costume locket I wear on fragile days, containing miniature oval representations of my parents in their thirties, attractive, sunned, seeming to gaze lovingly at each other even though I cut their faces from separate photographs.

Mr. Marekki's door is shut. I blow in nervously, jolting them from conversation. They're sitting by the only window, Mal hunched forward.

"Why, Miss Austin!" Marekki says, grinning, as if I've caught him doing something he shouldn't.

"I'm sorry! I was just so surprised when I didn't see the cart downstairs!"

"It is we who are surprised," Marekki says with avuncular calm. "Aren't we, Malachi?"

Mal smiles. "Indeed."

"The Libation Bearers" lies open on the movable tray table between them, attendant notes on a pad beside it.

"Don't let me spoil your lesson." I see to Marekki's book supply, holding up a Mary Higgins Clark, to which he assents with a bored shrug.

"You couldn't possibly," he says. "You *are* the lesson! Isn't she a picture, Malachi, having crawled up from the building's depths to deliver news. Now, if it were bad news she was bearing, to whom might we liken her?"

The question hangs. Mal's mouth twitches as he gives it thought.

"Clytemnestra?"

Marekki's eyes do the dancing his pendulous arms and miscreant legs will not do. "And what might the bad news be, that our Clytemnestra has raced to the scene to deliver?"

"She's saying that her husband Agamemnon is dead, and that the gods will not hold her responsible."

He lifts empty palms in response to his own brilliance. I sit on the edge of Marekki's bed, something I wouldn't dream of doing were he in it.

"To whom is she delivering this business?" Marekki continues in his expectant monotone. I can see how a younger boy might be cowed by his intensity into Classics worship.

"To her son," Mal says, looking at the dingy, speckled linoleum.

Marekki brings his boxer-mitt hands together to thunder out appreciation. Mal conceals laughter with a cough.

"Ah me," Marekki sighs. "I do miss the teaching."

"I can see how it must miss you," I say.

Heaving himself forward, Marekki paws one of Mal's comparatively skeletal hands. "So, my boy? What do we know about *The Oresteia?*"

Mal dramatizes thought by probing his chin with the hand he's withdrawn, bringing the other behind him to finger his neck philosophically.

"Blood's thicker than water?"

Marekki nods acceptance. "And."

"What goes around comes around."

Marekki looks at me. "It's a start."

"We done?" Mal says, rising, a skyscraper in a strip mall.

"For today. Next time you'll do me the honor of having drunk of 'The Eumenides.'"

"Yeah, but I'm starting work, so I can't come in Monday."

"You'll call me, in that case. The hospital is generous in its visiting hours. We'll make another appointment." He pushes at his bifocals, then closes the book.

Only a man doomed to an eternity of nothing to do could appear busy in this context. Only Marekki could invent and justify a connection between people who have simply collided.

At the pastry shop I order us baklava and ask Mal what he wants to drink.

"Coffee. With milk."

"Since when?"

"A while."

Since a while with Jessica, the urban sophisticate.

"To stay or to go?" the owner asks.

"To stay."

"Is this your son?"

"In a way."

Mal stiffens, his eyes bugging out. "Yeah. In a *way*." Like, not in a million years.

"Take these," I say, holding out the small plates. I carry the coffee, and we sit at a table in the back.

"Talk to me." I won't waste another second eating, fighting, lecturing, mothering him unless he's honest with me. "Tell me what you're doing."

"I'm getting a life," he says. How dumb can I be? "That is, if Dad will float me the loan."

"Did you talk to your mother?"

"Yeah, I talked to her. And just like I told you, she said no. She says I need to learn how to make my own way." He brings his hands high, as if to receive a pass to shoot. Then he drops them.

"Far be it from me," I begin, "but I think that stinks. If I had a kid, there wouldn't be enough gold on the planet. I mean, *like unto bullion.*"

He laughs. "You sound like Marekki."

"He'd know where it was from, chapter and verse. It's Melville. *Billy Budd,* I think."

"Does that mean you'll loan me the money?"

"No."

He rocks back, frowning. "Great."

"Eat," I tell him. "I won't *loan* you the money. I'll *lend* it to you."

"You're kidding, right?"

"No," I say again. "I'm not kidding."

"I thought you were so pissed at me," he says, digging into the dessert.

"I was," I say. "I am."

"So what's the catch?"

I brood, have more of the pastry. It might be the closest I'll ever come to thinking as a parent. What catch *could* there be? What condition should I place on this advance of money? That he'll pay it back by Christmas? That he'll clean my house weekly? It seems a preposterous, uncivilized way to proceed, to give something away and demand something of the recipient at the same time.

"There's no catch," I say. "I'll just give you the cash, and when you're gainfully employed, you'll pay it back."

"Really?"

"Really."

"Why?"

It's in him, to reason the need. To push like this. He gets it from Dorothy, her penchant to nail everything down.

"Because I want you to have what you want. And you can't live in a college dorm when you don't go to college."

He drums on the table, looking to the front of the shop. "Sounds good."

"What's her name?" I ask him.

He looks at me sideways.

"The girl. The bare feet."

"Hilary."

The name strikes me as incongruous for the creature it belongs to. I expected Chelsea or Amber or Gabriella, something to designate beauty or call up an exotic world people would voluntarily suffer to lay claim to.

"Is Hilary part of the quad?" I ask. "In the apartment?"

"Yes, ma'am, she is." He salutes me proudly.

"Forgive me, Malachi, but I don't think living with your girlfriend at your age is a good idea. There is a fairly good chance that it won't work out between you, and you'll have already paid rent and you'll have to move out. Trust me when I say that you won't enjoy that process. I know whereof I speak."

I did it once, premarital cohabitation, with an actor named Peter. Without knowing much about him other than the fact that he had an agent and came from Vancouver, I moved into a studio apartment with this man, who turned out to be a television addict and a layabout with absolutely no theatrical ambition beyond acting in commercials for jeans and underwear. Mother called Peter an opportunist, Diana said the only roommate that would suit him was a mirror, and Daddy nicknamed him "six-pack" for the speed at which he consumed beer on the one day we were invited as a couple to sail on the Sound. On top of these few disappointments, Peter was cheap, a firm believer in the Dutch treat. When I gathered my things to return to Mother's apartment, six weeks after moving in with him, I was so overjoyed I bought theater tickets and took her to a show he'd never heard of.

"She's not my girlfriend," Mal says, without interest.

"Oh, but I thought—"

"I don't have time for serious romance right now," he announces. "Neither does she. She's pre-med."

"*Pre-med?*" I squeak. "And she's attending *pot parties?*"

"It wasn't a *pot party,*" he scoffs.

"Oh yes it was. I almost had to go out to the all-night drugstore and buy an inhaler. Really, Mal, why'd you do it? Have all those people over to our apartment and let things get so out of hand? I know you're angry, but at *me?* I can't tell you how much effort it takes to get the place to look like more than a cave. And there you are, wrecking it."

"Doyle kind of took over. He brought some guys with him. Jessica left early, and Hilary just hung around to talk to me."

"You *let* Doyle take over. And you stretch the definition of *talking* by a long shot."

"I was kind of *involved.*"

"With your non-girlfriend," I snap. "Not good enough. You can't do this to me, to your father, I don't care how mad you are. If you want me to give a damn about you, which I do, then you have to give a damn about me. That's the way it works."

"I *know* that!" he shouts. Some people at the counter look over briefly, then go on ordering. I'm not sorry I've worked him to a pitch; it seems a logical part of the reciprocal arrangement I'm trying to illuminate for him.

At Citibank I take out the maximum, giving him four hundred and keeping one, while he towers over me, bodyguard, thief, and accomplice all at once. I feel ice in the air. It will pelt us later, as hail or stinging rain. It will change the city's mood, make everyone race for cover or the travel agent.

"Come with me," he says. "I want to show you the place."

"I think I'll wait on that. You get settled."

"What, you don't want to see where your money's going?"

"I'm leaving that up to you," I say, unhappy with the topic. "I really like it that you go and see Marekki. You can't imagine what it means to him."

"Whatever."

"I'm only on you about Hilary because I don't think you need a breakup right now."

"Will you stop *worrying* about that? I told you, we aren't going out! And anyway, I drive her nuts. She calls me the Cling-on."

"I should give her more credit, then."

"So are you coming?" He's tugging at me.

"I don't really want to see it yet. You all get it together over there, and I'll come along in a while. Who are the others anyway?"

"Two guys. One goes to Juilliard. He plays piano. He's hooking me up with some people."

"God, how does she manage?" I ask, shivering. If I lived with three men in their twenties, I'd spend my days in perpetual defense.

"Who? What?" He too is dancing with the cold.

"Nothing. I'll see you." I back away to get a look at my project. Will he remember half of what I've said to him? Or will ours be another in a series of households he'll rearrange, then leave?

He takes a pen from his back pocket, grabs my hand, palm-side up, and writes the address on the flesh. "In case you change your mind."

Then he hugs me. "Thanks, Paige."

"You're welcome."

Within seconds he's a third of the way down the block, loping along, rent pocketed, plans made, love ahead. It's appalling how very much I covet looking forward to things, as he is now.

❧ SEVENTEEN ❧

"Are you *sure?*"

He's packing the drums into their made-to-order carrying satchels. I'm trying to get him out for a walk.

"I'd be lousy company," he says.

"Wouldn't it make you lousier to stay here? There's nothing more to clean, Ian. And we have to get the Halloween candy at *some* point." I like to offer a lame alternative to whatever Ian's in the middle of, just to get him to return to the moment, get a look at his obsessive, stubborn self.

"I'll find something to clean," he mutters.

"I saw him, you know."

"Where?"

"At the hospital. He'd already taken the book cart out when I got there. He's really getting attached to Marekki. He does *homework* for the man."

Meddlesome Athena again, trying to offer the brightest picture possible. I'm not mad for myself in the role, but it's an ends-justify-the-means thing.

"That doesn't exactly go with my current image of my son," Ian says, zipping the last of the drums away and stacking it on top of the others. "The idea of his doing *anything* for *anyone* just isn't credible."

"Well, he is. You can trust me on that one. He got a job." The darker he gets, the brighter I go.

"Right, and right now he's at the Water Club."

"Who told you that?"

"His mother."

"His mother, who won't give him rent money and will spend it instead at the Water Club so she doesn't have to cook."

"Yes, *that* one."

He starts straightening things on the desk, piling up newspapers to recycle.

"Ian, he's been kicked out of everywhere. How's he supposed to *live?* How's he supposed to get started?"

"By finishing," Ian says. "By finishing school."

"Well, he didn't finish school. We can't do anything about it now except help him get back on his feet. He is who he is!"

"I don't know who you *mean!*" Ian cries. "I don't *know* who he is! One day he's winning for the basketball team and taking a prep-school band to Boston. The next day he's selling pot to his friends! One night he's running an escort service out of our apartment, the next day he's ministering to a diabetic in the hospital! You tell me who I'm supposed to think he is!"

"He's *you,* Ian!" I shout back, never so angry. "He's a watered-down Scot! In Glasgow drinking himself blind one

night and in Edinburgh the next day, prosecuting! What can
I tell you? The two of you are nearly impossible to keep track
of! For all I know, you're going to have tofu with Paula
tonight, not that it would send me over the edge!"

Ian flops into the armchair as gracelessly as a cartoon
character. "I'm not going to have tofu with Paula, that I can
assure you."

If he wanted to go to her right now, I'd send him with
blessings. For all I know, he does.

He looks at me in profile. "You look different," he says.

"How so?"

"Impish, I think. Young, and impish. Yes, that's it. Have
you been up to something?"

"*Young!* I couldn't feel *older!*"

"Tell me more."

"He's living with that Hilary creature."

"Not for long," Ian says. "Not without rent money. He'll
be back."

"For his drums."

"Oh, Paige," Ian says, rubbing his face. "You gave him
the money, didn't you?"

"Your half, and Dorothy's half."

Ian looks pained. "How is the kid going to learn *anything*
if we keep fueling his whims like this?"

"I gave the money to him on the condition that he pay
it back," I fudge.

Ian laughs out loud. "And you think that's going to
happen!"

No matter if the prediction is for sunnier times, Ian will
be forever on the periphery with his umbrella pointing to the
clouds: *Nevertheless, it's raining.*

"I don't like not knowing what he's up to," I say. "I can't
think you like it either."

"The kid lands on his feet, don't you worry."

"That is so *smug*," I say. "And I wish you'd stop calling him *the kid*."

I return to the West End, which is lively with television, guaranteed to take the edge off. I sit at the bar, order the only white wine they have, and half-listen to the local news. I try to picture Mal much younger, standing between his warring parents. But I can only project my own history, see Daddy in the front hall, waiting to take me to lunch. We'd come here usually, settle into the oakey décor and the smell of grilled onions, order omelets, and go over the week. Then he'd give me a wrapped present. When Audrey started joining us for Sunday lunch he'd give me the present the minute he picked me up, as if it would cause him a galaxy of embarrassment were Audrey to discover our little ritual.

"She doesn't like Audrey," Mother reported to Daddy when I decided I didn't want to see him on Sundays anymore. "What did you expect?"

"Another," I tell the bartender.

"Comin' right up," he says.

I watch him get it, one two, easy, no spills. I should have a job like that.

"We've got a dinner special tonight," he says. "Shepherd's pie with the house salad, five ninety-five. Interested?"

"That does sound good," I say. "My son was supposed to make dinner, but he got held up. So, yes, I'll have the special."

Bars. You can be anyone in a bar. You can sit right down and be anyone.

I find a pay phone, dial Dorothy's number, which, though I've never used it, I know by heart. Find her in. In the grand scheme of things, what effect do one person's actions have on anyone, I'm thinking. Drunk or not, I'll have no cause to regret this. Wreckage is wreckage, no matter what you add to it.

Dorothy answers roughly, par for the course, and takes the information that it is I on the other end with business aplomb.

"I wanted to report on Malachi," I tell her.

"That's okay. I've seen him." Oh yes. The Water Club.

Crying baby, sirens, running water. Odd, that a Brooklyn apartment should be noisier than a Manhattan street.

"So you know where he's living."

"He's with his friend Jessica," Dorothy says sharply. "Look, is there anything wrong? Did he do any more damage to your apartment?"

With the eloquence of a person who knows she's had too much to drink, I state, "Quite the opposite. And he's *not* with Jessica. He's got a spot in an apartment with his girlfriend Hilary. Lovely girl. Couldn't be lovelier. And he's got a paying job. Music retail. In his spare time he's taking an independent study in Greek drama and volunteering at St. Luke's."

"The drama part's a little hard to believe," Dorothy says caustically. "The kid has such performance anxiety."

"Oh really, Dorothy," I chide, "all he does is *perform!* He's a complete ham! You should hear his recitation of Hamlet's great soliloquy. In fact, now that I think about it, you should just start listening to him in general. Looking at him. Thinking about him. He's a wonder, and there's no reason on the face of God's earth that you should be in the dark about this, as his mother and all. I think he's such a total dream that I gave him the rent money you refused him."

I'm completely out of breath, holding the receiver away from my mouth so Dorothy won't hear me gasping.

"Paige, maybe you should talk to Ian about this. He's got a responsibility to the kid too."

"Stop calling him *the kid!*" I shout.

"Call your shrink, Paige," Dorothy says, and hangs up.

As I have no current psychiatrist, I think to call other people, confide, vent, but this is, after all, a street corner. And there's a limit to consolation anyway, how much of it is available, what it can do for anyone in the long haul. The women I know well have enough on their plates. And I'll see them soon. I draw up the zipper of my jacket and head back to the hospital.

Marekki is on his side, dozing. I'm embarrassed to see him like this, his large face slack against the pillow, mouth slightly ajar, his intellect absent. As he is not expecting me and ours is a formal relationship, I go to the desk and ask the floor nurse if he might be up to receiving visitors again this evening.

"His pressure's sky high," she says, exasperated. The floor is fairly quiet, no call buttons lit above the doors, but it's the end of her shift, nearly eight o'clock, so any request is unwelcome. "The doctor upped the beta-blocker." She gives me a threatening look over the top of her glasses. "You'd best go on home. I don't think he's up to much conversation."

"Right," I say officially. "Well, that's too bad. But thank you."

"You bet," the nurse says, back to paperwork.

Outside, the city, shrouded in rain, seems a great mistake in planning. How, in the end, does anyone think all this garbage, loosely stored in tin and rubber, can be collected and disposed of? How, given the random nature of *everything*, is it possible to keep to form and schedule, to remain civil, to make informed and wise decisions? How does one keep one's temper, not lose one's mind?

The reproductive endocrinologist didn't tell me to stop. She simply said, "*You* know your limits."

I'd endured laparoscopy (twice), hysteroscopy, endometrial biopsy, and between the two IVF attempts an ovarian cystectomy which made the second even more complicated. Gamete Intrafallopian Transfer: GIFT.

"No more," I said, when I got the results.

I stop at Woolworth's, where I fill a cart with Halloween candy and several packages of decorations to stick on the door. The cashier picks up one of the bags of candy.

"Fun size," she says. "What's fun about it? My kids don't think it's fun." She lifts her eyebrows at me, as if we're in collusion about this, mothers of unappreciative young people hip to the cheap instincts of their parents.

"Maybe it's fun because you can eat them so quickly," I say.

"May-*be*," the cashier says, then announces the total.

I watch her bag the items, too many for just me and Ian. Few people come to the door anymore, what with longstanding rumors of wicked people concealing razors in apples, poisoning deftly opened and resealed packages of candy.

I examine the address scrawled across my right palm, remember him holding my wrist, writing.

❧ EIGHTEEN ❧

The building, between Broadway and Riverside, has an unmanned entrance. We gather in the small space between glass doors, Lambchop/myself, Pocahontas/Winifred, Baby Spice/Electra, Peter Pan/Kyle, Surgeon/Ralph, Bumblebee/Anthony. I pray to the Great Pumpkin that Malachi will have seen fit to buy a few Milky Ways, but no matter if he hasn't. It's still before four, and we've got blocks to go before we're done.

"Yeah," he answers gruffly. A response suited to someone delivering a cocaine shipment.

"Trick or treat!" we all shout. "It's Paige," I add.

He buzzes us in. What there is of a main hallway is shadowed, the elevator dingy and scratched.

"What a dump," Ralph says. He lives on Park Avenue.

When we get off on the eleventh floor he's standing at

his open door, where a cardboard skeleton dangles from its tiny neck.

"Holy Toledo," he says, for Ralph's benefit.

"Trick or treat!" they all scream.

We file past, into the front hallway, which is frugally decorated with a table, a vase of dried flowers, two bicycles. The hall gives onto rooms that promise space.

"Do you got any candy?" Kyle asks.

"Sure do," he says. He points to two bowls behind the door, and they descend.

"Where are the troops?"

"Out," he says.

"Trick-or-treating?"

"Ha ha."

I can't tell if he's disappointed to see us or just weary.

"The kids were dying to see you," I say.

He shrugs. "What are you supposed to be?" he says to Electra.

"Baby Spice."

"Isn't she white?"

I reach for Electra, try to shield her from what's already been said.

"So what anyway," she says.

"How come you live here now?" Ralph wants to know.

"Because I like it," Mal says. Hardly credible.

The others take over the living room. As with the hallway, the décor of the living room is sparse and functional. I look out of one huge window, at the lit city, a slice of river. I love the carpet, plush and dark, and the pile of *Architectural Digest* plunked by the sofa. I envy these young people their surprising taste. At their age I lived in rooms that I wouldn't have wanted people to visit. I was continually catching up, drained by all-nighters, poor choices in bedfellows, the awful eating habits Mal has been quick to notice.

"What were you doing?" I ask him.

"Just hanging out."

"What about the job?"

"I don't work today."

"Can we stay here for a while?" Winifred asks.

"Can we stay here *forever?*" Kyle is bounding from sofa to carpet repeatedly.

I tell them we can stay just a little while. "We have to get back for the trick-or-treaters in my building," I remind them.

"Can we come back?" Ralph asks in a tone too plaintive for a surgeon.

"Maybe," Mal says.

I look at him. "Can't you just promise them one afternoon? They're really very anxious."

"*Whatever,*" he tells us.

"Are you mad at Paige?" Winifred asks him.

"No," he answers.

"She's mad at you," Ralph shrugs.

Kyle breaks in with "The good thing about Paige is that she mostly lets us do what we want."

"The bad thing is that she gets really mad sometimes," Winifred says.

"That's because she expects too much of people," Mal says.

I take a step back from the pack of them. In my Lambchop getup I couldn't feel more foolish.

Electra comes out from behind one of the speakers. "*Shut up,*" she says loudly.

Mal does the worst thing he could do, and that is laugh. She bursts into tears on cue.

"The truth is," I pitch in, "I expect too much of *myself*. That's the trouble with *me*."

This seems to satisfy the small boys, who nod, while the big one regards me with what I can only imagine is disdain.

"Lies," he says.

"What?"

"It's a *lie*, Paige. You're *lying* to yourself. You're just sad, is all. You're so sad you take care of these kids, pretending they're, like, *yours*."

I keep a firm hold on Anthony and Electra, who has taken to picking at the cotton balls I stuck all over a pair of tights.

"I don't understand you," I say blankly, then make haste for the door.

They clamor, confused, not knowing whether to follow. Somehow, one takes the lead and they all follow.

"I don't understand how you could say a thing like that to me."

He keeps the door open with the toe of his sneaker. "And I don't understand what you want from my life."

They wait for a sign to keep faith in me. I know they've heard what he said, but I can't tell if they know what he meant, whether they're offended or just afraid. I want to cup my hands over their little ears, too late, wake them from this bad dream and at the same time wish someone else would do all this for me. I want the perpetrator to take responsibility instead of acting like a doorstop while we all try to rescue ourselves from sudden damage.

As we get on the elevator, I let myself look once at him. I've become, in a second, what I've been trying too hard not to be: someone he can't trust, can't love, a person who lies to herself and, thus, to others.

I feel weak. Changed. Not since Daddy died in front of

me, and not ever in my life besides that one time, have I wished I were somebody else, anybody else with a different set of difficulties, who has no idea what it is to be Paige Austin MacGowan of New York City, who'd pass me on the street in my Lambchop costume without giving me a second look.

I'm listening for a difference in the way he closes the front door, a new weariness. He stops in the kitchen, takes in that I'm working. Really, I'm only considering it, having lined up the collated sections of *Tom Sawyer* for a tight back. I have no intention of getting to the stitching tonight. My hands aren't steady enough.

"What made you do it?" he asks blandly.

I look at the book, flat and open on the table, then at him. "*Do what?*" I ask. "Dress up for Halloween?"

"Leave my dealings with my ex-wife to me," he says. His voice is without inflection, as if he's just instructed me about where to dump the trash, were I a maid.

I should feel relief, and it's possible that I do, but any feeling of reprieve is swallowed by astonishment. *So what? So what* if I called Dorothy? *So what* if I've meddled? Haven't they, as the parents of this boy come to live in the apartment where I live, *asked* me to meddle? I can't fathom that they can't see this.

"Then leave me out of his life," I say. "I don't want to do this anymore. I don't want to keep hoping there's some reason for me to pay any attention at all. There's no return but disappointment."

Ian puts his hands in his pockets. "I'm sorry you feel that way."

I stand, attempting a like pose, measured, adversarial. "I can't do it, Ian. I just can't do it."

"We have to talk about it," Ian says. "At some point."

The sex, he means. "I know."

"Five months is a long time."

"I *know*," I repeat. I don't mean to sound churlish; I'm stalling. I have no desire for him, he knows it, and things are bound to explode.

"Are you *trying* to push me away?" he says. "Please tell me, Paige."

It occurs to me I might be doing just that. I stay at the table, terrified.

"I just can't," I begin, "I can't find the right feelings."

"That's all you need to say," he tells me flatly, sets down his glass, and goes in the other room. I wait for the paralysis to pass, for the right words to come and fix this, but they don't.

We have a round table in a windowed corner. We're talking about the snow, which started as I was waiting for the bus to come uptown.

"Happy Thanksgiving, travelers!" Patty says menacingly.

"We never go anywhere on Thanksgiving," Toni says. "We just invite everyone to come over and go nuts at *our* table."

Diana groans. "I'm supposed to drive my mother out to Sleepy Hollow, come back into town for the others in the afternoon, then drive back out."

"Can't Tod use the company *jet?*" Toni whines.

Patty and Bibiana laugh, but I fail to see the humor in it, as there really is a company jet.

"What will you do, Paige?" Bibiana asks. "For the holiday?"

"Go to my stepmother's," I answer. "With my mother.

The three of us plan to stand over a large pot and put hexes on everyone."

"Sounds fun," Toni says. "What about Ian?"

"We're going to try something different this Thanksgiving," I say.

"Uh-oh," Patty says.

"How are you, sweetie?" Diana asks, pouting for me.

"I'm fine," I say. "I think." I glance at the sky, spotty with snow. "It's beautiful up here."

"Deep end," Patty surmises.

"You think?" Toni challenges. "She looks so together. Do you eat anymore, darling?"

"Carrot and celery sticks," I tell them, happy to switch gears. "And four gallons of water every day. My goal is to become more and more hated as I waste away." I cover my face in mock shame, shielding myself from their attention, although I love it. Need it.

"Dare we ask?" Toni ventures.

"He moved out," I say.

"*Grazie a dio*," Bibiana blurts.

Patty holds up a victorious fist. "Believe me, you couldn't ask for a better solution. It just can't work, out of the blue like that."

"Wait a second!" Diana tells Patty. "Did you stop to think Paige might not feel that way?"

"Let the woman *speak*," Toni orders.

I'm more interested in the roasted garlic appetizer and the pâté, but I thank them for the floor. "I'm not sorry, really. I think I can do this better from a distance."

"She's *tough*," Patty says. "I'd be in the loony bin, thinking it was all my fault."

Patty is too quick with the disclaimers. She's quietly

accomplished, in areas the others of us aren't. She does needlepoint and goes to art classes and keeps her out-of-town stepchildren apprised of what's going on at the city museums, which she supports in every way possible.

"Don't we know it," Toni says.

"I'd be writing poems, then tearing them up," Bibiana admits.

"I'd have probably gone with him," Diana says. "At this point."

We wait for an explanation, but she waves away concern, saying we should order.

"The truth is," I go on, inspired, "I like him. I never thought that would happen. I figured I'd start to get to know him and he'd be just like *her* and I'd spend entire mealtimes loathing every word that came out of his mouth because it would be like having her at the dinner table. But it isn't. He's neither of them." I think that if I say this with enough conviction I can go back to my original hopeful feelings about Mal. That I can justify having let him lay siege to my heart, eclipsing Ian's need for my attention.

"Wow," Toni says. "Are you telling me you might get a happy family out of this scenario? It might be too much to bear!" She clutches the table's edge, as if in the throes of a stroke.

"Ian must be singing your praises to the heavens!" Patty says.

"Ian's not an optimist," I say, even though one night he did that very thing.

"If the fathers of these children were more optimistic about how we raise them," Bibiana says, "the job would be so much easier!"

"Nice idea, Bibi," Toni quips. "Now, get *real*."

"It's just a matter of a little spoken appreciation," Patty reasons.

"Is *anyone* hungry?" Diana asks fiercely. "Could we focus?"

"It'll be fine," Toni whispers. The others are doing holiday anecdotes. Tears come to my eyes, wildly inconvenient. I can't help them. Tomorrow I'll be raising a glass at Audrey's table, in thanksgiving.

❧NINETEEN❧

*B*ecause of the snow that has amassed in drifts around the fire hydrants and parked cars, Mother and I take the train out to Audrey's. We have to stand all the way, Mother straddling a shopping bag from the Vinegar Factory, full of things to contribute to the meal and other holiday entertaining Audrey might have planned for the next month.

"Isn't it odd," Mother says quietly, as if anyone would object to her saying "no men this Thanksgiving."

"A little."

I didn't figure on our not getting seats. I anticipated a civilized, chatty trip into gray Connecticut. Something cozier.

"What do you suppose she'll have done to the house this time? Every time I've been there someone's knocked down a wall or added a pool. Maybe she'll have one of those at-home movie theaters in the basement."

"I don't think so, Mother. She likes to keep things dreary."

"Oh no she doesn't," Mother says. "You've got her all wrong. She spends a fortune on fabric."

"I have to forgive her that," I say. Everything looks so crisp there. It wouldn't work for me, such a look. Yesterday, when the littles and I were gluing feathers on cardboard turkeys, glue got all over the sofa. As has recently become habit, Ian said nothing about the new crusty surface.

"I know. Poor soul. I'm mean about her. But she can be so irksome. At times I'd have liked to shake some sense into your father while she was out chipping away at his pension at ABC carpet."

Mother would have a field day at ABC carpet. Sometimes I think she'd have made a better second wife, and Audrey, who is serious and inward, a better suffering ex. Take away the covetousness, the two women might have combined to make one perfect wife for Daddy, no divorce necessary.

"Do all the children have adequate Thanksgiving plans?"

Mother likes to know about them, their families, whether there's anything peculiar to report on as far as their home lives are concerned.

"Ralph went to Florida. They picked him up on the way to the airport. Kyle and Anthony are going to Johanna's mother."

"That father doesn't seem to do a *thing* for those kids," Mother observes. "What about the little girls?"

"Winifred does something at her church, and Electra's gone to Baltimore on the train, I think. I never get the complete story on that one."

"Oh dear."

Because it's too painful to speculate on Electra's home life, whoever it is that uses the language she fears and at whom it's directed, I leave go the topic.

"Holidays can be so beastly," Mother says. "Everyone under such pressure to have a good time!"

The loaded train jangles to a sloppy stop at Norwalk and we get out. I lug the bag of jars.

"Hoo hoo!" Audrey calls from her post at the hood of the Suburban. "Over hee-yer!"

"Oh, blast her," Mother says. "She's driving that Safari car. It's so hard to climb into that thing."

"You didn't mind it when Daddy drove it!"

"Don't be silly. Of course I did."

"Look at *you!*" Audrey squeaks as she hugs me, leaving Mother to make her way into the front seat.

I climb in back, feeling more than the usual holiday drowning of spirits.

"I've gone and bought the most enormous turkey there was so we could all have leftovers," Audrey says as she pulls out of the lot. "It's over twenty pounds!"

"I don't know how you *dared!*" Mother says, disguising her disapproval very handily. "I've always been afraid to cook a turkey that big. How did you ever *lift* it?"

"I've been walking with weights, you know!" Audrey says, shaking her arm free of the steering wheel to make a muscle that no one can see through the fur sleeve.

"You don't mean it!"

On and on to the house, which appears over the rise of paved drive, neatly stuck between towering maples, the paint still new, the lawn prim. It's not the monstrous size Mother described the first time she went out to see Daddy, then in bed after his first round of chemotherapy. But it's certainly larger than necessary, like the car. I've spent so much time here I've ceased to think of its superficial qualities, although the pool did help me through the summer weeks before Daddy's death. For me the house is full of his things, his moods, the voice I can no longer hear except out of context, when it comes back to me, nearly full strength, catching me unawares in places where it is mortifying to let oneself cry.

The smell of the roasting bird sharpens my hunger, and I take a cracker topped with speckled spread without thinking to wait for the champagne.

"Sorry," I tell them. "I raced out this morning and didn't have breakfast. I'm completely famished."

"Oh please go ahead," Audrey insists. "You've gotten so thin. You too, Frannie. You must be starved."

"Oh no, I'm perfectly fine," Mother sniffs. She's sensitive about her size as compared with Audrey's. Mother's rounder than Audrey, but most human beings are.

"So, it's just women today!" Audrey crows. "Won't we have fun. No men around to please, we'll just have to please ourselves!"

It must be because Daddy isn't here that Audrey sounds more than ever as if she's coming unglued, making stabs at hilarity when she feels none.

"Where are the men, anyway?" Audrey asks me. "Your mother said there was some trouble?"

"Nothing too unexpected," I report. "Mal was kicked out of school. Then he was kicked out of our apartment. Ian's guarding the fort against further infiltration."

"Oh well," Audrey says. "That's boys for you. And *stepchildren*. It can only get worse!"

I swallow, wondering what terrible pain I've caused Audrey to make her say such a thing.

"The thing that *I* think is so interesting," Mother

interrupts, "is that Paige was all for the boy coming to live with them. *She* didn't want him to leave. It was Ian's doing."

Mother's voice has the snap it gets when she feels I've been wronged.

"Fathers are sensitive about their little boys," Audrey professes over the spitting turkey. "Almost done!"

Not all fathers! I want to scream.

"Shall I open this?" Mother has pulled a bottle of Veuve Clicquot from the refrigerator.

"*Mais bien sur!*" Audrey says in her terrible French.

I don't believe there's enough champagne on the planet to get me through the meal, which, despite Audrey's disclaimers, is outstanding. There's excited talk about the next baby to arrive in Audrey's family, and corollaries to that concerning what Audrey will be buying and knitting for the child. No one raises a glass to Daddy, as this, all of us know, is bound to stir up sadness and ruin pie and coffee. Not to mention that he'd have hated a eulogy at the holiday table. I contribute details about Mrs. Alderman's book project and Mother narrates the itinerary she's drawn up for her trip to England in the spring.

Then Audrey says she's filled the guest room with things of Daddy's she thought I might want and when we've finished dessert maybe I'd like to have a look.

I look at Mother, who says nothing.

"I don't feel much in the mood for sifting through heirlooms today," I say.

"It's been over a year, Paige," Mother says.

I want to get up and run, but I'm nailed to my chair, staring at the dessert plate I've scraped clean. Audrey is looking at me as well, bewildered, not having anticipated any problem over this.

I turn to my mother. "Daddy is dead," I say. "That's as much as I can manage for the moment."

Mother cannot make me laugh over Audrey's hand-weights or verbal gaffes or at the two of us, traveling home at dusk on a dour Thanksgiving train like people in an English novel who have lost their prospects and station and are being shipped off to a gloomy future with poor but affable relatives.

"Oh, sweetie, you have to be able to see past it at some point," she finally says to me in despair.

"I'm trying," I say. "I'm really trying."

"You have your work," Mother says. "You do gorgeous work, and those children love you. And you're a beautiful woman, and you have a good husband."

"Come on, Ma," I say. "I'm not beautiful, and you can't stand Ian."

"That's simply not true," Mother tells me. "He's pretty contrary, but he's got good humor. He's a lot like your father. So when I see him acting like your father I get worried. I think of myself in your shoes. I couldn't live with your father, and so I naturally assume that you won't be able to live with Ian. It's idiotic, how my mind works."

I smile at the logic, at the person who thinks so protectively. "It's not idiotic. I'm not having the greatest time. I keep wondering why I'm not having more fun. And then Mal wanders in to remind me of what is and isn't fun. And then he leaves. It's all making me feel horribly old."

"You!" Mother roars. "I'll tell you about *old!*"

"I keep wishing for romance. As much as I wish for a baby. As if that will keep me going. Talk about idiotic." When Mal was in the house, I wanted to keep the feeling of not wanting anything further than that. For those few days I *had* what I wanted.

"Who doesn't?" Mother begs. "Lord, if we thought it was all over at forty, we might as well pitch ourselves into the sea like a troupe of lemmings. Can you imagine? All married women over forty can give it up right now, the idea of being swept off their feet by some gorgeous creature? Paige, honey, I really think you're too hard on yourself."

"That doesn't really change the facts, Mother."

"What facts? What facts are you talking about?"

"That I'm childless. That every day I'm challenged to find ways not to let that bother me. That three hours each weekday is the extent of my ever having any children."

I keep my eyes on the suburbs swimming by, densely purple and gray.

"I'm not surprised," Mother says. "He's part of why you're feeling bad. Just by being there, he brings it all up. It's probably not too easy for him either. And who knows? Maybe he feels all kinds of things about you. It's understandable."

"What is?"

"Maybe he feels a connection with you that he doesn't feel with his mother. But if you want to know *sad*, try having a head of white hair."

"Your hair isn't white." It's gray *and* white.

"It may as well be. And we won't discuss anything south of it."

I suppose I could start bucking up by realizing I have a great mother who is, thankfully, alive.

"Anyway," Mother says. "There've been days when I'd have lain down with the doorman, given the chance."

I burst into loud laughter, to the brief interest of some teenagers riding a few seats back. "Now there's one I hadn't thought of!"

"Yours is awful," she goes on. "He's not like Stuart. Stuart missed his calling. He should have been a male escort."

Stuart has about ten years on Ramone and the English accent.

"I can see you with Stuart." Odd as that would be, I can.

"Oh well," Mother says. "In heaven. After we're all dead."

"How do you keep your spirits up?" I ask. "*How?*"

Mother shrugs. "I don't think about it. For me, it isn't really optional. I just have to stay active. Stay alive. I don't expect to feel great all the time, so I don't always think about it."

"I think about *him* all the time," I confide. "I can't stop. He made that much of an impression. I imagine him as a baby, as a little boy. We've got pictures, but they don't tell you anything."

"That's not necessarily a bad thing. Consider it a wonder of sorts, that he moves you like this."

"I don't have anything left, it seems, to give Ian."

"That comes and goes," Mother says. "Anyway, if you worry, you won't be able to enjoy things! Think of it this way: You love this boy! Have fun with him! Forget his parents! They've dumped him into your life. It's better that you *do* like him. He'll bond with you. It can't hurt."

"Mother, did you say *bond?*"

"I did. I can be quite mod, you know. Quite up on things."

"Truly."

I settle back next to my mother, accept the night sky over the buildings as something less than tragic. "I'm sorry for what I said at the table."

"Don't be. It was stupid of Audrey to think that Thanksgiving was a good time for a yard sale and stupid of me not to tell her so."

"You're a great mother," I say.

"Now stop that talk," Mother says.

* * *

At home Ian has work spread out in the living room. "How went the war?"

We're speaking, at least.

"No war," I say. "Just inanity and a lot of food. Shall I fix you a cold turkey dinner?"

"That would hit the spot."

I fix him the dinner, bring it in, then say, "I'm going on vacation."

I want it out between us, said, open, whatever the price. Mal has told me I can't live in untruth.

"Now?"

"In about a week."

"Why didn't you tell me?"

"I thought you might disapprove."

"Why? Are you taking someone along?"

I laugh, although it isn't funny. "Like who?"

"I don't know. Some young stud?"

"What young stud would have me?"

"You're serious. You're going on vacation by yourself."

"I knew you'd be too busy. And I need it."

"Of course you do." He means this, I know. It's odd, his complacency about the whole thing. Easier, but somehow not right.

"Shall I tell you where?"

"That would be helpful."

I get the brochure out of my bureau drawer and bring it to him. Cross-legged, amidst all the papers and open texts, he looks like a student awash in finals stress.

"It really threw you, this thing with Mal," he says, studying the pool and the beach beyond it.

"It brought a lot of things to the fore," I say. "I want to sort them out."

"You don't have to apologize for that, Paige," he says. Then he starts eating, telling me how good it is.

In the morning I cab over to Mrs. Alderman's with half of the Mark Twain set in a canvas bag. I've made the appointment to assure myself as much as Mrs. Alderman that the project is moving forward with due speed.

"Mrs. Alderman can't meet with you," the housekeeper says.

"I phoned yesterday, and she thought this would be a good time."

"She's not herself," the housekeeper tells me. "I'll take the books to her later."

"That's all right. I wanted to point out a few things to her. Is there another time I could come back and do that?"

She shakes her head no. "I'm sorry."

"Has Diana been here?"

"Early this morning." The housekeeper fumbles with the miscellany in a flat ceramic dish on the hall table and brings up a small envelope.

"Miss Alderman did the books before she left. She told me you were coming."

"Thank you," I say, and ring for the elevator.

I open the envelope the second the elevator door shuts. The check, for four thousand dollars, is eight hundred dollars over the estimate I gave Diana's mother. Mrs. Alderman's signature is stamped in the corner.

"Thank you, Diana," I whisper into the holy vault.

I spend the rest of the day at the kitchen table reinforcing the most fragile pages of *Connecticut Yankee* with coated paper. By evening, when Diana finally calls, my fingers are raw from the effort.

"What happened?" I ask her.

"My mother's having a million tests. She doesn't know where she is."

"This is awful," I say.

"You're telling me."

"Where are Robert and Lydia?"

"Robert's in cyberspace. Lydia's been with me all day, my right arm. She's telling me everything will be fine."

"She's terrific. And Tod?"

"Oh, please."

I ask how I can help, and Diana says she has to stay at the hospital.

"Honestly, Paige, I knew I was headed for something like this, some kind of rock bottom, but I really wish that I didn't have to meet my mother in it. When I got over to the apartment this morning, she looked like some freak of nature, a child draped in wrinkles! She said she wanted to go horseback riding. She'd found Daddy's old jodhpurs in the bureau and she was trying to get them up past her knees."

"God in heaven. Do you want me to visit her? I'll go tomorrow instead of you? You'll have to take a few seconds off, Diana, or you'll go mad."

"It doesn't appear I'll be able to do that for a while, but thank you. Mother would love to see you, I know she would. But of course she wouldn't know you if she fell over you. And I can't *not* go in there myself, not with all this shit happening at home. Tod's been staying in a hotel. He comes home for dinner, to see Robert and Lydia."

"Why didn't you *say* anything, Diana?" I whine. "The other night, when we were all sitting around talking about *me?*"

"I did," Diana says. "Sort of. I just don't want to talk about it. It's too—*actual.*"

"Well, can't Tod stay with both children while you go

back and forth to the hospital? I mean, under the circumstances, Diana, he really ought to."

I feel myself getting worked up, the way I did when I phoned Dorothy from the street, minus the pleasurable influence of wine.

"I know," Diana says. "But I don't want to talk to him about *anything*, so I'm limiting my exposure. I think I'm starting to hate him."

"Me too."

"You know," Diana says shakily, "you're really great. You know that? You're a good friend."

"I get paid well for that."

"I'll call you." She clicks off.

I wander into the living room, where Ian's dozing in front of a PBS series about a Welsh doctor.

"What was that all about?" he slurs.

"I think Tod and Diana are getting divorced," I tell him.

"Christ," he says. "When will it end."

❧TWENTY❧

"You seem tired, Ms. Austin," Marekki says.

"I have a vacation coming up."

"How long will you be away?" he asks.

"Just a week."

"I'll have to shore up reading, then," he says. "Is there anything new under the sun on that wagon?"

"There's a le Carré," I say, searching. I glanced at it downstairs, thinking it might please him.

"Twist my arm," he says, which is unimaginable. "What else?"

"Another book on the Kennedys."

"No. I don't understand the fascination with that family. We lack royalty in this country, so we subject ourselves to focusing on the mediocre and inflating it with undue references to King Arthur. We are not poised as a nation. We insist on being the most elegant, the most aristocratic, the most glamorous, and we are none of these things. We suffer from hyperbole. The Japanese say 'Too much is too little.' Do you agree, Ms. Austin, that we dwindle in comparison to a wise nation like Japan or a poised nation like Britain?"

"At times, yes," I lie.

"I'm glad to report that Malachi will be paying me two visits during your absence. He has become enamored of the character of Telemachus, a point of view I very much share. Of course, most young men do identify, but I find his interest quite poignant. The poem seems to call up much for him."

Marekki pauses to puff heavily as he shifts under the blanket. I have never really focused on the length of his legs. They don't reach much farther than the position of the tray table, in the middle of the bed, and while I know he can walk, it saddens me to think of their limited use.

"Has he been in to see you a lot?" The usual: untie the child and watch him run. I feel Mal's absence in my gut, a scary space there.

"No. He's employed in a record emporium, so we've been communicating by telephone. We've actually managed all four books of the Telemachy in some depth. Of course, one could not scratch the surface if one had a year."

"Of course not."

Marekki looks at me without expression, a great, blank Buddha swathed in hospital linens.

"Your name crops up with some frequency."

"Does it?"

Now he smiles. "Come, come. Surely you aren't surprised."

I bring a chair over from the window. As long as we're doing life secrets, I don't need to stand at attention by the book cart.

"Frankly, I am," I admit.

Marekki laughs hoarsely, then coughs. At one point he must have smoked. "Silly woman," he says.

"Why do you say that?" I ask, mildly offended.

He narrows his eyes. "Ms. Austin, the drama is inexorable. It will continue, on course, no matter where one flies off to. You surprise me. You're a student of the Classics! How has this truth escaped you?"

"It hasn't," I insist. "I was hoping against hope, I suppose."

"Hoping *what?*" he demands.

"That there'd be some sort of reprieve. Some *likelihood* of friendship."

"Love will kill us all," Marekki professes. "Not illness." He indicates his own girth with a graceful sweep of fleshy forearm. "My glands won't mutiny. It's my heart that will get me."

Were he someone else, I'd reach for one of his hands. "Do you believe that, Mr. Marekki? Do you?"

"I don't *believe* it, Ms. Austin," he says faintly. "I *know* it. There's a difference, of course."

"Of course there is."

"Age is not always a good teacher, Ms. Austin," he says. "Age does not direct the heart. The heart rebels, like a young man."

"Or woman," I throw in.

"In any event, the rebelliousness we see in Malachi now will furnish him later on with a sense of responsibility and mission. The fervor Odysseus has for war and conquest is later replaced by a fervor to get home. I'm attempting to subtly introduce to Malachi that Odysseus' journey is always toward home and community, so perfectly objectified by the motif of the winnowing fan."

"I've always been a great fan of the winnowing—well," I say, grasping at levity.

"You *are* clever, Ms. Austin," Marekki says, puffing. "Recall that at the bourne of ocean, Teiresias foresees the planting of the oar in the mainland sod. Then later, in Book Twenty-three, Odysseus himself speaks of it, so convinced is he that this oar pitched into earth will serve as a mark of his contribution to his family and people."

I nod vigorously, although I don't remember the passage at all vividly.

"Then death will drift upon me / from seaward, mild as air, mild as your hand / in my well-tended weariness of age, / contented folk around me on our island. / He said all this must come."

Marekki sighs, then relaxes into the pillows, ennobled.

"I love that," I say.

"Yes," he says.

The nurse comes in to take him for dialysis. I hurry to collect the week's books and replace them with the le Carré and Russell Baker's autobiography. Marekki is too immersed in the misery of moving from bed to wheelchair in backless hospital livery to notice the second choice.

"That's it," the nurse says.

I wish him a good week.

"I'll be here," he assures me, "awaiting the denouement."

At five A.M. on Sunday we join a crowd of people, lots of children, in front of the baggage check of what promises to be a lesser airline. I ask a man trailing scuba gear if this is the line for Club Med.

"It better be," he says. He exhales disappointment, over the length of the line and its members, I suppose. I can't be helping, with my contributions of Electra, Winifred, and Kyle. When I told them I was going on vacation Electra refused to look at me for three days, and Winifred said she hoped I'd have a bad time and come back early. Kyle couldn't come up with "the good thing" about Paige going on vacation. So I approached their parents with the "kids go free" ploy in a big hurry, after I made sure it didn't matter whose kids you brought.

"No can do," Ralph said, when we started planning. "I'm in Florida that whole week."

"My dad's grouchy in the morning too," Winifred says to the scuba diver, coaxing a smile out of him.

"These three all yours?" he asks me.

I look from kid to kid. "In a manner of speaking. This week anyway."

"She's our baby-sitter," Electra pipes up.

"Well, she's not exactly a *baby-sitter*," Winifred counters.

"Is too."

"Nuh-uh."

"Girls, please," Kyle says. "I've really had it." He covers his eyes in exasperation. There will be moments of total despair for him this week, being the only man on board, no Ralph as backup.

"You've got your work cut out for you," the diver says. "So much for R and R."

"Just letters," I say.

"One letter," Winifred corrects.

"There you are!" the man laughs.

We check the bags, hit a few of the eateries, and finally gain access to the plane.

"We get our own table?" Winifred says, amazed.

"Yes! And you each get a seat you're meant to stay in for five hours!"

"My dad said there's a movie. Where is it?" Kyle demands.

I point to the impossibly tiny screen several rows ahead.

"I won't be able to see," he decides. "No way."

I tell him we'll put blankets under him, he won't miss a single gunshot. Winifred settles in with her book immediately. The minute the engines begin their roaring, Electra throws up.

The bus bumps over undeveloped, arid terrain whose only promise is the glittering ocean at its distant edges. After seven hours of travel, inclusive of a stop in Martinique to load on drunk collegians, the children have become hostile. They blame me for their discomfort, and I can only make promises that I find inspiration for in the brochure: riding lessons, go-carts, circus training, windsurfing.

"Look!" I cry. "It says here that you'll be doing all these things!"

I could kill James for not telling me about Electra's penchant for motion sickness. I've seen her queasy on buses, but the relentless vomiting has put me in mind of more serious medical difficulties, such as an inner-ear imbalance, something Dr. Eisman could easily diagnose. Winifred is merely bitchy at this point, denying that there's any virtue in the view. Kyle feels betrayed, his good-thing-bad-thing having mutated into bad-thing only.

We pass through gates which give onto an instant horizon of pleasure, enhanced by booming reggae and an array of model types, dressed identically to those who saw to the busing, all doing a line dance. We all accept frosted cups of something pink and fruity handed us by a young man I could only have conjured in a daydream.

I drink the concoction in the line for room assignment, bid the dancers a happy farewell, and find our room, where I tuck the children in, filthy as they are, unpack in a blurred hurry, then collapse on the bed.

*   *   *

I wake at sunset, to blaring noise: more of the same music and a man's voice announcing the evening's events in French, then English. Electra wakes up for a second, looks at me with eyes that suggest she might be sick again, then rolls back into sleep. I take a shower in barely warm water and put on a summer shift which makes me look ghostly and drawn. I rouse the weary three, get them in the tub for an acceptable number of minutes, then lay out shorts and T-shirts for dinner attire. Hunger drives us through a maze of outdoor stairwells and hallways to the main entrance, where I ask for the dining room. The snappish French receptionist points to a wide staircase, its banister dripping with leis.

Upstairs is a sea of people, clanking dishware, and food so various and plentiful that I doubt it can be any good. I manage to find chicken nuggets and fries for them, some grilled fish that is adequate, and vegetables that aren't too poached, and we sit with a family who have almost finished eating. The mother, already blotchy with sunburn, says it's the fifth Club Med they've been to.

"This one's supposed to be so good for single parents," she says, "but my kids won't leave me alone long enough for me to find that out. What about you? Are you going to try to get to some of the night activities?" She nods at the kids. "Or do you have help with these three?" She's already accepted that I am the adoptive mother of at least one of them.

I skimmed the bit in the brochure about the effort made at this particular club toward single parents. Since I'm neither single nor a parent I didn't give it a second thought.

"I'm signing them up for the camp."

The woman grimaces. "*Don't.*"

"Don't?" I had counted on a few hours in the morning off-duty, as per my usual schedule.

"It's *terrible*. My kids won't go." She hikes her burned shoulders up, then releases them, hopeless. "There go my chances to mingle."

"Well, they must like the beach, at any rate," I say.

"You can't sit on that beach!" she says. "Look at me! I was out there for ten minutes this morning!"

The oldest of her children, a boy a few years younger than Mal, looks up from his untouched plate. "Way to go, Red Lobster."

"My" children are rapt, eating, watching the Red Lobster relate her woes. Her children are older, and the girls roll their eyes, pick at their food or their corn rows, seem to resent the very fact of sitting here.

I'm irritated enough by them to ask her if her husband is here.

"My *ex*," she clarifies. "Back in D.C., living the life of Riley. Where I'd be if I didn't have to be here. What about yours?"

"Back in New York, defending xenophobes. I'm married actually. These aren't my children."

"Who are you, the Pied Piper?"

I make a silent, xenophobic vow that we will not sit at dinner with any more strangers, so much do I not want Winifred, Electra, and, most of all, Kyle to have to listen to people like her.

"In a way, I guess. I take care of them in the afternoons." She nods a few times, like a doctor sizing up the degree of my insanity. "Finish up, you three. I saw some ice cream up front for dessert."

After ice cream we stand in line for the phone for a while, then give up and walk on the steep beach, letting our feet sink into the sand, warm water washing over them. Marekki wasn't completely correct in his declaration that I'd be unable to escape what's bothering me. Here, with an unobstructed stretch of night to peer into and three of my closest friends clamoring around, love can't pull me all over the planet.

"Paige!" Kyle calls, scattering phosphorous from his heels. "Look! It's beautiful!"

"It sparkles!" Electra screams.

"Oh my God!" Winifred is fast after them, her wake lit, arcing behind her.

If I could preserve any moment, it might be this one, of watching the three of them flailing down this beach I've brought them to, where I can let them go.

"Do you miss me?"

"Give me a couple of days, Paige!" he says. "I've scheduled my week's watching and eating based on your absence. I was sort of getting ready to have fun!"

"Thanks a ton." Absence helps, bringing back humor and laissez faire.

"Hey, you need to let loose. Put those kids in day care. I'm trying to recover from trial, which won't be possible. We've got snow again."

Nevertheless, it's raining.

"I'll call you after those couple of days," I promise.

I don't even ask how Malachi is.

I write a postcard instead, about my enviable surroundings, the human scenery he's missing. Smoothing things over, as if he never said what he said, as if our not having seen each other or spoken in weeks is accidental.

It's only eight in the morning by the time we drop the cards off with the cranky concierge. Each of theirs has under six words on it, the same words on every one.

As we troop over to the kiddie camp, I promise them they'll have fun. I attempt to make one of the day-care affil-

iates understand that I'm to be alerted in the event that one
more of them gets upset about *anything*. At the swing set I
give a merry good-bye to all three, who regard me with fury,
now certain they've been left to the wolves and won't have
fun again in their entire lives.

"Just give it a chance, guys! You want to be in that circus, don't you?"

Well, yes.

"So this is where you have to come to learn how to use
the trapeze!"

Horrified by this possibility, having noted the height of
the circus apparatus, I make my way to the pool to join the
water aerobics class. Into the pool I wear a T-shirt over my
one-piece, also sunglasses and a tennis hat.

"You got enough on there?" the woman we met at dinner
says. Again she's thrown caution to the wind and worn nothing more than a bathing suit, and not the one she originally
fried herself in.

"Pull and drag," I explain. "The more resistance, the
more calories you burn."

"Pull and drag as much as you like!" she says. "There's
just too much to eat here."

I fear I've begun to understand her ex-husband's escape
into the life of Riley. I try to move to the music, not that different from what was blaring at Malachi's party, but it isn't
easy, and I feel and am certain I look clumsy. At the end of
the class I go dripping over to the main desk to see if I've got
any messages from the day-care center.

The cranky concierge reminds me that the children have
only been in camp for half a morning. I thank her, wishing
I'd never put them in it, then wander over to the beach. The
club's signature dolphin is coursing back and forth in the
shallows, looking for friends.

I'm interested. I've heard people in the dining room talking about the creature. I'm not mad to touch him, but I wade in anyway. The sun off the water is so blinding I have to shield my eyes. I can't see the animal. Then he bumps into me, not hard, but suddenly enough to knock the wind out of me.

I don't know what to do, whether to race back into shore or put my hands out for him, so I freeze, waiting for the next step in the game. He comes barreling back for more fun, so I float my hands out, touch his rubbery flank and he's gone again.

I put my face in the water, then go completely under. Submerged, I hear him talking, short squeaks that are too cute for the bulk of him. I stay there, my eyes wide open to the stinging salt and the misty underworld, waiting for him to come back because now I'm ready for him. When I can no longer hold my breath I surface and swim toward the space he's vacated, investigating the water with my arms.

"He went back out," a man wading nearby says. He points to the fin making its way into deeper, darker water.

"God, that's a shame," I say. I still have the feel of him on my hands, and I've memorized a whitish scar somewhere on his belly.

I proceed from the infirmary to pickup at four-thirty. I've got all the sunburn medicine they have, mostly aloe products, some Benadryl. All I can comfortably wear is a sari I had to buy for fifty dollars at the boutique. I fell asleep on the beach for a fierce hour and a half after lunch, and even though I lathered up with Coppertone Shade, the sun showed me little mercy.

They're animated, gleeful, happy to see me but not thrilled.

"Are we coming back here tomorrow?" Electra asks.

"What did you *think?!*" Winifred quips. "Like, *duh.*"

"Ladies," Kyle says. His face is red, from running and sun, his hair slick with sweat.

"So I take it you had a good time," I say. "That it wasn't solid misery from start to finish."

"It was grrr-eat!" Kyle says. "I won in the go-carts."

"I went on the tightrope," Winifred announces.

"What happened to your arms and face?" Electra asks.

"Sunburn," I say. "I hope none of you has one. We should stay out of the sun the rest of the day."

"You look funny," Kyle says. "Like somebody fried your face!"

"Some*thing*," I correct. "That being the sun."

By the stables, we watch an inexperienced rider dig her heels into a horse's side, and the animal takes off comically, trapping the woman between the forces of gravity and speed.

"I'm glad I don't have to carry *her* around," Winifred says.

This breaks the other two up.

"What'd you do all day, Paige?" Kyle asks. "Besides lay out?"

"Exercised. Played with the dolphin. That sort of thing."

I don't want them to know how at moments I worried, how I almost hoped that there would be cause for me to go running to the camp and save them from inattention on the parts of the counselors, from boredom and fear.

"You played with *the dolphin?*"

I beam, miraculous again, a poached superhero, ready to swoop in and stop crime and illness and cruelty and whatever else their divine little minds can conjure in the danger department.

"Sure did. Tag, I think it was. He won."

* * *

The good thing about vacations like these, Kyle might say, is that the days are fairly well mapped out, and it's easy to fall into the recreational routine. The bad thing, all too obvious, is to overdo any one aspect. Now that I'm burnt to a crisp, it's harder to join in the fun. I make a good Ferdinand, sitting under my tree, providing my own distraction, willing the hours to pass a little more quickly until the littles are released from their regimen. Each afternoon, I walk them by the riding ring, the tennis courts. We swim, eat dinner, then head for the phones. There's a video playing for them at night, and they fall deliriously into bed by nine-thirty. I have a drink or two at the bar, book always in hand, and talk to people, men and women, whose names I won't remember.

They fight about tans, who's got one already, who's never going to get one.

"Black people don't *get* tans," Winifred tells Electra.

"White people do. And then they get cancer."

Electra's in the best shape of all of them.

"Oh, *Lord*," I carp, trying to squeeze the last bit of Kids' Coppertone onto Kyle's shoulder. "Isn't your generation supposed to be color blind?" I ask. It's been a week. I've been letting myself go in the speech department. I didn't anticipate that spending so many days in a row with them would turn me into a harpie. At the same time I'm amazed we've survived this long, in one room, no TV, without serious battles or homesickness, or sickness in general.

Electra moves her bathing-suit strap aside to prove Winifred wrong.

"The good thing about a tan is you look better," Kyle says. "The bad thing is . . . " He points to me, "RED LOBSTER!"

"Let's do our best not to hurt each other's feelings in this beautiful place where we've *really* got no excuse to be mean." Singsong it, and they'll listen. "Winifred, say something nice to Electra."

"*Sorry, Electra.*" She draws it out with a sneer.

"Something nicer than sorry."

"Really sorry?" She taunts me with laughter, then stops. "Paige, do you love us?"

Caught unawares, I'm flip. "Of *course* I love you. Would I have brought you here if I didn't love you?"

"If you love us," she continues, to the fascination of the other two, "they why do you always tell us what to do?"

"Because I love you," I say. "Now let's go to breakfast before they run out of Froot Loops."

The single mother whose children hate the camp comes up to me in the crowd gathering for the circus on the last night.

"I see your kids are in the show."

"They've been practicing all week."

"They must be pretty well adjusted to have stayed in all week," she remarks. She strikes me as a permanent moper, a bit like Ian but without the humor.

"They're good kids," I say.

"No issues," she adds.

"Plenty," I tell her. "But they've had a good week."

"What about yourself?"

I think this over for a second. "Yes," I say. "It's nice to see them so excited. I don't think they'll ever stop talking about it."

"You didn't meet anyone?"

"I met droves of people!" I say, trying to turn my hours at the bar into gold. "I just don't remember who."

"Yeah," she says. "Me neither."

I go and sit in the front row as the music starts. Winifred said I'll love the costumes, and Kyle said I'd be scared watching him swinging on the trapeze. The little kids, for which my three qualify, have the first number. An acrobat named Georges, about whom I've heard all week from the girls, hangs upside down from the trapeze, waiting to sport each child across a net-bound space, low enough to keep the parents in their seats but terrified all the same. Winifred, Kyle, and Electra wear spandex suits, half white, half black, swirling with red sequins, and black ballet shoes. They are gathered with several other young children in the same attire, all responding with glamorous poses to the glory being dished their way by the French announcer.

Of the three, only Winifred falls in the net, and she gets another chance to show off later, in the ribbon-dancing and gymnastics numbers. The final act, where all the children in the camp sing "We Are the World," has most of us in the audience in tears even though we all must have heard it a hundred times before. Afterward, I race up to the littles the way the other parents do, squealing over their success, squeezing them to bits.

"You were just *wonderful*," I tell them, handing each a stuffed dolphin from the boutique and suggesting we go get in line to order photographs from the show and have them sent home. Winifred says she's mad at herself for falling during the trapeze number, and Electra is crying because she wants to keep the costume, but Kyle is ecstatic over himself, over circuses in general, over tropical islands and French people and warm air and water in early December.

"I have to tell you something else," I say, down at their level, getting the last sandal buckled.

"What now," Winifred moans.

"It's this: I'm really happy I got to see you in that circus."

"Yeah. We don't get to do stuff like that every day," Kyle says.

"Like, *duh*."

I find a free phone and get Ian after the first ring. "What's wrong?"

"Your friend in the hospital died," he says. "Mal's out of his mind. He went in after work apparently and the room was empty. Then he went to patient information and found out the man had a heart attack."

"He knew to do that?" I can't get myself to focus on the right thing. What Ian has related is like TV news, something to hear, barely react to, then forget.

"Give the kid a little credit," Ian says miserably.

I sink to the floor of the booth. "When did this happen?"

"Yesterday. I didn't find out until this morning when Hilary called and said she couldn't wake Mal up. The kid was so drunk I had to give him an emetic. Paige," he says. "I can't do this alone. I just can't. I don't *know* what to do."

"Of course you can't," I say. Which is the sort of thing I've always said to Marekki. Marekki gone, his bed a blank shrine, his room empty of disciples.

"He kept asking where you were, in between vomiting sessions."

"Tell him," I begin, then pause to cover the shake in my voice, "tell him I'm coming home."

❧ TWENTY-ONE ❧

*T*he flight home is laughable, delayed for hours. All night I sat up in the room's one chair, looking at the grass leading to the luminous sand and the flat black water beyond. I listened to Winifred's snoring, the softer versions of the other two. I remembered Mal's asking me what I was going to do when the kids got too old to come to me in the afternoons, how flip I'd been. The truth is, I don't know. I don't know how I'll bear the difference in my days, once the mighty four move on. And now, Marekki. I have never once connected Marekki with the actuality of death, never once had to struggle with his image as close to it the way I had to struggle to separate my father from it. I keep trying to think about everything as Marekki would have, with the dramatist's ironic distance, eyes keen to foreshadowing and logic, brain shielding heart. But I'm not like him. I'm more like my mother, who lets herself be stunned and upset and will say so to anyone, who has always let herself love people past the point of safety.

We eat, watch the movie, talk about the circus, color in their new tropical-fish coloring books. They're not saddened by the end of the vacation, more excited to tell their parents all about it, get home with their loot, be Odysseus returned.

We blow kisses at the baggage belt at JFK, and everyone thanks me effusively for transporting their treasures home safely. I am offered a ride back into the city by both Johanna and James, but I decline, invoking the children's need to be with their parents alone now, to let them tell the story themselves.

I get my own cab, get caught in traffic, spend every last dollar, dread the reentry.

Ian says Mal won't come over, that Mrs. Alderman is home on bed rest. We're messengers, he and I. That's all. We could go work for Western Union.

I try to reach Diana, with no luck. I call Patty instead and ask her what to do about Mal, what I should say to him.

"What would you say to me if a friend of mine died?" Patty asks.

"I'd say I'm here if you want me."

"So say that." She sounds exhausted. "As tough as he can be, if you befriend him, he won't resent you. It's important, now and later, not to have that on your head."

"I thought I'd sort of done that," I say.

"Then you've done all there is. See how frustrating it is? You get to know the child a little bit, think you have a handle on him, even *want* to have a handle on him, and he's totally out of the realm of your control, because he isn't yours."

It's too much like infertility. You can try everything, after you've been drained by all the testing, all the invasion. You can go on the goddamn Internet and chat with others who have been similarly disappointed, whose lives have been altered by soaring and dashed hopes. Then you have to stop yourself from trying, from all the talk, from even thinking about it.

The difference is that I won't stop thinking about him, talking about him, trying.

He says Dorothy's found a shrink for Mal, a Dr. Esslin in the west Sixties. "She wants us to meet," he goes on. "You, me, Jeremy, and herself. To discuss what to do about Mal."

"She wants to meet *now*? After *all these years?*"

"It's a start," he says.

"It's as if she suddenly looked at her son, saw he was frowning, and decided we should all help her make him smile."

Ian sighs. "True, but—"

"Ian," I bark, "I'm *not* doing it. I don't need Dorothy to tell me how to handle Mal. This is a mother who jets in for dinner and won't give her kid rent money. *You* go eat with her. I know I couldn't keep my food down."

"She just wants to have a discussion," he says.

"When will you wake up? When has there ever *been* a discussion? Dorothy gives orders. That's all. And those who won't follow them can't have dessert."

"She's actually very upset too."

"She should be."

I busy myself with unpacking. The day of the circus I had our laundry done to unfathomable expense, so there isn't anything to dump in the hamper, just folded clothes to put in the drawers. Drawers that now seem as out of context as the ones at Club Med.

"He actually hit me."

Ian pulls back the sleeve of his work shirt to display a dark fist-sized patch on his bicep. "He throws a pretty mean punch."

I touch the bruise, which feels warm. Then I put both arms around him. "I'm so sad about all this," I say.

"Me too."

"Are you going to meet this doctor?"

"Eventually," Ian says. "Dorothy's going to the first session."

"And you're going to the second?"

"That depends on the doctor, what he thinks needs work."

I close my eyes, trying to recapture the tranquillity of the beach, my spot under the palm tree. Carefully, I say, "I think it all needs work."

"I'm very aware of what you think, Paige," he tells me. "But we can't always rally immediately to your view. There are other factors involved."

"I see only one factor," I say. "And he needs help from both of you. You can't take turns for the sake of convenience. Or because some doctor you've never met or heard of says you should."

"That all?"

It occurs to me, looking at him in profile as he waits for my next barb, that the only thing that will cheer him is sex. I sit down on the bed next to him, reach over, lace a finger into one of his belt loops.

"What?"

"Just—nothing." I smile. I'm curious. I really want to see if we can still do this, still love it.

"You really want to?"

"It's now or never." I think I mean this. I kiss him.

"Whom should I thank?" he asks.

I put both hands on him, delight at my findings. I help him off with his jeans, his sky-blue boxers, and he attends to my clothes. We fall into it, one-two-three. I'd forgotten how nice it is to have him on top of me, his wonderful weight, his face out of a fairy tale but soft about the eyes.

Afterward, he looks as disheveled as his son and proud of it.

We stroll down the aisles of trees, finding something wrong with every one. I want a balsam, the kind Birch insisted on. They're the most expensive, and the ones in shortest supply.

"They look so scrawny," Ian complains. "Are you sure?"

"There's space between the branches," I point out. "If you string white lights on them they look so pretty and spare. And then when you hang the ornaments there's air around them."

"She wants this one," he tells the clerk, who looks like a woodsman.

"These are good trees," the man says. "Come from Canada."

Ian helps the man net the tree, then counts out the cash.

"You folks have a good holiday."

"You too," Ian says.

"Oh, I will," the man says. "I'm gettin' it together. Gettin' the whole thing together, I can promise you that."

He makes me uneasy. He sounds like Mal.

We're doing an early Christmas for them, cooking a turkey, priming the tree for trimming. I had to wait to get the tree until this evening, a Friday, so the kids wouldn't stage a war about decorating it. Ralph's father made me promise not to let him hang ornaments on the tree, and Ralph is out of sorts as it is because, it would appear, we had a better time on our vacation than he did.

"Does Malachi seem a little disaffected to you these days?"

"I'm not sure how you mean."

"Sort of right-hand-doesn't-know-what-the-left-is-doing."

"Well, that's *always* the case with him."

"He seems more so to me, just from his tone. When he said he was bringing Hilary with him, it was as if he meant to say he was bringing a dessert along."

"Maybe that's what he meant!"

"Ian." We're flirting. We're finally lovers again, and we're flirting.

Ian shrugs. "Maybe it's best not to trouble trouble."

The old box of ornaments Mother never uses stands by, waiting to be plundered.

I hang one gleaming red ball on a low branch as a suggestion. There are presents under the tree. We bought Hilary some bubble bath and Mal some CDs by groups with purposely misspelled names. I'm anxious, not having laid eyes on him in weeks, and I want to get out of the apartment for five minutes. I tell Ian I'll wait for them downstairs, if he'll keep an eye on the potatoes.

"No problem," he says, "*tiger*."

It is a ridiculous misnomer, I think, laughing, sallying forth in my Christmas red from Chadwick's.

In the lobby the devilishly handsome progeny of Diana's friend Neil attend two luggage carts full of duffel bags and ski gear. I sit on the center sofa. The boy with the darker hair is pacing and the other one is busy with a Donkey Kong game. These are kids like Diana's, used to going to far-flung slopes, and there is no excitement visible in either one.

Neil charges out of the elevator bearing three or four large decorative bags of presents. He's alive with purpose, unlike the day we saw him at the Whitney. The man follow-ing carries his share of similar bags.

"Any word on the car?" Neil calls out to Ramone as he and the much younger man behind him breeze by.

"Five minutes, sir. He got stuck on the bridge."

"Ah," Neil says. So arch, on the surface.

He joins his sons, attempting to pile the smaller bags on top of the bigger ones. His friend helps with the arranging. The dark-haired son watches this procedure with a sneer that betrays his disgust. The other son keeps his focus on the noisy Kong game.

"Kellum, get your jacket on," Neil tells this boy.

He looks up. "Why? Car's not here."

"The car *will* be here," Neil says.

"But it isn't here *yet*, Dad," the other kid warns.

"Yeah, *Dad*," the seated one says, glaring at the man Diana had referred to as "the boy toy," who reaches out and steadies Neil against the instinct he must have to slap the kid from here to kingdom come. And in this ges-ture I see myself, reaching out to do the same for Ian on the few occasions when Mal's behavior has become insup-portable.

I walk over to the boy who has just spoken.

"Hi."

He looks at me as if I've stepped on his foot.

"I'm Paige. I'm an acquaintance of your father's?"

"So?" He's laughing to himself as he says it.

"I heard what you said to your father," I say.

"And?"

"You know, things happen to people, things they can't

help, and no amount of meanness on the part of those who claim to love them will change it."

"Okay," he says suspiciously. "What else."

I glance at Neil and his friend and at the other brother, who has stopped his pacing to hear what I have to say.

"That's about it." I nod and go back upstairs.

❧ TWENTY-TWO ❧

When Ramone announces them over the intercom, I open the front door. I want to see his face, his eyes, get a handle on the evening before it begins.

Hilary gets off the elevator first, looks the wrong way, then fixes her dark gaze on me. I don't remember one thing about her from that evening of wreckage. Mal ushers her along, hand on shoulder. His jacket hangs open, exposing de rigueur jeans and a basketball jersey. He holds a bunch of carnations by the stems downward.

"Hi there," I say.

"Hey," Mal says. In lieu of further greeting he extends the flowers, which I take with an appreciative sigh.

"Wow," he says flatly, when he gets a look at the tree and the table set for dinner.

"For you to decorate," I chirp.

"Good to see you!" Ian says too loudly. "Give me your coats." He averts his eyes from her alien beauty, pretends not to be amazed.

"What can I get you to drink?" I ask them.

"I'll take a beer," Mal says. "Hil?"

"Beer's okay."

I don't wait for Ian's permission. I take out the beers, open them, and pour. When I bring in the tray, Mal and Hilary are sitting on the sofa, opposite Ian, silently. I push the two bowls of nuts their way on the coffee table. The honey glazed are Mal's favorite, and I calculate that a human stork like Hilary probably knows enough about protein to appreciate blanched cashews.

They take up a few each and munch.

"You don't like beer?" Hilary says.

"Not much," I answer.

"She only drinks water," Mal says, smiling at Hilary. "And coffee. Which is really water."

Never mind that I'm fast becoming a wino.

"What a mind, right?" Hilary says to me.

"Mal tells me you're reading *Ulysses*," Ian says pleasantly. "How do you like it?"

"Mn," Hilary begins, clearing her gums of nuts. "It's, like, really tricky. I think when he wrote it he was playing some kind of psycho game with words. It's a great puzzle, I guess. I don't know. Some of it's funny. He could think about punctuation a little more."

"Good point," I say, nodding firmly.

"So, do you, like, teach English? Mal said you know everything about books." She seems to be composing a list of features that will make up the whole of me, to be judged on completion. And for a girl purported to be brilliant, her speech is about as polished as Electra's.

"I'd like to," I say. "I've thought about it. There's a school a couple of blocks from here. Sometimes I imagine myself inside, in front of a bunch of kids who'd rather be drawn and quartered than have to listen to me. But I have too many other commitments at the moment."

Mal swigs a third of the beer, then wipes the smear of foam off his upper lip with his shirtsleeve. There are reasons beyond danger on the roads that underage persons shouldn't drink.

"I'll say," he says acidly.

"Whoa," Hilary says, pushing back the denouement with her long, flattened hands.

"I'm sorry about your friend in St. Luke's. Poor thing," Hilary says.

Poor thing? "You can't mean Marekki!"

"A guy who'd been on dialysis that long?" Hilary says. "The treatments weaken the body, you know. He shouldn't have made it as long as he did."

I stare, disbelieving. *Shouldn't?* Can a mere girl embarking on medical study dole out the assignments of who *should* and *shouldn't* live? No wonder I have such antipathy for doctors. "What a creepy thing to say."

"I just meant it's amazing he *did* live that long," Hilary says casually.

"Does anything need doing in the kitchen?" Ian asks, darting up.

"The peas," I say. "On."

"I'll keep you company," Hilary says, rising, brushing at her hips, brushing away the altercation, as if it has engendered no feeling in anyone. She swishes into the kitchen, wide-leg jeans and needless heels. I take a seat next to Mal.

"Are you all right?" I don't think I've ever asked a question this stupid.

"Sure." He's staring off, not all right, his eyes dull.

"What can I do?"

"Go to the hospital and ask them how to get hold of his ashes," he says. "They won't talk about it to me because I'm not an employee."

"They probably won't release that information," I guess. "I'm not an employee either. I'm just a volunteer."

"You have a badge, at least," he says harshly. "The guy put our names on his Living Will."

"How do you know that?" At least neither of us has to exercise that sort of authority.

"When I went and asked about when he died, they said go to Patient Information, so I went there, and I said I was his friend."

"You were."

"Yeah, so I asked them what they were doing about the funeral, and they told me all they had on him was a Living Will. They said only people whose names were on the Living Will could get a copy, so I asked them whose names were on it. And guess what I found out? Yours and mine."

"Did they actually show you a copy?"

"No, but when I said who I was the lady remembered that Marekki just redid his will. He left instructions about the ashes, so you have to get them."

"What instructions?" I brace myself for the moribund.

"We have to scatter them," he says. "In the river. He was really into rivers."

He says this from such a distance, as if he, like Marekki, has left instructions for a Malachi facsimile to conduct all of the absent Mal's quotidian business while he soars away, finally free.

"I feel so bad for him," Mal says.

"I do too." I feel worse for Mal, but I can't say so.

"Come," I say, heading for the tree. "Let's fix up this scraggly old thing."

He follows heavily, fingers some of the ornaments.

"They want dusting," I apologize.

"*Do* they!"

"Hand me a cocktail napkin. The angels you can just go ahead and hang. I can't possibly get them clean."

He rustles in one box, pulls out a nearly decapitated angel made of tin. "Out? Maybe?"

"She goes on the top," I instruct.

"Doesn't that, like, send the wrong message?"

I ask him what he means.

"Well, are angels supposed to look like they're suffering?"

I think about this. "Christmas isn't about *looks*, Malachi."

He laughs at me, so serious about this holiday that will never be serious for him.

"Anyway," I say more lightly, "the littles *love* gore. We'll end up writing a story about her, what mistake she made in her angel life before someone tried to chop off her head."

"I *know* them, remember? You don't have to tell me what they love."

"What they'd really love," I say in an attempt to dilute his irritation, "is to come over and spend an afternoon at *your* house."

"We'll get to it," he says, back in outer space.

After dinner Ian gets out the photo album that features earlier stages of Mal's growing up. I exempt myself from this audience because I don't enjoy looking at pictures of Dorothy as a young mother next to Ian, who wears the same beatific expression in every picture. Mal offers to help with the dishes.

"She seems quite enamored of you," I lie.

"Whatever *that* means," he says.

"Is she still *not* your girlfriend?" I hand him a rinsed plate.

"I'm seeing a couple people." He shrugs. "You meet anyone interesting at Club Med?" His tone borders on the accusing, as if I've wronged his father.

"A woman with mean kids. An acrobat named Georges. He took quite a shine to Kyle at circus practice. They had a wonderful time in that circus. I was scared to death watching them. By the end of the five days they were doing *frightening* stuff. But it looked so pretty, all of it."

"I don't want to hear about it."

"You don't want to hear about their *having fun?*"

"I just don't want to hear about it."

"Oh." I try *him*, as a topic. "How's the shrink?"

"He's an idiot."

"How so?"

He frees himself of dishes, sets up for the explanation. "I come in, he points to the couch, which, of course, is too short. I lie down, and then he says nothing for an hour, and I say nothing. A hundred and fifty bucks."

I don't try to disguise my irritation. "I thought your mother was supposed to go with you."

"She did!" he says. "She waited outside. You know, got work done. I could hear her talking on the phone."

"Oh, for God's sake. And she thinks this will help?" I finish up the rinsing, then look straight at him.

"Paige, please. I'm *fine*. I'm getting stuff together. I told you."

"You're *not* fine. You're binge-drinking and getting into fistfights with relatives and for all I know, making two dollars an hour doing menial labor."

"Five," he corrects. "And I got drunk *once*, after someone died, someone *you* made a huge deal about me meeting. *Don't disappoint him, Malachi. Don't you dare disappoint my friend Marekki.*"

His voice rises with fury, and I fight the impulse to shout back my defense, all in the name of his reformation, which I never should have taken on in the first place, according to the degree of his appreciation.

"The point is, I'm not buying it. You don't have to *do* this with me, put on the big act. That worries me more than the drinking. You know, Mal, you really —"

"Mal! Oh my God! You have to see this!" Hilary calls from the other room.

"What? Say it, Paige! What do I do to you?"

I fold the dishtowel and hang it from a magnetic hamburger clip on the fridge.

"You scare me."

They leave about midnight, after an obligatory round of Scrabble, which Hilary wins using medical words that I'm surprised Ian allows are legal for the game. I pack some leftovers and put them in a bag with the opened presents.

"Smart girl," Ian says, after the elevator door shuts behind them. "Hope he can hang on to *her*."

I wheel. "I can't believe the way you talk about your son."

"Now where did *that* come from?"

The wine bottle, no doubt. I know this, but I continue.

"As if he's some kind of stranger you're allowed to pass judgment on. As if he's a big flop who couldn't hang on to a girl if his life depended on it! And who wants him to anyway? She's about as warm as an ice storm, she's totally other-directed, witness all that stuff about my friend in the hospital. Typical doctor's mentality—already! Looking at the human being as if he were on display in a textbook. I'm also amazed that you think some Freudian who doesn't speak is going to help him! I haven't seen this much bullshit fly since we were listening to the doctors tell us we could freeze embryos and make a family."

"I thank you for saving that diatribe for the end of this evening, which up until now I thought had gone rather well."

He strides to the hall closet, pulls his parka off its hanger, and slams out.

Right now, we can have tantrums without worrying so much about their consequences. Another advantage of having resumed our sex life.

I'm cleaning the cover of *Tom Sawyer* for gilding purposes when Diana calls to tell me Lydia broke her leg.

The long and short of it: Tod took the kids to Cervinia to ski, Lydia fell down some sort of ravine, broke her leg in two places, they had to change their flight home, they got in this morning, no one has slept, Lydia is beside herself, she won't be able to skate again until next fall.

"But how is she feeling? Is she in bed in a cast?" In an insomniac haze myself, I take in the drama of Diana's household as an extension of that in my own.

"She's in traction at Lenox Hill," Diana reports. "I'm going over there now. Will you come with me? I don't know why, but this undid me. Worse than the business with my mother. I don't want Robert over there with me, so Tod said he'd stay home. Lydia's so miserable, and I'm not good at making her feel better. I thought maybe you'd say the right thing."

"Me!" I'm intensely flattered. Overreacting, no doubt.

"Yes, *you*."

"Of course I'll come."

Diana says she'll be along in half an hour, in a cab. I search the apartment for something cheery to bring to Lydia, but there's nothing suitable in either the food or literature departments, so I settle on a trip to a hospital gift shop where, again, there'll be nothing suitable, but at least whatever I decide to pick up will be new. I regret not being able to finish applying the gold leaf, as it constitutes the last hurdle in the Alderman project and it has kept me up through dawn. But the idea of Lydia on her back, her leg plastered and strung above her, is almost as distracting as Mal's shuttling between earth and the moon last night.

I dress warmly and go downstairs, where Ramone approaches me in haste, smiling. "Thank you," he says, "for your card."

The card featured Breughel's ice skaters, and inside I put thirty dollars, a large tip considering I never ask him to so much as hold a door for me.

He asks if he can hail me a cab. "No thanks. A friend's picking me up."

Diana is along shortly, opening the door from the inside, shoving over to make room. She looks awful, her eyes ringed with exhaustion, her face pale.

"She's going to be fine," I say. "Remember that you're very tired. It colors everything."

"I know she'll be fine. I know that. But this comes at such a difficult time. Too many other things are going wrong."

Nearly at the hospital, I tell Diana I'm going to the gift shop. "Then I'm getting you coffee. Then we're going to sit down until you've caught your breath. Then we'll go to Lydia. Deal?"

"Deal."

I buy Lydia magazines, candy, a teddy bear that says I LOVE YOU.

"She'll hate that," Diana carps.

"She hates everything!" I say lightly.

"Oh God, I know!"

I get the coffee off a cart in the lobby, and we sit in square vinyl chairs, puce-colored.

"Tod's been seeing someone for several years. She lives in Paris. And she's an American. At least he could have gone for a French woman."

I'm anything but shocked. "How did you find this out?"

"Oh, I've known about it for a long time. I just figured it was one of those things all the guys who travel so much do. And I thought it was for money. But the kids met her when he took them skiing. I thought *that* was a little de trop."

I swallow some of the urn coffee, which lives up to its half-dollar price. "You thought Tod was sleeping with a whore? Jesus, Diana. You could *catch* something."

Diana smiles for the first time this morning. "No. I couldn't catch anything. We don't—"

"You don't?" I cross my sexpot legs.

"Not anymore. *No.*"

"And you found out how?"

"Bills. I went through the credit-card charges. But that was a while ago."

"And you let it go on."

"He thinks I'm not interested," she says.

"In him? Well, why would you be, if he's sleeping with an expatriate? Helped an awful lot by the image of a roaring fire and two snifters full of the finest brandy and the latest in rear-entry ski boots lined up on the hearth. Gee, Diana, can't say as I blame you!"

"When it happens to *you*, you can't believe it," she says.

"So they were skiing in Italy, and this American French woman appeared?"

"Large as life, in a banana jumpsuit. She's a fucking ski instructor, to quote Lydia."

"What are you going to do?"

"We're getting a divorce."

She gives up on the coffee, setting it on a low table. She rests her elbows on her knees. The bones of her wrists jut out.

"Let's go," I say. I virtually pull Diana to the elevators. *Too many hospitals. I've been in too many hospitals.*

We hear Lydia crying from way down the hall. "I can't take it."

"Yes you can. You have to. She's not dying, Diana."

Lydia is in a private room. The cast isn't exactly above her, as I'd imagined, but straight ahead of her, strapped into a mechanism that looks like it might be more useful at Cape Canaveral. Her toes, their polish chipped, poke out. Her face, creased with fatigue and stained from crying, is more upsetting than the architecture of her cure.

"Mom, I want to go *home!*" Lydia wails, and when she says this I think morosely of what that will be like for her, to go home with a broken leg into a beautiful land of an apartment besieged by infidel parents.

Diana kneels by the bed and smoothes Lydia's greasy hair back with her skeletal hands. "I know you do, Liddy," she says. "I know you do. But for a while, you have to stay here, where your leg can get better faster."

"But I don't *want* to lie on my back anymore!" Lydia shouts hoarsely. "I want to sit up!"

"The doctors say that will take a while," Diana says.

This news sends Lydia into fresh agony, and they go back and forth, back and forth, about getting better here and getting home soon. I don't think I can bear it, watching Lydia deny her mother, as I've so often done to mine, when Diana wants nothing more than for the world to be right for Lydia, for it to treat her well and keep her safe from this sort of thing.

They finally get to a calm place where Diana says that I've brought her something if she'd like to have a look.

"O-kay," Lydia hiccups.

Diana shows her the things.

"Thank you," Lydia says to me, taking the bear, wiping at her face with its paw.

She really is a beautiful child, strip away all that has spoiled her. Or, she's beautiful because of it.

"Could you bear to be read to?" I venture. "I don't want you to go hungry for star gossip. Or new cures for acne and cellulite."

Lydia smiles for a second. She is plagued by neither of these, at least. We read.

"One would have thought," Alice says, "this would be automatic. They *know* you here." She wags her head at bureaucracy. "The man is *dead*, after all. The way they go about these things. Honestly."

It's the first time I've heard Alice express irritation about anything. She hands me the letter vouching for my character, which will eventually authorize me to collect the urn from the funeral home. I exchange this, at Patient Information, for a permission form and the Living Will.

"Are there any other papers?" Lest I have to tangle with these folk again, I feel the need to be thorough.

The woman behind the desk levels a look at me that

seems to suggest, in its obduracy, that this is not the time to get greedy.

"I just wondered what happened to his things," I say cheerfully. "There were some books and photographs."

"Ask the floor nurse."

More organizational insouciance. The morning Daddy died, Mother and Audrey and I were asked by an orderly to remove ourselves from his room so it could be cleaned. As if a few minutes shorn from the room-assignment schedule would have caused any more havoc than is typically available in a hospital.

I decide against quarreling over Marekki's effects and take the #4 bus down to the funeral home, collect the urn, and walk home. I banish the quick image of him lying in state, his spirit adrift. Marekki would have found humor, I think, in the idea of himself being carted through the park in a paper bag. We might have had quite a discussion about this. Alone, however, I'm aware of my mission as distinctly somber. And with Mal in Florida with Dorothy, Jeremy, and the infant king, even more of a desolate undertaking.

❧ TWENTY-THREE ❧

"*I*t's brilliant," I tell her. Mother has given me business cards, mailers, and stationery with BOOKS BY THEIR COVERS stenciled across the top.

"You think?" Mother asks, delighted. "I took a chance."

"I really like it."

"Good! Then Christmas has been a success this year."

We're having leftovers in the kitchen.

"The thing I've always believed about Christmas," she says, "is that it's a great pain in the rump. But this year it's just easy!"

"Are you saying you don't miss Audrey?"

She laughs. "Well, now that you mention it. And what about Ian? You've said so little."

"We sort of did Christmas all week."

"Is everything all right with the boy?"

"My feeling is no."

"Well, how could it be, after all."

"I think you're right about that. But there's not much I can do from a distance."

"I think you've been an absolute *saint!* Some people would just look the other way and say 'It's not my problem.'"

"It would be easier if I did that."

Mother sighs, finishes her champagne. "Well, I love my scarves," she says, holding them up against her sweater.

We call Audrey at her son's house.

"I want all his books from childhood," I say. "And his telescope. And all the pictures I ever gave him and the ones of the boats. Anything to do with boats that you don't want I want."

"You don't have to do this, Paige," Audrey says gently. "Really, I felt so bad that day. It's not necessary now. This can wait."

"I'm just telling you those are the things I want. Just don't give them away, okay?"

"I wouldn't dream of doing that. Now tell me, have you had a good Christmas?"

I say that yes, we have. Very good indeed.

A few days after Christmas I take them to see the Angel Tree at the Metropolitan Museum. I got a special dispensation from Ralph's father, citing the Neapolitan derivation of the ornaments, the value of the Nativity *as story.* We make an evening of it, the viewing, meandering through other exhibits and then dinner in the cafeteria. I load the tray with peanut-butter sandwiches and six cookies the size of pancakes. Anthony is now an official toddler and can trail me through the line with panache.

"He was really born in the summer," Ralph orates.

"Says who," Winifred challenges.

"Historians," Ralph tells her. "People who *know.*"

"The good thing about Jesus," Kyle interrupts, "is that he said you have to love your neighbor."

"Our neighbors don't speak English," Ralph says. "They speak *Farsi.*"

"*So?*" Winifred says, as if this is grounds for some sort of envy.

"The bad thing is he died on the cross for our sins."

I don't know who's pumping Kyle full of liturgy, because neither Johanna nor Carson seem pulled together enough to get themselves, never mind the children, to church.

"My dad says the cross is just supposed to scare people."

"All right, you two," I say. "Maybe he was born in the summer, but as you know, in some parts of the globe, it's summer in December. Now, could we eat?"

"Are angels real?" Winifred asks me.

"What do you think?"

"I don't know. You can't see them."

"Maybe they don't want to be real," Electra says, right next to me. I help her unwrap her sandwich and jam the straw into the milk carton. Maybe *Electra* doesn't want to be real, I can't help thinking.

It's a tough week, the one after Christmas. Slow, a little aimless, a letdown, even for Ralph, our resident Maccabee. There's no school, so the kids are with me all day. But I need them to boost me up as well. We stay in the cafeteria until closing, until I see their eyelids start to lower and Anthony hangs on me as I imagine Jesus must have done on Mary.

"My mother died," Diana says.

"Where are you?" The news balls up, sticks in my throat.

"With Lydia." Her voice is faint, small. "Can you call everyone?"

"Of course," I tell her. "Then I'll come."

I've never been on the phone so much. I've never taken so many cabs in my life.

I find Diana in the hallway outside Lydia's room in the hospital.

"My mother! That was *my* mother! I can't believe it! I can't believe she's gone!"

"It's all right," I say, hugging her. "Oh, really, it's all right. You don't have to believe it now. You don't have to do anything, Diana. You can stop now. Just stop. It's all right."

"She always hated Christmas."

Some nurses flutter around. I let them know, with a gesture here and there, that there isn't anything more to do. I hold on, for whatever it's worth.

I pile them high on the kitchen table, the books I've rescued. I'm hungry for them, wanting to reread them before I go to work on them. I want to read them to the littles, who have only so much patience (Anthony, none) for chapter books. What better way to celebrate my father's and Marekki's life than to honor books, to worship words, as they did? Books take you in, adjust to what you want of them, make room. Like water does when you plunge in, like families do at their best. I should be able to do as much for Mal, to be the book he can lose himself in, the water around him.

I pick out Daddy's King James Bible and read Malachi. I remember Marekki saying it's as dark and hopeless as Job. *So little light. So little light.* The Lord is angry and demands to know of his priests *if I then be a father, where is mine honor?* He threatens them, issues conditional statements and absolutes, reminds them of his covenant with Levi. But by the end of the short book, the Lord promises righteousness and healing to those who fear Him. I do not see the same thing as

Marekki did. I see hope in the Lord's promise: *And all nations shall call you blessed: for ye shall be a delightsome land.*

I call him. I want him back, close, the way he was that short time before we fell off course. I reach Hilary.

"He's not back from Florida yet. I think he's coming back tomorrow."

Don't you know? I want to ask. It bothers me, not having been able to assess Hilary's status in Mal's life. It seems that two people who cohabit ought to know when the other might come home.

Instead I ask Hilary how she is, what she's doing hanging around the apartment instead of skiing or sunbathing in the tropics.

"Chemistry," Hilary says, her voice deep with importance.

I have to be impressed by Hilary's tenacity. And by her will to be alone studying on a vacation.

"There are a million things going on," I say, mentally referring to death and work and change. "Could you tell Mal I want to talk to him?"

"I'll tell him," Hilary promises, nothing-guaranteed.

We drive out to Westchester, a train of limos. The landscape is a ruin of snow darkened and eroded by rain. Lydia sits beside me, her crutches at her feet. Robert and Tod ride in the car ahead with Diana. Somehow, Lydia conceded to ride with me. She didn't want to be with all of them in the first car. Up there, she'd have to sit in the front seat with the driver so her remaining family members wouldn't crush her.

I can't say how nice it must be for Lydia to be out of the hospital and home again; instead, I ask about schoolwork.

"There must be a lot to catch up on," I say.

"I did most of it in the hospital," Lydia said.

"While you were on your back like that?"

"They let me sit up in the end," Lydia explains. "And it was mostly reading anyway."

"That's amazing."

We're on our way to a cemetery in Tarrytown, and afterward there will be a reception at the house in Sleepy Hollow. I ask about the house, whether Lydia still likes going there in the summer.

"It's pretty boring sometimes, but I like it if my friends are around. Next summer I'm going to Europe with my dad, though."

"Really?" Diana hasn't said anything about this. "Will Robert go with you?"

"Dad wants him to. But I don't think he wants to go. He's got a girlfriend."

I don't know whether Lydia was referring to Robert or Tod.

"I didn't know that," I say.

We ride in silence for a while; I ogle the stately homes. In the rain they look like fortresses, their owners safe somewhere deep within their vast holds.

"Granny wouldn't like it," Lydia says.

"Wouldn't like what, love?"

"All the stuff that's going on. It's really sad when grandparents die because they're the only ones that stay together."

"It seems that way sometimes," I say. Birch was too elegant, or too mortified, to discuss my grandfather's waywardness.

"I'm never getting married," Lydia says.

"That's what my stepson Mal says."

I stand among strangers at one end of a shallow ellipse of people around the grave. The minister, imported from St. James in Manhattan, recites the burial rites to minimal effect, and then the coffin is lowered by a hoist that wants greasing. I watch Diana throw one yellow rose down on top of it, and then Robert and Lydia do the same. The ground is soggy from rain and melting snow, and Lydia's crutch tips sink down so far she can barely get back to the car afterward. She'll accept help only from her mother, and it is decided on the spot that Lydia will ride to the house with her mother and Robert, and Tod will go with me. "Remind me that I have something to show you at the house," Diana says brusquely, and then she turns to help Lydia into the car.

Tod offers a share of his umbrella as we walk back to the other car. Politely, I take his arm. "Infernal, isn't it," he says.

I assume he means the drizzle and, by consequence, the footing. "Yes."

"It makes the whole thing worse."

I don't think it could get worse, for Diana, drizzle or no. We pull into the slow line of cars leaving the cemetery. I don't want to talk about the funeral, or anything connected to Diana, with him.

"Lydia tells me you're off to Europe for the summer," I say, for lack of anything else.

"Did she!" He nods good-for-her.

"She did. She seems hopeful but dubious about Robert's going along."

"We haven't worked out all the details," Tod says edgily. "You know what that's like."

Funerals, like weddings and occasionally births, bring out the worst in everyone, I remind myself. "Yes, I suppose I do."

"So we're all in the same boat then," he concludes. He checks his watch.

"Woman overboard," I say, certain that were this a fact, if Tod were watching me flail in the sea, he'd send no one to rescue me.

For the rest of the ride we say nothing to each other. I avoid him at the reception. It's easy, as everyone who was in the church is here except for the truly infirm. Diana whizzes by again and again, seeing to specific requests, losing herself in duty. Somehow the grief hasn't worn her out completely. She manages to look younger than ever today, crisp in black trousers and Mao jacket, her fine hair wisping up off the back of her neck. She looks like an athlete in finery, all the more stunning.

Robert shows me the library, large enough to require ladders on runners. I look over the leather-bound works, collections of James Fenimore Cooper and Hawthorne, the *Oxford English Dictionary* bound in vellum, a set of Shakespeare's plays. All these, just behind the desk. I am moved to realize that Mrs. Alderman was among the truly bookish and not just playing at it to suit her circle.

"Granny read all the time," Robert says stoically. "Whenever we came in from playing or being out on the river, she'd be in here reading. It was her favorite thing to do."

"I think that's wonderful," I say.

"Well, stay here as long as you like. I better go back and talk to people." He glances at me imploringly, wish-I-could-stay. In ten years there won't be any question as to his eligibility, his standing. He'll be written up in social columns and in the business section, and the line of women will grow.

"Thank you, I will."

I look out at the slope of lawn that has lost all its snow except on the far edges, where a stone wall separates this terrain from some more exactly like it. I feel a peripheral part of the saga of a great family, not unlike the Marchmains of Brideshead. And, as Charles does in some of the most wrenching scenes, I allow myself a few minutes of solitary contemplation and then go back into the fray of the livelier

rooms, to freshen my sense of who they all are, and, by association, who I am.

"I want you to do all of it," Diana says in the library.

"Diana, let's wait until things have settled down before
you hurl yourself headlong into this one," I suggest. "A lot of
these books are in terrific shape."

"You're not listening. I'm not telling you to cover them
with far-out fabric."

She says that her mother would have wanted the books
restored to mint condition, and by God she's going to get it
done. It will be half a life of work, and it will keep the wolf
from my door.

"Just say when."

"Today," Diana says. "You can start with the Coopers.
There are boxes on the side porch. We'll put them in the car
this afternoon."

She's doing that impulsive thing people do after a death,
boxing things, moving them out of the way, as if this will
ensure a clear view past the grief. Exactly what Audrey did
the days following Daddy's death.

"All right," I say. "If you're sure you want to go back
today."

"I'm not staying in this house tonight," Diana says.
"Lydia can't get up and down stairs."

"Whatever you like."

"So, I'll get those boxes," Diana says.

People are in the hallway in coats, saying good-bye to
Tod and Robert. It's dark now, and when the guests open the
front door to leave, the cold wind cuts through the front hall
and into the adjoining rooms.

"I'll get them," I say, although I don't know which porch
she means. "You go say good-bye."

Diana goes and stands next to her husband and treats the company to more of the lie that now holds up this house. She has to do it for her mother, this last time.

Neil sidles up, smiles hello.

"I'm sorry if I appalled you in the lobby that evening. I know it wasn't any of my business," I say.

"On the contrary!" Neil says. "You deserved an ovation. It had gotten way beyond tolerable in our house. I didn't realize you were in the building."

"Five years. How are things now?"

"No different, except the boys are back in school. Terry is being very patient. I don't know how he bears them. I can't bear them, most of the time."

"Don't you find that interesting?"

"That I can't bear them?"

"That so much of the talk is about how unbearable *we* are?" I say, daring to include myself among actual parents. I have a momentary pang about Ian, all the nagging I've done to sway him to my questionable view of what Mal needs.

"All *we* do is err," Neil reminds me.

"Cheers," I say.

"To you," he says.

❦TWENTY-FOUR❧

I start with *The Last of the Mohicans*, the only book of Cooper's I was ever able to get through. It's more ragged than the others, probably for just that reason. I observe a regimen that allows me only two outings per day, one in the morning, for errands, and one after the littles are picked up, for exercise, and I get the set done in twelve days, to the tune of five thousand dollars. News of Mal working at the music store and napping in Dr. Esslin's office reaches me one night, after he and Ian have dinner. The one time he calls for his father I tell him I'll see him soon, when I get through some of this work. It's almost February.

"Are you sure?" I ask Diana, re: the money.

"Have I ever not been?" She's smiling, finally.

"What's going on?"

"I got served papers."

"He served *you* papers?"

"Yes!" she laughs. "Can you believe it?"

"So why aren't you upset?" I glance around for signs of Tod's bailing, but the apartment, at least from this vantage point in the wide entrance hall, looks exactly the same.

"I met someone."

I wondered about the dearth of phone calls from Diana after the funeral, chalking it up to abject misery.

"Where?"

"He did the food for Mom's reception," she says. "He's to die for. A Cordon Bleu graduate. He built his business up from a kitchen in Ithaca and now he's in the city, delegating from Park Avenue. It's fantastic, what he's done. And the funny thing is, I've known him, however vaguely, for years. I always call him when I've got a party to do!"

"What's his name?" I feel unpleasantly surprised, in the way I do when other rivals get mentioned: Paula, Hilary.

"Gary. He lives near you, actually, not too far from the school. I've completely flipped. I drop the kids off, and if he's got a morning, I go straight there. Of course there aren't too many of those, given his hours and mine, settling the estate, but it's just about the best I've ever known!"

Diana hugs me, and I try to respond with something other than stiffness.

"What's wrong, sweetie?"

"Nothing! I just had no idea!" I say. "I'm happy for you."

"But—?"

"But nothing!" I'm ashamed of my lack of exuberance. "Have the kids met him?"

"Oh sure. They think he's a friend helping Mom through a rough spot. They're just glad I'm leaving them alone and not crying all the time. Lydia thinks he's the best cook on the planet. We all went to the Ice Capades last weekend!"

Replaced on all fronts, I think. But it's better to see Diana this way, animated by love. Crazy over someone.

"And Robert?"

"He asked Gary if he'd ever been a model."

"He must be absolutely beautiful!"

"He's pretty dishy!" Diana admits, blushing.

"So when do I get to meet him?"

"Soon. Some weekend when the kids are with Tod. In fact, he's getting married in a month. It seems the French whore/American ski instructor is pregnant."

"The speed of him!"

"Hey, the faster he's gone, the better for me. I look at him now, and I can't believe we were married for twenty years. I think to myself, 'How did I do that?' He's probably thinking the same thing. The nice thing is, I don't care what he thinks. As long as he's good to the kids, which he's always been, I don't care."

"When are we all getting together again?" I ask. "I feel deprived."

"Next week. Bibiana's taking us downtown. For *real* Italian. Did I tell you Lydia's walking cast comes off today?"

"Tell her congratulations for me. Tell her I said hi."

Outside Diana's building I stand still long enough to cause the doorman to ask if I want a taxi. I say no despite a mean wind, wrap my scarf tighter around, and head directly into it.

Our February program includes making valentines and papier-mâché masks for our trip to the Village on Mardi Gras, a number of dreary days in the apartment treating various stages of strep throat, and one visit to the Museum of the City of New York for their special exhibit on circuses. The cost of taking all five to the actual circus at Madison

Square Garden is prohibitive. I try to explain this to Kyle without bringing up the subject of either parent.

"Now that you've actually *been* in a circus, watching one may not be as fun," I say.

"You're just saying that because you don't want to take us."

"Oh, no, I do want to take you. It's also very expensive."

Kyle mopes. He mutters something about his father. I ask him to repeat it, even though I don't want to know what it was.

"He probably told you not to take me!" Kyle screams.

"What are you getting so bent out of shape about?" Ralph complains.

"Ralph, please." Sometimes I wish he'd just hurry up and *be* his father so I wouldn't have to admonish him about the awful way he talks to us.

"The bad thing about Daddy is he never gives us any money."

I could throttle both of them, Johanna and Carson, she for badmouthing him, he for being bad enough to badmouth.

Electra comes forward with her Esmerelda wallet. She slips out two bills and holds them in front of Kyle. "Here. Now you can go to the circus."

"It's not enough!" he screams.

"Sweetie." I can't stand it. I pull him onto my lap. "I'll get the tickets. I *will*."

"*Yes!*" Ralph hikes victorious fists into the air. "Nice work, Kyle!"

"Can we sit up close?" Winifred asks. "It's really hard to see from high up. My grandmother took me, and we had to look through binoculars, and then we had to leave anyway because she has asthma."

"*What?*" Ralph says, annoyed by the non sequitur. If only

he could peer into his future of annoying everyone with non sequiturs. If only I could convince his doctor father to get him tested.

But I can't think about "if only." Things for these children are as they are, and there's only so much I can mitigate. The same with Malachi. I'm tired, I realize, from the effort at making things better. I would like to believe that improvement will come of its own accord, that Ralph will survive his ADD, that Kyle and Anthony will be well taken care of, that whatever struggle is going on in Electra's house will stop, that Winifred will find friends, that Malachi will find hope. What I want most is not to have to want all these things.

Bibiana says she would have told us at the last dinner, but she was afraid she might miscarry.

"So how many months *are* you?" Toni asks, prosecuting.

"Almost four." She holds in the joy, but it brims in her face, in its high color and fullness.

"I don't believe it!" I say, worried that the happiness I feel for Bibiana will momentarily give way to solid, unforgiving envy.

"*Un miracolo*," she suggests, gesturing helplessly at the ceiling.

"Let's kill her," Patty says, smiling. "Do the boys know?"

"Not yet," Bibiana says firmly. "I don't want to tell them until it becomes obvious."

"You shouldn't," Toni advises. "You don't want their reactions *now*."

"Maybe ever!" Diana says. "Oh, I can't get over it! It's too wonderful!"

"This is crazy!" Toni howls. "All this *stuff* that's happening. We're having a baby, we're in love, and beyond *reach*, I

might add." She shoots a look at Diana. "What's happening
on our end, Patty? Paige?"

"I'm an old bore," Patty says. "I'm going to work for Erica
Wilson."

"I don't think that's boring," I say.

"I do!" Toni says. "Jesus, I have to think of something.
Oh yes, Olivia finally got her period. She's in heaven, ailing
gracefully, and all of us are in hell."

"You know how much they love you, those girls," I say.
Toni finds something of interest in her lap, then looks up,
her eyes shining.

"I suppose that's true," she says.

"What about you?" Diana asks me. "How is that handsome nonrelative of yours? How is he managing?"

"He's *getting a life*," I say, my voice approaching the depth
of Mal's. "He's working at a record store."

"*And?*" Toni prompts.

"He's got a dreadful girlfriend."

"Part of getting a life," Diana reminds us.

"They do that on purpose," Patty says. "They date dreadful people to bug you."

"He *lives* with her," I clarify.

"Better she than you!"

"I don't know, Patty. I don't think so." I'm a-dither, with
all of our living arrangements, Bibiana's news, the depend-
able flux of day care. But two things stand out as clear to me
tonight: Mal is headed to no place good, and I can't help him
with that.

"Make us a promise, Bibi," I blurt.

"*Dimmi,*" she says gently.

"No matter how sick or tired you feel, you won't miss our
dinners. If it gets ridiculous for you to come out and meet us,
let us come to your house."

Bibi laughs, throaty, more gorgeous than ever. "*Vi prometto.*"

I walk home, on changed streets. I try to sort things, put the deaths in one compartment, my husband and stepson in another, the littles in another, the books in another, but it's a stifling effort. How do I do all of this, remain sane, when I can make sense of nothing?

"Put your arms around me," I tell Ian from the middle of the living room, my coat still on, damp and smelling of the city in rain.

"What happened?"

"Bibi's pregnant."

"Oh," he says. He hugs tighter, knows what I need, wants to give it to me. It's as much as I can ask from him, only just now it doesn't seem enough. I weep quietly into his shirt.

"One by one," I say, "people are leaving me. That's what it feels like."

"Can I say something?"

I nod miserably, wipe my eyes on his tie.

"I'm not."

"No matter what?"

"No matter what."

"What if I don't get over these things?"

"Who says you have to?"

I married Ian, I think, because *no matter what* his level of oblivion about external issues, when it comes to me he knows what to say. His big Scots brain may be in a permanent fog about Malachi, but about me he's clear.

"I really wanted him to be a part of us."

He draws back, holds my head. "That you can't control. But if it's any consolation, he called. He wanted to talk to you about bringing the kids over one afternoon next week."

I hop blithely back on the roller coaster. "He did?"

"Honest!" He hugs me again. "Even the ones you think are leaving aren't, you know. You've got no idea what a magnet you are."

"A geek magnet." Mal's phrase.

"And that makes me—"

"Right."

"Go call."

I race to the phone, get him at home. We settle on Wednesday.

"I'll bring things for them to do," I say. "We won't stay too long."

"Don't worry about it," he says. He sounds tired, for a change, and as if he's been talked into this, although Ian wouldn't have done so.

"We'll be there around three-thirty."

"*Whatever.*"

❧TWENTY-FIVE❧

*I*t's a good fifteen blocks to Mal's building, but Anthony's got a new stroller, and I promise them we'll stop and rest on benches in Riverside Park. The afternoon is cool, startlingly clear. I have a backpack full of the usual junky sustenance and art distractions, this time green construction paper and gold sprinkles for clover cutouts for St. Patrick's Day. I'll attempt the parade, if the weather holds, which it didn't do on Veterans' Day, a "real bust," to quote Ralph.

"Shall we practice our formation?" I ask, once we're in the park.

"You can't just decide to march in a parade, Paige. You have to get permission from the *mayor*."

"I'm not talking about marching *in* the parade, Winifred," I say. "I'm talking about marching *alongside* it."

"Like that's fun," Ralph says.

"Come on," I beg them. "If we're orderly about things, we'll get there faster."

I plug Anthony, whining in the stroller, with his binky, assign the proper rhythm to the pace, and pray that the others will follow my lead. Kyle zigzags ahead, his towhead white in the brilliant sun, while the girls keep close to me. Ralph puffs along a few yards back, cursing me in his head, no doubt.

"There's nothing worse than a surly cadet," I toss his way.

"There's nothing worse than marching for no reason!" he screams.

"Is Mal still sad because the fat man died?" Winifred asks me.

"Let's not call him 'the fat man,' okay?"

"But wasn't he *fat?*" She's doing this on purpose, so Ralph will hear and be hurt.

"He had a weight issue, yes. It had to do with his being *sick.*"

"What should I call him then?" she says.

"Mr. Marekki. That was his name."

"Mr. Mar-icky!" Winifred cackles.

I did not bring them to meet Marekki for just this reason. I knew they would be unable to contain their curiosity and comments, and why should they?

"I'm hungry," Ralph pipes up.

"Speaking of *fat.*"

"All right, let's stop."

We gather at a bench so I can dispense Rice Krispies Treats and juice, partly so Winifred's mouth will be full of something other than insults. I can see tears welling in Ralph's eyes.

"If you were fat," I tell Winifred, "you wouldn't want people to say so. And if you were mean, you wouldn't want people to say so either."

I bite savagely into a Rice Krispies Treat, to be sure she's gotten my drift.

"But she *is* mean," Ralph states boldly, the tears willed away.

"I am not!" Winifred shouts. "I'm a child of God!"

"God wouldn't *want* her," Ralph says.

"God doesn't want *you*," Winifred shrills, "because you're fat!"

I eat, stay out of it. Sometimes I just can't reel them back. I watch Kyle, the wisest man this afternoon, trying to share his Rice Krispies mess with an interested squirrel. Kyle reminds me of the squirrel, still for a second, then flying crazily off to the next thing, unconscious with speed, more elemental than material.

"Okay, gang. Onward."

We drift north, lazy from the snack, ready for something different. When we get up to the apartment, he's got the TV on, which doesn't please me.

"Can we switch this to Channel Thirteen. *Arthur*'s on, at least."

"How about cartoons?"

He's presentable enough, but bent on a challenge, it seems. All of today is challenge, I decide.

"Yeah, yeah, yeah, cartoons!" Kyle yips.

"Do you want me to stay?"

Ralph leaps to answer me. "You can go! We'll be fine!"

"Are you sure you're up to this?" I ask Malachi, worried, because now I can see the purple crescents under his eyes. "Have you slept in the last week?"

"City that never sleeps," he mutters.

"I think I should stay here."

"They'll be *okay*, Paige," he says, more reasonable. "Go do errands or something. Come back in an hour."

"I'm taking the baby," I say. Anthony, fast asleep in the stroller, won't have opportunity to balk.

I leave uneasily, thinking this is an instance where perhaps I should have stood my ground and not let them get away with what they wanted. I'm not sure what to do in terms of errands, so I resort to a bookstore where I can bring the stroller in without issue, where I know I won't spend money and something is bound to catch my eye for the required time period. It may be good for him to try and figure out what to do with them. It might get him out of himself for an hour.

At the corner of 112th and Broadway, there are two fire trucks and several police cars. Regular cars are crawling past the commotion. For a second I imagine myself in one of them, annoyed by the snag in my afternoon.

Strangers are clumped by the building, gazing up. Someone shouts into a megaphone, and there are police and firemen everywhere, some in the lobby, some out here, some moving between the two camps.

"What's going on?" I ask the first officer I come to.

"Kid on the roof," he says, squinting up at the trouble, pointing. "You can see him. Got little ones with him."

I don't look. I wheel Anthony, waking in all the hubbub, to the entrance, which is roped off.

"I'm sorry, ma'am," another officer says. "We can't let you inside."

"I think that might be my stepson," I say. "Please. At least let me find out."

He lifts the plastic yellow band across the entrance.

"Mama," Anthony says.

"You'll see her soon, sweetie," I tell him.

All the way up in the elevator Anthony cries for his

mother and I pray. The Lord's Prayer five times over, then I fly down the hall of the uppermost floor to the open door at which two more officers are standing guard. Beyond them is another man in plain clothes, talking to a female officer who's got Electra, Ralph, and Winifred in a huddle beside her. They are all wailing, which sets Anthony off. I leave the stroller with the two at the door.

"These your kids, ma'am?" the man says.

"Yes! Yes!" I cry, my voice stringy. "Where's Kyle? Oh my God, where is he?"

Outside, a policeman is kneeling in the center of the tar, about six yards from Mal. Mal straddles the two-foot-high brick divide separating the rooftop from the air. He's got Kyle perched on it. Kyle is shaking, from tears or cold or both, I can't tell. If there's been any physical struggle, he's given it up.

"That's right," the officer is saying. "That's exactly right."

What could possibly be right? I want to scream. I gather from the cagey tone of the officer that a dialogue has been established.

"Malachi was telling me," the officer says with terrifying formality, "that Kyle wants to learn how to fly."

"*Paige!*" Kyle screams. Mal jerks him to his senses, a firm hold on one small arm, and Kyle screams again.

"I was just trying to convince him that a flying lesson here would be a big mistake." There is no inflection now at all.

I hear everything, the girls wailing for Kyle, Kyle's whimpering, even the stir below, but loudest is my heart pumping furiously against this.

"Mal," I plead. "Let Kyle come to me."

He ignores this. "I'm tired," he tells me.

"I know that."

"There's no place left," he says. He shows us the emptiness of things with his free hand. The officer comes up off his knees, ready to lunge, but I grab his arm.

"No." I turn to the officers nearby. "Have they got something set up down there? I didn't see anything on my way in. One of you needs to go downstairs and make sure there's a net or a goddamn reservoir!"

"They've got it set up," the man in plain clothes says. "But anything you can do to keep them both up here with us would be better."

I turn back. "What do you want, Mal?"

Mal is smiling out into the air, letting his head dance as he considers the vast world of his wants. Kyle is stiff with fear. I thank God for his rubber soles. If my heart pounds any faster, I'll be dead.

"There's nothing left!" he shouts. He seems to want us all to celebrate that discovery with him.

"I want my daddy," Kyle sobs.

"Can I come over there, to where you are?" I ask, my voice loud.

Mal doesn't answer, instead keeps looking out into what he must at present think is freedom. I go ahead. Behind me, I sense the officer standing up.

"If I put my arm out, would you grab it?" I ask.

Again, nothing. Kyle's eyes beg me to move faster.

"Keep it steady," a man's voice comes from below. "Hold on to the kid."

I hear Ian behind me. Hilary must have come home, gotten nervous and called him. She knew enough to do this, at least. He takes my hand and grips it and says, "How about it, Malachi? One of us puts an arm out and you grab on and you give Kyle to the other one?"

Mal faces us, looking from one to the other, trying, try-ing to get from us an answer, a way to proceed. *Us. The wrong people.*

"Tell me what you want, son," Ian says.

Mal laughs, a sardonic bark of a laugh. Hollow. "You tell him," he orders me.

Ian looks at me too.

"*Tell him,*" Mal urges.

"Paige?" Ian says. "Speak?"

"Love," I say weakly. "He wants love."

Mal leans out, the arm on Kyle straightening.

"*Steady!*" the voice below booms.

Mal jolts to attention. I shut my eyes. Kyle's fallen, or they both have, I know it, and if I open my eyes I'll be in a world that will be unlivable.

But instead I hear Malachi moaning, from some deep place no one should have to know about, and then he's off the brick divide and in his father's arms, and Kyle's in mine.

⚓TWENTY-SIX⚓

Pieces of what went on after that stay with me, and I lose others. Ian's face, that of a person who might have opted for death over a life that contained an incident like this one. The shape of Ian and Mal, huddled against all that happened and didn't. Kyle's reunion with the others, with Anthony. Hilary's ravaged face in the back of one of the squad cars. The terrible duty of telling Johanna and the other parents. The wait I've endured since, not knowing if they'll be back, the knowledge that, for the most part, I don't deserve to have them back.

A reporter asked if I was a relative. I might have said yes or nothing, but I don't remember which. There was loud, late telephoning between Ian and Dorothy, he obligating her to keep Malachi's name out of the papers, and, by association, mine.

It's almost like someone dying, this. You don't recover.

You have to learn to live differently. Tonight, our future stretches across the bedspread, out into the city, ending in colorless water. I don't believe I'll get to him again, or know him anymore. The most terrible thing is I'm not even sure I want to know him. He'll be guarded by the unimpressive shrink and by his frightened parents. I curse myself for not knowing more about him, for not seeing this wrong turn coming. I curse my thankless position, this role I accepted before knowing what it required of me.

Anyone can set up a life. But is it the right one? That you can't know.

In tears Ian begs to know why Mal said what he said on the roof, why he thought I'd know the answer.

"Why didn't he think *I'd* know it was love he wanted?" Ian cries. "Does he think so ill of me?"

"I'm an outsider," I say. "I don't know what he thinks of you."

I've rehearsed for such a question, uselessly.

We deal separately with tears, he with his handkerchief, I with a wad of paper towel.

"What *happened?*" he insists.

"I think," I say finally, "I disappointed him. I was around for a while, crowding him, meddling. Then everyone started dying, Marekki, Diana's mother, and I just didn't seem to be around anymore. But I *meant* to be. I wanted to give you room, all three of you. I wanted you and Dorothy to tend to him. I didn't want him to think I wasn't paying attention. God knows how I think about him all the time. I think he was jealous of the kids."

"It has to be more than *that!*" he says.

"Why? Why does it have to? I disappointed him, like you and Dorothy did."

"You really believe that?"

"I don't know, Ian. I've lost too, in all this."

He sits down again, cradles his head in his hands. "I know you have. And I'm sorry. I've been terrible, and I'm sorry for that too."

I stay apart: *But what will that do?*

Johanna brings out two chairs. It's cold on the terrace, but we're going to eat there anyway. She's made fennel soup, and a warm chicken salad. It's all beautifully presented on her best china, but I don't feel like eating it.

"I'm slowing down," I apologize.

"You're entitled." She serves us both some soup from a Limoges tureen. "This is all our wedding stuff. At least Carson's not getting *that*."

"You got what matters," I say, of the boys.

Kyle comes in with a plate of cookies. "Can I have one of these?"

"Take the whole plate," she says. "Give some to your brother."

I try a little of the soup, but the fennel is so strong I don't think I can go on with it. "It really does taste like licorice."

"I'm one of those people who thinks candy should be featured in every meal."

"That's because you're brilliant," I say.

"I've got something for you."

"Johanna, it's enough already."

She holds up a finger and goes back inside. When she comes out she's carrying a glazed creature, brightly colored. She sets it beside my soup dish.

"It's an elephant," she says nervously. Why she should be nervous in my company is beyond me. Of all people, I should be kissing the ground she walks on.

"I can see that!"

"To cheer you up. I know how much you miss them."

"Oh Jo." It's slightly larger than an adult hand, intricately fashioned out of clay. Its yellow drape and red saddle and matching bridle gleam.

"I love elephants," she says. "They were my favorite part of the circus."

"Me too. We always had one in our parlor."

"We come from the same family."

I tell her that if there was anything I could do to have them back in the afternoons I'd do it.

"As soon as my paperwork comes through," she says. "Carson's watching everything I do right now. I'm a bad judge of character and you're the negligent nanny I chose. *We almost lost our little boy because of you,* he tells me. I can't wait until he has to listen to a judge talk about abandonment. Let the authorities remind him his kids need to eat."

"You're the only one who will talk to me. James went completely ballistic, telling me, skillet calling the kettle black, that Electra wasn't safe with me. Winifred was swept off by her hurricane of a mother and Ralph's dad said I'd be hearing from his lawyer. You're the one whose kid was in danger, and you're feeding me lunch."

"April is the cruelest month," she says. "Maybe some of this will pass."

Understandably, I have lost my nerve. I tell her as much. I give the boys their books, *Peter Pan* for Kyle and *Goop Tales* for Anthony (when, Lord help us all, he gets bigger), kiss them, and go home, where I sit at the card table by the living-room window at the telescope.

I angle the telescope so I can get the largest spectrum of stars, available above the lowest building. Then I glance over a section of text he marked with dark brackets. *The distance*

*traveled by an object may depend on the time elapsed since it left
a specific point.*

It's easier, to think of us all as traveling.

"Ian?" I say. "Look at this."

He comes in from the kitchen, leans down, looks into
the eyepiece.

"Beautiful," he says, turning to me.

"No matter what happens," I say, rushing, afraid that
if I don't speak fast enough this thing I want to say, that
I've thought of because of the stars, because of Daddy, will
fade, "I love you. I do. I love you. And if we can't all get
back on course, you *have* to know that! And you *have* to tell
Mal and make sure he knows it! Please promise me that!
Please!"

He puts his arms around me. "Okay, Paige. Okay. It's
going to be okay. Somehow, you're going to be okay. We all
are."

"No!" I cry. "No! I don't believe you."

"Believe me," he says softly, not letting go. "Believe."

Functions, limits, continuity. In his calligraphic script
he wrote "key" in the margin, which seems profound. Not
that he wasn't as deep as the sea, but indulging in the collection of philosophical chestnuts was not his style. He
preferred levity, banter. Only once, when he was expiring
from cancer, did he tell me that he loved me and Mother.
My heart, knocking with fear, felt unwieldy, and I was
unable to speak. Right then, I gave him nothing in return,
and he went knowing this, leaving me his marginalia to
steer with.

"He's doing better," Dorothy says. I'm as stunned by this as
I am to be sitting across from Dorothy in a restaurant. But if
this is her attempt at apology, I'm going to take her up on it.

She fiddles with a heavy gold bracelet, helping it to tour her bony wrist. "Anyway, he wants to see you. Dr. Esslin has him on Paxil. To even things out. So far he just seems his usual, smoldering self."

"I want to know what made him take those kids I love up on that roof."

"He was jealous. He wanted you to pay the same kind of attention to him."

"Bullshit. He wanted that from *you*."

Coarseness is an asset, in this case. Dorothy lets go of herself for a second, losing the forward, gripped posture.

"He'll be okay," she says. "He has to. I can't live with him being so unhappy anymore. He told me he hated me the other day."

"He doesn't hate you," I say. *Whether or not he should.*

The waiter brings blintzes, and Dorothy thanks him. We're at a Russian restaurant midtown, near Dorothy's work.

"Try the food," Dorothy says, pointing with her knife. "You're thinner than I am."

This is true. I've been too awash in all of this to eat, even to drink.

"I've been sitting in on classes I'm supposed to start teaching for a woman who's about to have a baby," I tell Dorothy. "I look at the kids, who are only a couple of years younger than Mal, and I think I should know their every need. But I don't."

Dorothy sets down knife and fork. She eats the European way, with fork in the opposite hand and knife the active partner. "I know I'm part of the reason he got himself up on that roof. And if you think it isn't killing me, you're wrong."

She dabs at tears. Oddly, her makeup doesn't streak.

"I wish you had a kid, Paige. I really do. It would be so much easier for you. For all of us."

Blintzes are not really made for chewing, but I chew hard. Ugly as it is, I've come here to settle a score.

"You know what your problem is, Dorothy?" I say. "You're indestructible."

Groundwork, this is. *Part of mothering.* Believing despite the evidence. Breathing easily, contrary to fact. Because you have to.

❧ TWENTY-SEVEN ❧

"*P*eople?" I call. This is how Mrs. Lerner addressed the students, her basketball stomach resting on the desktop. The kids quiet down, some reclining arrogantly in their chairs, some leaning on their hands, waiting for some impression to cross their view.

I write "tragedy" on the board.

"Here we go again," Elizabeth, the class loudmouth, says. They've been tossing the term around with Mrs. Lerner all semester, but I haven't seen it defined anywhere, on any of the Xeroxes accompanying the text.

"What about it?" D.C., the closest to obtaining a prison record, demands.

"Tell me what you think it means," I say.

D.C. beats out a preamble on the desk, to the amusement of some of the others. "Means something's over," he says.

"Right," I tell him. "And how do you know it's over?"

He grins at my obviousness. "Because you see it."

Elizabeth rolls her eyes, and Adriatic, in the front row, the most diligent of them all, mans his Bic, gleaning more in notes from the discussion than it can possibly be offering him.

"If you *see* it, how is it over?" I ask D.C. He shakes his head. *The bitch can kick it,* I overheard him say a couple of days ago.

"You watch it happen."

"Apply it to the play," I say.

"You watch them all die," Elizabeth says triumphantly. "You watch them go from being a normal family to this group of liars and murderers. And then they all end up dead!"

"Sort of like your family, right?" Elijah, class clown, teases.

"Eat it, Eli," she tosses back.

"Hold on, folks!" I order. "Don't murder the messenger here."

D.C. again, confused: "*Normal family?* That's a joke! The uncle's doing his sister-in-law, the kid's in love with his mother, you got this fool behind the curtain tryin' to get in everyone's business. They're all nuts!"

"Don't go over *his* house!" Elijah warns. "Ain't no better over there!"

"The point is," Elizabeth says, "they're supposed to be like that. Or you can't have the tragedy. It's a setup."

"Brilliant!" I crow.

"You crazy," D.C. says, to both of them.

"You stupid," Elijah counters.

The bell, loud enough to signal a fire, sounds, and people start to gather themselves noisily to the task of moving on to the next class.

"Wait! Homework! I want a page on tragedy. You define it and give me an example."

"What about Act Four?" Elizabeth moans. "I already read it!"

"Act Four isn't going anywhere," I say. "They've been waiting to die for centuries. They can wait until Friday."

"*Está muy loca*," Enrique says fondly.

"*Loca en la cabesa*," D.C. agrees.

I make my way downstairs, my new popular self. Mal is outside, as promised. I have the urn with me, in the same paper bag. "Let me look at you."

He presents himself, bowing like a courtier, then pivots, as if to pass to the outside.

"You look better," I say. He does. His shoulders aren't slumped. He's holding himself up. None of that weary distance in the eyes.

"So do you."

"I feel okay," I say. "Better, I mean. I love this place. I love the class."

"Told you," he says.

"I know you did," I say. "Ready?"

"Wouldn't be here otherwise."

We take the subway downtown and walk west to the Circle Line terminal. I buy two tickets to go as far as Spuyten Duyvil.

"Good day for it," the ticket master says.

"Isn't it?" I say brightly. It's cool and clear. Mal lopes along beside me on the ramp.

"Let's stand at the back, don't you think?" I say to him. "There are chairs there, and, I figure, we don't want to throw ashes into wind that will blow them right back in our faces."

"Sure."

There is just one other group of people on the boat so far, speaking a language I don't recognize. They keep solidly to themselves, without taking much interest in the shore or the water. They don't need either, finding themselves in talk. I wonder about myself and Mal, who we are in the eyes of these strangers. A young man. An older woman, mother-aged. A person halfway to the end, to whom graceful men and women have left their legacies of brilliant words.

"How do you feel?" I ask him.

"About what?"

"Anything," I say.

"Worried," he says.

"I wish I could help."

"I don't," he says. "Then I'd just worry some more."

"Why?"

"Because that's the way I am. I worry all the time. I make myself sick."

"Are you worried now? About me?" I can't stand it, the idea of his worrying about me for a second.

"I'm worried about you and Dad."

"Don't," I order. "We're okay. You made us think about things we weren't paying attention to. He's all right, and so am I."

"Then I won't ask you what I was going to."

"Ask me what?"

"About coming back." He's looking away, waiting for me to get a clue.

"You can't be *serious*."

"I can't?"

"Why would you want to do that? Move in where you moved out of? Does your dad know you want to do this?"

"No," Mal says, laughing. "I figure you'll tell him for me."

"Give it some more thought," I say. "I will, too." I want to shout for joy.

"I'll pay my way," he says.

"I don't want her living with us," I say.

"Who?"

"*Hilary.*"

He smiles. "Why do you hate Hilary so much?"

"I don't *hate* Hilary. I just think she's mean. She's not right for you."

"Oh! Is that it!"

"Yes, that's it," I say.

"I miss you," he says. "I miss—fun."

I say nothing of the epic proportion of this, the nightly prayers, the manic work on Daddy's books, all rebound and delivered now. Ralph got the *Treasure Island*; Winifred, *The Princess and the Goblins*; Electra, *A Child's Garden of Verses*: all of which he read to me in their entirety, sitting in the rocker in my room.

"Dr. Esslin wrote all their parents letters," he says.

"What? *Why?*"

Signature shrug. "Because I asked him to."

"Saying *what?*" I'm unnerved by his further messing with the trembling structure of it all.

"That it wasn't your fault," he says. "That I snapped."

"The fault will always be mine," I tell him. "Anyway, enough on this."

"He's got me on this drug that supposedly keeps me from doing crazy shit," he says. "I won't bug you. I promise. I'm really getting back to music and I'm going to take a writing class with Jessica. I want to show you some of my stuff, when I get it written."

"I'd like that. I mean, I think that would be good."

He looks at the water. "My mom told me you let her have it."

"She had it coming," I say. "But who am I? I've got no business letting people have it."

He smiles. "You sure do tell it like it is."

The foghorn blares, and the boat eases away from the dock. As soon as we're midriver and gaining speed, I lift the urn out of the bag at my feet. "Shall we get this part over with?"

"So we can get to the fun part?" he teases.

"Exactly."

"You first," he says, after I open it.

"Thanks," I say. "A ton."

I dip my fingers in. The ashes are lumpy. They feel sort of wet. I don't want to think about why. I throw a fistful out over the churning water.

"He'd probably have wanted me to say something while I did that."

"You did!" Mal says. "Here, give me a handful."

I hold out the urn for him. It is truly ugly, a sin of a thing, bronze and squat, with careless detailing. It doesn't do Marekki justice.

"Where are you, man?" he says, digging around.

He throws the ashes, full force. "Bye, friend," he says. Then he turns and asks me, "How was that?"

I shake the last ashes out, watch them disappear in the air before they ever get to water. Then I put the urn back in the bag.

"Wonderful," I tell him. "It was wonderful."

What I want to say is that *he's* wonderful, that it can work, that maybe I don't need nine jobs for life to seem worthwhile, for my contribution to seem enough. But there are laws about what you can say and when, and they're determined by more than one person.

"It moves so slow," he says. Of what, I'm not sure. The boat, the water. Time, maybe. "It's kind of nice."